The Devil's Own Angel

Book Two of The Bounty Cove Chronicles

Brenda Tetreault

PublishAmerica
Baltimore

First printing

Hardcover 978-1-4512-2683-6
Softcover 978-1-4512-2684-3
PUBLISHED BY PUBLISHAMERICA, LLLP
www.publishamerica.com
Baltimore

Printed in the United States of America

To Mark and Harry—

I love you guys!

Evette—

Thank you part 2!!
It was so good to see
you; thanx for braving
the traffic!!

— Brenda

25 Sept 2010

~ PROLOGUE ~

She sat alone on the beach as the coming summer storm drove the masses of sun worshippers under cover; not everyone could appreciate the feeling of absolute *lightness*, of release and relief that came with sunbathing as a summer storm brewed. The ocean was a muddy turquoise expanse topped with ruffled whitecaps, and the bruised sky had lowered to the horizon as thunder rumbled and lightening flashed. The storm had circled from the north, its edges just brushing the stretch of pale sand beach where she sat, and she laughed quietly to herself as the summer rain began to fall softly, bathing her body in warm wetness and washing away tension. The sun continued to shine upon her, though, causing fragile tendrils of steam to rise from her warm body. She reached a lazy hand down and closed the zipper on her beach bag, preferring not to get her book and clothing wet, and leaned her head back, tipping her face to the sky. She sighed gustily with a measure of contentment and let the sound of the ocean and the storm carry away her concerns, and allowed herself to simply *be* for a short time.

The gentle wash passed as quickly as it blew in, and gradually, she heard the chattering crowds return, and gave a bemused shake of her head. She knew the storm hadn't spent itself; she could feel the energy gathering in the center of her being, and in a short while, they would be scrambling for shelter again. When that happened, she would join them, knowing the next wave would be much angrier and more violent than the first; she could feel the power of Nature gathering in the way her skin prickled and the sense of tense awareness that awoke in the back of her skull. Determined to soak up as much of the early summer sun and the clean ocean air as she could, she retrieved her book from the depths of her bag, and leaned back as her skin puckered with goosebumps from the cool breeze that had abruptly shifted to blow in from the water.

She returned to her story and listened with half an ear to the increasing sound of thunder and the increasing sounds of warning and consternation coming from her fellow beach goers; briefly it occurred to her that the crowds were beginning to sound like chickens who'd become flustered. Glancing up, she noticed one woman, plump and sunburned, fussing and clucking to her children as they hurriedly gathered their belongings. The woman's children, a boy and his younger sister, were doing more protesting than actual cleaning up. From the look on their mother's face, the children were in imminent danger of pushing her past her limits of patience. Those limits were well and truly exceeded moments later when the little girl suddenly sat down on the sand, her legs and arms crossed, a petulant expression on her face, and announced loudly that she *wasn't* going home to take a nap, and her mother *wasn't* going to make her. Carrying a clearly harried and harassed expression, the girl's mother snagged an arm around her daughter's waist and hoisted her up and, toting her daughter under one arm and several beach chairs under the other, called to her son to get their small cooler. Moments later the little family was under way, picking their way through the crowds to the boardwalk, the little girls' cries and screeches of protest trailing after them. Sending the beleaguered mother a thought of commiseration and patience, the young woman returned to her book.

Tension steadily wound itself in her belly, and as it reached an unbearable point, she sighed heavily and packed her belongings; she was safely in her car by the time Mother Nature unleashed her tempest on the beach. She drove through rain whipped by fierce wind to a vantage point, and watched the storm swirl around the peninsula, thunderheads piling up faster and faster as the wind picked up, and drove the rain almost sideways.

Far out in the distance she watched a large freighter as it chugged, undisturbed, through the rain bands, lightening licking its deck. She gave a salute of farewell as the storm overtook the large vessel and it disappeared like a ghost ship into the teeth of the storm. She returned to her car and sat, the rain pounding on the roof and blurring her sight through the windshield. Then, just as quickly as it had blown in, the storm had passed. She stepped from her car and walked to the edge of the bluff, overlooking the beach far below, the stormy sky clearing. She placed her forearms along the top of the wooden safety rail and leaned on them, breathing in the fresh salty tang of the breeze as it teased her short blonde hair. Her silver eyes reflected the distant flashes of lightening far out to sea. As the clouds parted completely and the sun came out again, a rainbow painted itself in a sweeping arc across the northern sky.

She stood there, still and silent, as the evening twilight faded into full dark, reluctant to return to her hotel room. She tried to ignore her conscience that told her

Nicodemious would want his evening meal, telling it the fat cat could wait a little longer, and that he wouldn't starve if his plate of leftovers were a little late. As if thinking of her feline companion could conjure his presence, she saw him clearly in her mind's eye. She saw him pacing in agitation in front of the door, and heard his demanding mew. With a heavy sigh, she left the vantage point and crawled into her car, not caring that she got the upholstery a little damp, reluctant to leave this spot where she'd found a small measure of peace.

The drive from the state park to her hotel took only minutes, the beach traffic now gone. She slowly climbed the stairs to her floor, digging her room key from her beach bag. She could hear Nico meowing impatiently on the other side of the room's door. She stuck the key in the lock and gave a sharp twist of her wrist, pushing the door open as she did so, her foot automatically shoving between the door and the jamb to prevent her furry companion from escaping. The main road to the ferry and state park ran in front of her temporary home, and she didn't want him squashed flat by a car. The fishing party boat docks were just a hundred yards to the right; there were strays there who prowled dockside, looking for a hand out from the myriad of tourists and locals who came and went four times a day from the boats and the restaurant those boats supplied with the catch of the day. Though Nico was a city cat, she imagined he fancied himself a tough guy who could take any of those ruffians on and win. Not wanting to spend another night pacing with anxiety, or another day wrestling the large feline down to medicate his wounds, she bent down and pushed him back, her palm cradling his furry face.

"No, you don't," she told him sternly as she closed the door behind her.

She moved across the room to the bathroom vanity and pulled a foil packet from her bag. Nicodemious' nose started to twitch, and the tone of his voice changed from demanding to pleading as he jumped up to try and sneak a piece of crab cake off the plate. With a chuckle, she pushed him gently off, and finished arranging the leftover crab cake and shrimp Alfredo on his plastic plate, garnishing it with a sprig of fresh parsley. Most would find this an eccentric touch to a plate of cat food, but Nico loved the herb, and as a result, he tended to have sweeter smelling breath than the usual feline. She quickly policed his litter box and left him to enjoy his meal in peace.

Angeline Carston sat down on one of the double beds and stared at the phone, watching the red message light blink off and on. Tension knotted in her belly and her hand shook, her hard won serenity lost, as she grabbed the receiver and dialed the message line. She breathed a deep sigh of relief as she heard her grandmother's voice, calling to make sure she was all right; Angeline had been worried the message would be from her ex fiancé Chris Jessop; that he had tracked her down yet again. Her cell phone trilled in her bag as she hung up the phone, and when she checked the caller id, her blood drained to her feet. This time, the caller was Chris; for a moment she debated ignoring it, but finally sighed and flipped open the phone.

"What do you want this time?" She asked wearily by way of greeting. The connection wasn't very good, and she initially had trouble hearing him. Finally, the line cleared and she felt a shiver of revulsion at the sound of his voice.

"I want you," he told her, his voice strained, "to get your ass home. Don't make me come after you."

She closed her eyes, and clenched her jaw. Chris was an attorney, and came from a large moneyed family; he was accustomed to getting his way, and responded belligerently when he didn't. For a short time, she had imagined herself in love with him, and had gladly accepted his marriage proposal; three weeks later he had beaten her senseless over a trivial matter. In the three years she had known and dated him, she had never seen this violent side of Chris, and she had decided she wouldn't be sticking around to witness anymore. She broke the engagement and gave back the ring. Chris hadn't taken the break up very well, and had stalked her for six months until, no longer able to feel safe in her own home, and unable to get the proof she needed for police protection, Angeline had sold everything off, including her veterinary practice and home, and had gone on the run. Her grandmother had told her to go with her blessings, stating it was time for Angeline to go out and find her destiny.

So here she was, in a little coastal town in southern Delaware, as far away from her home in Oregon as she could get without leaving the country, and still Chris was calling her to harass her. She listened with half an ear as Chris continued to demand she return to Oregon and marry him. When she didn't respond, he resorted to threats and name-calling. She hung up without a word and ignored the phone when it began trilling again immediately. She glanced across the room at Nico as he paused in his after dinner washing ritual to give her a steady look. Angeline read caution his yellow gaze. "You're right," she sighed heavily and started throwing things into her beach bag and suitcase. She already knew she was running again; the phone call had spooked her, just as Chris had wanted. She took one last look around the room, shoved Nico into his carrier, and began loading him and their belongings into the car. Twenty minutes later, she was on the highway and driving south, trying the still the tremors in her hands and calm her racing heart.

Two days later, she pulled her overheating car into a parking spot along Main Street in a little town called Bounty Cove, a small coastal town in North Carolina.

The Devil's Own Angel

Book Two of The Bounty Cove Chronicles

~ CHAPTER ONE ~

Angeline sighed wearily as she killed the engine. Her forearms and hands ached from gripping the steering wheel tightly for so long, her backside was so numb that she felt as if it had fallen off the sensory map, and her eyes were hot and gritty from driving since the crack of dawn. When she'd left the hotel in Lewes, Delaware a day and a half earlier, she hadn't had a destination in mind, just a deep-seated need to find somewhere to disappear. Now, somehow, she found herself sitting in front of a small bed and breakfast, looking up at the welcoming sight of a VACANCY sign hanging over a wraparound porch and gardens behind a white picket fence. She felt a smile beginning to grow on her face as she noticed the white rocking chairs on the porch, just calling to a weary traveler like herself to have a seat and forget her cares for a little while. Sighing heavily, and feeling a small measure of hopeful peace working through her, she turned to look at Nico sulking in his carrier in the seat beside her.

"This looks nice, doesn't it?" She asked the cat. The only reply she got was a long, drawn out yowl that sounded rather pathetic; Nico hated travelling, and only did so with ill grace and kitty relaxants. Sighing again, Angeline opened her door and managed to drag herself out of the car, her legs and back stiff. Despite the weariness she felt, however, a sense of excitement had begun to tingle up her spine in an almost premonition; she could start over here, reset her life and finally begin living the way she had imagined she would when she was younger.

Nick Damien—Devil to his friends because he shared his surname with a character from a series of Son-of-Satan movies from the seventies—watched the small stranger literally crawl out from behind the steering wheel and stretch, her motions slow with evident exhaustion. She was slim hipped and small breasted in her white shorts and pink tee shirt, and her hair covered her head in a short and wispily curled cap and was the color of the old gold coin he kept in his pocket as a good luck charm. A large pair of dark sunglasses covered her eyes, but he thought they might be blue, to go with her blond hair and fair coloring; to his appreciative and practiced eye, she appeared no more than eighteen years old, at the most. He watched as she went around the car to the passenger side and opened the door, his attention so concentrated on her that he could almost hear the slap of her flip-flops against her heels as she walked. She leaned down and into the car, and seemed to be talking to someone in the seat, but from his vantage point in the diner across the street, Devil couldn't make out who it was. He continued to watch her as she closed the car door and enjoyed the way her hips swayed as she jogged up the front steps of Aunt Blanche's hotel and disappeared inside. He monitored the front door like a hawk and was pleased to see her come tripping down the steps several minutes later, a smile on her face, and, it seemed, a renewed bounce in her step.

Devil paid his tab and left the diner, intent on introducing himself to the petite stranger. Why he felt compelled to do so, he couldn't say, but he didn't fight it; it just seemed to be the right thing to do at that precise moment. It was a silent, powerful compulsion that propelled him across the street and he was unable to ignore it; it was the same compelling sense of fate that had caused him to settle in Bounty Cove three years ago, despite having to give up a lucrative promotion at the architectural firm he worked for in Raleigh. Almost everyone who thought they knew him, or at least knew of his quasi-playboy reputation, had assumed he'd gone off the deep end when he turned down the promotion in order to live in Bounty Cove. Yet, the moment he step foot inside the town limits after an extended time away, Devil had felt as if he'd finally come home; something about Bounty Cove called to him on a level so deep that it was almost primitive instinct. He'd come to Bounty Cove to see his friend, Michael Kemper, and had found himself unable to leave when the time came to do so. He'd bought a three acre wooded lot outside of town, and built himself a house that, if he were honest with himself, was simply too large to be a bachelor pad; and though there had been several women willing to be called Mrs. Damien, he hadn't taken the hints, some of them not-so-subtle. Now, three years later, and that silent compulsion was calling to him again, and he wasn't about to be a fool enough to ignore it. He approached swiftly, a genial smile on his face, watching as she struggled to pull a large suitcase out of the trunk, admiring the lean lines of her legs. "Need any help?" He asked in a friendly voice as he neared. He was startled to see her shoulders stiffen. Her head whipped around and he felt the appraising look she gave him from behind her sunglasses; it was an almost physical sensation that he felt skitter along his skin and delve deep into his core. The impact of her regard was so intense that, for a moment, it halted him in his tracks.

Angeline watched the tall, dark haired stranger approach, a smile lighting his features, nervous caution screaming from every line in her small body. "No, thank you," she said, waving him away sharply and turning her back on him in an attempt to put him off, "I can get it." She gulped hard and tried to calm her erratic heartbeat, as she took several slow, deep breaths to keep from hyperventilating. The dark haired man's sudden appearance had startled her, causing a small, hot breeze to race through the flower garden of the bed and breakfast. With a desperate grab at control, she tamped down on her knee-jerk reactions; the last thing she wanted or needed was attention. She could already feel the energy straining to break free, and she didn't want to announce her arrival in town by turning loose a tornado in the middle of Main Street. She glanced over her shoulder and watched the man as he frowned at the tone of her voice and with a tightening of her jaw and holding her breath for a moment, she took herself more firmly in hand. Turning her back on the stranger, she reached into the trunk, wrapped her slender fingers around the handle of her suitcase, and with a grimace of effort, pulled with all her might, but exasperatingly, the luggage wouldn't budge. She tugged again, growling in frustration and swearing under her breath as the muscles of her forearms stood out with the effort. From the corner of her eye, she saw the strange man who'd approached her move closer, and she did her best to ignore him as she adjusted her grip on the handle and braced her legs to give herself a little more leverage; in her experience, if you ignored someone long enough and hard enough, they usually went away. A moment later, however, it was obvious the man wasn't going to leave and she stiffened as he leaned in close, his shoulder brushing hers. When his large hand closed over hers, she gasped as an electric tingle jumped between his impossibly warm fingers and her cooler ones. She froze instantly, suddenly aware of the heat and strength of his body and the clean, masculine scent of him. The hyper-awareness left her nerves feeling instantly stretched and vibrating, and she was unable to do anything more than watch as he lifted the stubborn luggage out with ease. Her hand was still trapped between his and the handle of the suitcase, and when he turned a toe curling, wit scattering grin on her, she felt the heat of a blush flood her cheeks and in a bid to lessen the impact of him, she yanked her hand out from under his as if he'd burned her. Then, wondering if there was any way to stop him, she watched as the stranger reached into the trunk again, snagged the straps of her beach bag, and lifted that out as well, hefting it to an impressively broad shoulder. An insane urge to giggle rose in her chest as a sense of unreality washed over her, and she frowned at herself in consternation as she quelled the giggles in time to gape at him further as, without saying a word, he headed for the front steps. Disbelief flooded through her as she watched his broad back head up the front steps of the inn, and shaking herself, she hustled to catch up with him, intent on recovering her baggage and sending him on his way. She found him in the front lobby, and pushed her sunglasses up into her hair as she sputtered at him.

"Really," she insisted with a healthy dose of exasperation, grabbing hold of the beach bag and tugging. "You don't have to do this. I can manage on my own."

Devil glanced down into her heart shaped face, and felt himself pinned in place by the silver depths of her eyes. He stared at her for several breathless moments, feeling like a goobering fool as he tried to think of something—anything—to say, and with immense effort, he forced himself to look away. He ignored her protests, and covering his unaccustomed moment of distraction, directed his look at Blanche, who hovered uncertainly behind the desk. “Which one,” he asked with a grin. As long as he didn’t stare directly into those quicksilver eyes, his equilibrium remained intact.

“Second floor, third door on the left,” she told him with a wink, “Melissa’s old room.”

Devil nodded and started for the stairs, almost dragging the girl behind him; she still had a firm grip on the straps of the oversized beach bag. He paused and looked down at her and watched as she let go of the strap and stood indecisively, twisting her fingers together at her waist and worrying her bottom lip between her teeth, obviously trying to decide what, if anything, she could do to stop him. She gazed at him with guarded, frightened eyes, and he heard again in his mind the reedy, high-pitched tone of her voice when he’d startled her outside, and realized without knowing how, that she’d been really, *truly* afraid. The expression in her eyes kicked him in the gut, and he felt an overwhelming urge to drop everything in order to gather her in his arms to protect her from whatever it was that haunted her. To hold her close and shield her from-

What?

Life?

The world?

The ghosts he’d glimpsed lurking in the starlight depths of her eyes?

He shook his head to clear his mind and frowned as something soft and binding slid through his chest, causing his heart rate and breathing to slow. Time itself slowed and stretched between them as their gazes met and locked. They stared at each other, frozen in a moment of silent communication, neither one breathing, as her eyes silently begged him to just forget about her and his answered that he simply couldn't.

Blanche scurried from behind the desk, waving the room key in her hand. "You're going to need this," she called, breaking the spell. Devil watched as the small woman flinched, her body tensing as if expecting a blow. She looked at him with large, haunted eyes, still afraid, still unable to trust. The disquiet and bone deep awareness stretched between them, and he knew it was up to him to dispel the unnerving tension; she was too wrapped up in her own uncertainty to do it herself.

Adjusting the bag's straps on his shoulder, Devil winked at the small stranger and gave her his best boyish grin—one that had never failed to charm the socks of women in the past—before indicating with his chin for her to get the key. He watched the woman blink slowly then turn to Blanche and hold out her hand for the key, almost as if she were in a daze. When he saw she had the key in hand, he continued up the stairs, trusting that she would eventually follow him.

Angeline stayed behind, watching him carry her heavy bags as if they weighed next to nothing. She honestly didn't know whether to stamp her foot and pitch a fit, or what; her natural inclination to avoid men had served her well in recent weeks, but this man had refused to be put off by her less than warm attitude, and had insisted on lending a hand. And though she'd wanted to stand her ground and tell the man to butt out, something inside her had prevented her from doing so; had caused her to stand aside after a show of token resistance and allowed him to help. What had happened or was continuing to happen, she didn't know, but it left her feeling shaky and uncertain. She flinched as she heard Blanche clear her throat and Angeline suddenly remembered Nicodemious. She hurried out to her car to collect him and his accessories, giving herself a stern talking to and rallying her defenses as she lugged the carrier up the front steps, through the small lobby, and up yet more stairs. By the time she gained the top landing, breathing heavily and perspiring—Nico was no lightweight after all—the tall, dark man was waiting by what she assumed was her door, a grin lighting his face. Grudgingly grateful for his unasked for assistance, and ignoring the way her heart leapt at the sight of him, Angeline thanked him and told him to leave her things on the floor.

"I can get it from here," she told him firmly, hoping he would take the hint and leave.

She darted a glance up into his face, felt a shock as something inside her flared hotly in the center of her chest, as if in recognition, and was dismayed at the way her heart picked up its pace and the hallway lights flared in time to its uneven beat over their heads. She pushed the feeling down, not in the mood to listen to Fate, or whatever it was that was playing tiddlywinks with her hormones and waited for the lights to steady. She noticed the dark stranger hadn't put her things down, and seemed perfectly happy to carry them inside for her, apparently oblivious to the lightshow. With a grumble to herself about unasked for chivalry, and doing her best to shake off the lingering effects of his touch and smile, she unlocked the door and swung it wide to reveal a small, tidy room done in tones of green with ruffles and lace that appealed to the romantic little girl that still lived deep in her heart. By contrast, the large man with his dark flashing eyes and wavy dark hair looked distinctly out of place; his large body seemed to crowd itself into the decidedly feminine room. Doing her best to appear unaffected by his presence, she stepped in behind him, and shut the door in order to let Nico out; the cat had reached the end of his patience and was loudly demanding release, his yowls becoming more strident with every passing moment. Devil cast a wary look at the carrier and asked in surprise, “Is that a bobcat?” as she unlatched the carrier door and Nico sedately made his entrance.

Angeline stifled a giggle; his wasn’t the first reaction of that sort she had received when people first met Nicodemious. “He’s a Maine Coon,” she said lightly, fighting the grin that threatened to spread across her face; this dark man was a stranger, and it wouldn’t do to become too friendly with him, yet she couldn’t help but enjoy his momentary astonishment at seeing her cat for the first time. Past experience, however, cautioned her to make sure he didn’t think she was laughing at him. “He’s still a baby yet; he only weighs about ten pounds. When he’s grown, he’ll weigh close to twenty.” She watched as Nico made his way to the man’s shoes and gave them a cautious sniff before he started winding himself around the man’s legs, rubbing his cheeks on his ankles.

Devil reached down and stroked the cat from head to tail, enjoying the silky feeling of the fur. A loud purr rumbled through the cat, and Devil felt the vibrations not just in his fingertips but radiating up his arm as well as they buzzed through the large cat. Nico stretched luxuriously, his front toes reaching up to anchor themselves in the denim that covered his knee. Devil hissed softly as the cat’s nails bit through his jeans and into his skin.

“He likes you,” Angeline said as she knelt and gently disengaged Nico’s claws. “He normally doesn’t like men, as a rule,” she explained, standing and holding the cat close, eyeing Devil as if trying to make up her mind about him. Finally, she stuck out her hand, realizing she simply couldn’t be rude and brush him off when he’d so nicely helped her out.

"I'm Angeline Carston," she said, introducing herself. "Thank you for all your help…" She let the sentence hang.

Devil collected himself; he couldn't help staring at her. "Nick Damien," he said slowly, dazedly, taking her hand and shaking it. He shook his head to clear it. "My friends call me Devil," he added with a mock leer.

Angeline smiled slightly, still cautious around this tall, dark and somewhat intimidating man with his easy smile and warm, laughing brown eyes. Yet, there was something about him that called to her at a deeper level that soothed and calmed her nerves, and she relaxed a little, as the warmth of his hand seemed to spread up her arm and through her chest. Her smile widened a little as she relaxed slightly and gave in a tiny bit to his charm. "Nice to meet you," she replied honestly.

"Are you planning to stay awhile?" Devil asked, still holding her hand and knew a moment later that he'd asked the wrong question. He watched Angeline's expression suddenly shutter again and wondered at it.

"I don't know," she said noncommittally, pulling her hand free of his. She set Nicodemious on the floor and walked to the door. "Thank you for your help," she said sincerely.

Devil knew a dismissal when he heard one, and crossed the room to leave. She opened the door for him, and he paused to gaze down at her, taking in her starlight silver eyes. He had never seen eyes that color before, and he found himself mesmerized by them. His gaze swept over her, taking in the smooth, round curves, and decided she was older than the eighteen he had originally thought. He realized he was staring and shook himself.

He shook her hand again. "I hope I'll see you around, Angel," he said softly. Then he turned and left, closing the door behind him.

Angeline stood, silent and still, staring at the closed door. Her fingers still tingled from his casual contact, and she wondered why her heart fluttered so unsteadily in her chest. It was several minutes before her brain kicked into gear again, and Angeline turned her attention to the now habitual routine of settling into a new hotel room, Devil Damien and his intoxicating smile put, if not firmly, at least temporarily, out of mind.

~CHAPTER TWO~

June melted into July and Angeline hadn't departed after a few days, as was her usual habit. She found that she liked Bounty Cove; she felt at peace and safe here. There was something soothing and calming about the small town with its quaint Main Street and small shops that lined it on both sides. Angeline especially liked the park at the center of the town, with its grassy lawn, tall oak and maple trees, and Victorian styled bandstand. With the days warm and pleasant, Angeline developed the habit of eating her lunch on one of the park benches. The park seemed to be a popular meeting place for the mothers of the town; each morning Angeline watched as they arrived and sat talking as their children ran and played. And though Angeline felt the curious looks the women sent her way, she didn't look up or make contact of any kind; she wasn't ready to let her guard down, even with women, and as a result, she was certain people thought of her as snobbish, but she was unable to take the next step; Chris hadn't tried to contact her again, but she was simply too afraid to relax. Afraid that if she grew close to anyone, if she started making friends, Chris would reappear and ruin everything. She didn't want anyone else to get hurt if that happened, so she kept to herself, her nose constantly buried in a book, that until recently, she had kept with her at all times. Now, however, her lunchtime reading also included real estate listings; there was a half-formed notion of perhaps settling in this peaceful, pretty little town and perhaps, reestablishing her veterinary practice. Even the lurking specter of Chris Jessop seemed to fade at the mere thought of spending the rest of her life in Bounty Cove; when she closed her eyes at night, she did so feeling safe and protected, as if nothing could ever hurt her again. And she awakened every morning with optimism growing and becoming more firmly established in her heart.

She'd run into Devil several times since their first meeting, and she was amused whenever he remembered to ask after Nico, though he often referred to the cat as 'the bobcat' when he did. And though he always seemed pleasantly surprised to see her whenever they met, Angeline had a sneaking suspicion that he engineered their meetings—she was fairly certain that by now most of the town knew she ate her lunch in the park everyday or that she always had a green salad, soup and a tuna fish sandwich for dinner every night at the diner, or that she was quietly talking with a realtor about homes in the area—so there was only a finite number of times Devil could 'accidently' run into her and she wasn't sure if she should feel flattered or concerned. And the way she found it difficult to draw a deep breath or think in a straight line whenever he smiled at her left her feeling a little panicky; the control she kept on herself during those meetings always became painfully shaky, and she felt a hot, electric stab of fear that her secret would be found out.

It was that panic that caused her to refuse any invitations Devil issued to join him and his friends in various activities. Though she hated how his face changed from carefully hopeful to clearly disappointed every time she declined, she told herself it was for the best. As long as she maintained a safe distance from him and his friends, no one would get hurt—least of all herself. However, Miss Blanche constantly urged her to get out and make a few friends. By the end of her second week in Bounty Cove, Angeline knew Miss Blanche's argument by heart:

"A pretty thing like you shouldn't keep to herself so much. It isn't natural; you need to get out and make some friends, have some fun, maybe even fall in love. You don't want to wake up one morning and realize you missed out on most of your life!"

Angeline let the little old lady have her say at least once a day, and made the appropriate promises to placate her, then went about her usual lonely business. And then one day, when Angeline wasn't looking, Blanche accepted an invitation to join Devil and several of his friends for a picnic on the beach one hot summer afternoon, having decided that she was finished watching Angeline ghost her way through life.

Angeline protested vehemently that she wasn't interested in picnics on the beach, but in the end, found herself seated beside Devil in his pickup, unable to withstand Blanche's near-constant badgering, and her need to remain distant thoroughly eroded by a deeper need for companionship and friends. She met Michael and Melissa Kemper, and their friends the Andrews, Jamie and Jessica, as well as the two couple's handful of rambunctious children. She grimaced in embarrassment and blushed when Devil introduced her as Angel, and muttered a quiet correction to Melissa and Jessica when Devil sauntered off to play touch football.

"I suppose he thinks he's being witty," she grumbled to the women over lemonade, "calling me Angel, when his nickname is Devil." She snorted. "Maybe he thinks we go together like salt and pepper," she continued in the same scoffing tone. Then she sighed suddenly, wistfully, and watched Devil, unable to help herself, while he played with the kids. "He does seem like an awfully nice man, though," she said thoughtfully, not noticing the smug look Jessica and Melissa passed between themselves. Angeline shook herself as she recalled that Chris, at one time, had seemed like a nice man, too. Unable to help herself, though, she covertly watched him from beneath her eyelashes. She flushed as Devil's gaze caught hers, and she turned away to hide her pink cheeks. She missed the look that passed between her companions; little did she know, but the two had already decided that Devil needed to settle down, and they'd picked her as the perfect candidate for him. Their matchmaking plans roared to life as they watched the hesitant fascination Angeline had for the tall, dark, and oh, so handsome Nickolas Damien.

Devil felt her gaze like a physical caress before he looked up and was disappointed when she looked away quickly as soon as he caught her eye; he had noticed the longer he was around her, the more aware he became of her, of the way the air moved around her. She had been in town for just a couple months, and he had come up with every excuse he could think of since their first meeting to spend even a moment of time with her; not an easy feat, considering how she kept to herself so doggedly; even when she was sitting on a bench in the park or sitting at a table in the diner, she seemed firmly ensconced behind ten-foot-tall privacy walls. Yet he persisted, and had managed to catch her unguarded a few times just so he could look into those silver eyes of hers, hear the light, husky timbre of her voice, and simply bask in her presence; he'd even managed to unglue his tongue from the roof of his mouth long enough to casually ask her out.

Until today, his only results had been cool rebuffs, even when she seemed to be warming up to him, and he found himself more often than not frustrated by her reserve. He told himself the fascination he felt for Angeline was simply because she hadn't fallen at his feet, despite his many attempts at charming her, the way other women had in the past. It was a singularly frustrating situation for a man so accustomed to not having to try very hard to receive female attention.

To say Devil had had his fair share of women in his time would be an accurate assessment; from an early age he'd found it very easy to charm women of all ages; most times all he had to do was smile at them. But it wasn't until college that he truly developed his love for women; the way they smelled, the way they laughed, the feel of their warm, satiny skin, all conspired to mold him into a willing connoisseur. During those handful of years, with Michael Kemper at his side, he'd cut a swath through the ranks of women, coed and professor alike, leaving behind a string of broken hearts and unfulfilled dreams. His tastes had refined during college, leading him to prefer tall, leggy brunettes with long hair like Connie Jackson, the woman that, until recently, he'd been seeing. The relationship had ended amicably when they both realized they were growing bored with each other and neither was in any hurry to stand before a preacher.

Angeline wasn't his typical flavor; with her short, burnished gold hair and tiny, compact physique, she was more a sprite that an Amazon, but there was something about her that he simply couldn't name nor ignore, and it drew him like a moth to a flame. She was so petite; there was an ethereal quality about Angeline, an air of delicacy, or perhaps fragility, that teased, tantalized, and made him want to gather her close and learn all her secrets even as he wanted to protect her. Yet, during the handful of times he'd 'accidently' run into her around town, he'd come to realize that her seeming vulnerability hid a stubborn streak a mile wide. He'd seen the soft line of her jaw set mulishly and her pointy little chin jut proudly when she dug in her heels and refused to be wheedled into a date with him. The recollections caused him to chuckle and shake his head at himself; it had been a long time since he'd done the chasing, and he wasn't sure he was doing a very good job of it. After all, it was obvious Angeline could have thought of a thousand things she'd rather do than go to the beach with him; she'd actually muttered something about root canals before finally giving into Blanche's badgering and his own cajoling. Now, here she was, looking slightly more relaxed than he'd seen her since meeting her, and—could that be a smile?—appearing to enjoy herself. Her laughter floated on the breeze to him, and the sound stunned him; it was the first time he'd heard her truly laugh and the sound left him wondering what he had to do to make her laugh like that himself. He didn't realize he continued to stare in Angeline's direction until the sound of Jamie's loud shout broke through the cloud of distraction that had settled in his brain. Looking up swiftly, he reacted in time to catch the football as it spiraled at his face. He grinned sheepishly, his face growing warm when he noticed Melissa watching him with a knowing gleam in her eye and a smug grin curling the corners of her mouth. Angeline, he saw, didn't look in his direction at all, almost as if she were avoiding doing so.

Melissa and Jessica announced lunch, and Devil and Angeline found themselves seated on the same rock, whether by accident or Melissa's design, neither could say. They exchanged a few minutes of stilted conversation before lapsing into silence. Angeline found herself watching Devil out the corner of her eye, unable to stop looking at him, but afraid to be caught doing it; Devil found himself in much the same predicament, but decided to take action. He leaned over until his shoulder brushed hers, and in a husky whisper, said in her ear, "The potato salad is very good, isn't it?"

Angeline gave a start as his warm breath sent shivers through her body. She fumbled with her plate, almost dropping it, and carefully set it aside before answering, "Yes, it is." She glanced up at him through lowered eyelashes, pink staining her cheeks. She saw him gesture to his cheek from the corner of her eye. She raised her head a little then drew back slightly as Devil ducked his head towards hers. "You have something right here," he said, his fingertip touching the corner of her mouth. Angeline had time enough to draw in a quick breath before his lips settled over hers.

The kiss was slow and surprisingly gentle, snaring Angeline's attention immediately. Her hands sat limp in her lap and his came up to frame her face. His tongue slid softly across the fullness of her mouth and her lips parted as a near silent gasp burst forth. He took advantage of the opening, and explored her mouth with lazy darts of his tongue, inviting her to join him. When he felt the first tentative touch of her tongue against his he had to stifle a groan; she tasted as sweet as he'd imagined she would. Just as he began to truly sink into the kiss, reality reared its ugly head as the sound of Michael's laughter at something Melissa said intruded, and Angeline tore her mouth away, wiping it with the back of her trembling hand almost guiltily. She looked at him with alarmed eyes and stood quickly, picking up her plate.

"Please don't do that again," she said, her voice quavering. She turned to walk away, but his hand manacled her wrist and he pulled her back, causing her plate to fall to the sand at their feet. She let out a soft gasp of shock and dismay as he hauled her down onto his lap and tipped her face up to his. “Why not,” he teased, his mouth hovering just above hers. “Afraid you'll like it?”

Angeline lay, frozen in his embrace, not fighting, not frightened, simply overwhelmed. This man was so full of life, so confident, so appealing, that he seemed to fill her senses and leave no room for anything else. Her heart thudded in her ears and she wondered what it would be like to have his kisses whenever she wanted them, to awaken in his arms, warm and secure, every morning, to be the complete focus of his intoxicating sensuality. A flash of heat burst through her at that last thought and she had to fight the urge to squirm. He grinned then, a grin so full of wicked promise than Angeline was positive her every thought was playing out across her face, and felt helpless to resist him when his mouth claimed hers once again. Her hands had been pressed against his chest, pushing weakly, but now her fingers curled into the soft fabric of his shirt as he held her easily and plundered her mouth over and over, stealing her breath and scattering her wits completely. Angeline felt heat rising through her blood, and heard her heart thundering in her ears. She unconsciously let her head fall back as his mouth explored her jaw line and tormented the sensitive spot below her ear. His hot breath whispered across her ear, causing shivers to erupt up and down her spine. A deep, steady throb began low in her belly as he captured her mouth once again. For a moment, she forgot who she was, where she was, forgot the secret she was hiding, and simply allowed herself to enjoy the feelings his kiss awakened in her body. Unable, and for the moment, unwilling to control her reactions, she threw herself into the kiss.

Devil gentled the kiss and pulled away several long minutes later, his body hungry, his mind stunned. He watched her face as she struggled to pull herself together, noting her silver eyes had gone the color of storm clouds. She drew a deep breath, causing her small breasts to press more fully against his chest, and he had to bite back a groan. When she finally looked at him, she wore a bemused expression. Her tongue darted out to moisten her swollen lower lip and his gaze narrowed on its pink tip, imagining the wild and wicked things it could do to a man's sanity. He noticed with amusement she seemed to be trying to speak, and couldn't seem to get the words out.

"Uh," she breathed, "I, um, don't think we should be doing this," she managed to stammer, and from the corner of her eye, she saw a mini dust devil of sand evaporate as she gained an upper hand on her control. She heard the voice that normally resided buried deep in the back of her head demanding she take everything he offered her body, give him everything he demanded in return, but did her best to ignore it; she really didn't want to think of what would happen if she completely lost the handle on her control, nor what would happen if Jessop suddenly turned up and found her involved with another man. Yet, at the same time, something deep inside her yearned towards Devil, yearned and ached to be a little reckless, to take a chance and see where it led her. That yearning was what frightened her the most and caused her to shiver in spite of the warmth of the day, in spite of the heat that curled through her; it gnawed at her, made her feel hot and cold in turns, made her want to surrender and finally share her secret with someone else other than her family. The thought of sharing her secret with Devil and the possibility that he would reject her, however, was stronger than any argument her hormones could raise, and it strengthened her resolve to keep her distance. She slid off his lap and stood, her emotions warring with each other in her expression. She gave him a look rife with pained confusion, then turned and hurried away as she recognized the signs of another sand cyclone stirring a few yards away.

A few moments later, Devil saw her speaking to Michael and Jamie, obviously asking a question. He watched as Michael nodded, throwing a thoughtful glance at Devil before turning and calling to Melissa. He didn't hear the words that passed between his friends because he was too intent on Angeline as she stood to the side, shifting her weight from foot to foot nervously. She had an arm around her waist, and had propped her elbow on that arm in order to chew on her thumbnail; Devil wondered what it was about him that made her so nervous. He watched as Michael turned back to her and whatever he said caused Angeline to smile, her relief palpable even at a distance. He heard Angeline call to Melissa and Jessica then turn and begin hiking up the trail to the cars parked on the cliff above, Michael following. He suddenly realized that she'd asked for a ride home and jumped to his feet to catch up with his friend. A few words to Michael, and he was following Angeline up the trail instead, having convinced Michael to stay and help Melissa clean up and corral the kids. They reached the trailhead quickly, and Devil continued to follow her to the cars, silent and intent. He increased his pace until he was right behind her, and when she turned at the sound of his footsteps on the gravel, he rushed forward and pinned her against the side of the car with his body, his fingers threading through her hair to cradle the back of her skull, and unable to stop himself, he kissed her.

Panic rippled through Angeline and she cried out, her whole body immediately going into fight or flight mode. She shrank back hard against the car and pushed as forcefully as she could against his chest. She was so surprised by his presence and the feel of him against her that she was unable to muster any more of a defense. "Let me go!" Her voice was pitched high with panic, and to her surprise, he immediately complied. She looked up, wary, as Devil took a few steps back, and she slumped against the car, trying to force back the fear that had sparked to life when his body had pressed in so close to hers. Gasping, she took several deep breaths as she struggled to calm her racing heart and push back the suffocating pressure that had begun to squeeze around her chest once he'd given her room to breathe. When she had gathered enough courage to do so, she looked up at Devil, expecting to see anger in his face. Instead, she found something else; he actually looked appalled by her reaction. Fear turned to chagrin and she found herself hurrying to reassure him.

"You scared me," she managed to say weakly, her fingers twisting together at her waist. "I'm sorry if I upset you." She licked her lips nervously as the gravel at her feet fell back to earth with a muted clatter. She scuffed the toe of her shoe and sent several pieces of gravel skittering away in an effort to cover the fact that the pebbles had risen off the ground and had begun to move in a circular pattern. It became easier to breathe when she realize that he hadn't noticed a thing and she relaxed a little more. As she calmed, the thought flittered through her mind that she hadn't lashed out at him in her fear, and she wondered at the fact.

Devil gave a short, surprised bark of laughter, drawing her attention back to him. "You're apologizing to me?" He asked, incredulous, "Shouldn't I be apologizing to you?" He watched a tentative smile waver at the corners of her mouth and took a step closer. "I didn't mean to frighten you," he said, his words low and soft. "I really couldn't help myself; I couldn't let you leave without saying goodbye." The soothing tone of his voice relaxed her an infinitesimal bit, and he slowly moved closer until he could touch her again. He frowned as she dropped her gaze to the ground, and her small body tensed all over again. It was then that he realized his whole approach to this tiny little woman had been all wrong; instead of simply thinking she wanted him as much as he did her and was trying to give the impression of resistance, she truly needed coaxing, needed to know she could say no without worrying about punishment. Her hesitant demeanor wasn't an act and was so opposed to what he was normally accustomed to, that it had taken him this long to realize he'd been gravely mistaken where she was concerned. She needed to be coaxed, seduced, and if there was one thing he was good at, it was seduction. Reaching out slowly, he tipped her face up with a long finger under her chin. He paused then, searching her silver eyes as his fingers curled themselves around her jaw. Leaning close, he continued to wait, giving her the chance to make up her mind.

Angeline's breath had locked in her throat and her heart beat erratically as large butterflies began to tumble in her stomach. She'd known this man for two months, and he'd been nothing but friendly and kind to her. Until today, he'd never given her any reason to believe that he was attracted to her; then again, she'd hadn't truly been paying attention until now. Until this moment, she'd done everything in her power to fight the fascination she felt towards him, had pretended she wasn't drawn to him, had convinced herself that any attraction between them was one sided, and that side had been her own. Even when he'd asked her out there had been an almost cavalier atmosphere between them that had made her think he was interested in simply being friends.

And now?

Now she was a hair's breadth away from kissing him or being kissed by him, and the blood in her veins was reaching boiling point; anticipation and impatience rose in her belly, causing her to feel the beginnings of frustration.

What was he waiting for? An engraved invitation?

Her lips parted of their own volition as his thumb brushed across them in a feather light caress. Back and forth, his touch tantalizing and light, until she was unable to help herself. With a little sound of capitulation, she closed the distance between them, throwing her arms around his neck and pulling him close enough to kiss.

The moment their lips touched, Angeline knew she was playing with fire.

Was flirting with danger.

She didn't care.

She welcomed the raging burn that swept through her and let it sweep her away; allowed it to incinerate everything but the sensuality of kissing him. Let it burn away the hesitation and the fear. A gnawing craving awoke in her, and she pressed herself as close to his warm, solid strength as she could. Without thinking about it, she twined her fingers into his dark hair, loving the way it felt against her fingertips and arched her body against his, seeking more of his heat, his strength, leaning up on her tip toes in an attempt to satisfy the sudden craving she felt for him.

Angeline was several inches shorter than he was, and Devil had to chuckle under his breath at the way she strained up onto her toes in order to kiss him. He lifted her easily against his chest and continued to kiss her, licking and nipping at her mouth as greedily as she was his. Devil liked her uninhibited reaction, and let her set the pace until it seemed as if they would both be consumed by fire where they stood. His hands roamed the contours of her back, learning her rounded curves until they were as familiar to him as his own body was.

The kiss end slowly as the first flames of passion eased and settled into hot, slow burning embers and Devil reluctantly pulled away. Angeline's body followed his naturally until she was leaning against him, her head lowered in order to rest her cheek against his chest. "I need to get back," she said quietly, "I need to take care of Nico," she added, using the cat as an excuse; what she *really* needed to do was step back and take stock before she found herself lost in something she would regret later. And she couldn't do that when Devil was kissing her and scattering her wits to the four winds. She kept her eyes down as Devil led her around the nose of his truck and held the door for her as she slid in, doing her best to not allow a single bit of her body to touch his; she hadn't imagined the sparks that jumped between them whenever they touched, and it was clear to her that with her control as shaky as it was, those sparks were very dangerous indeed.

They drove back to town, their conversation minimal as they each struggled to fill the tense, silent awareness between them. When Devil dropped her off in front of the bed and breakfast, Angeline watched him drive away, her mind a tumult of jumbled thoughts. She needed to talk to her grandmother, she decided, and quickly climbed the stairs to her room. She dialed the number, and waited on edge for the older woman to pick up. When she did, Angeline felt shock and surprise lance through her at her grandmother's first words:

"You've met him, haven't you?"

Angeline stammered. "What? Him? Grandmother, what are you talking about?"

Her grandmother's chuckle came loud and clear over the line. "I'm talking about the one you're destined for, of course." She paused to let her words sink in. "The one you've been waiting and searching for all your life; you've finally met him, haven't you?"

Angeline groaned. Why she was surprised that Constance knew more about what was going on than she did, she didn't know; her grandmother had always known more about things than she should. "No, Grandmother," she sighed, rubbing her eyes in an attempt to ward off the headache that was threatening to explode behind her eyes. "I mean, yes, I've met someone, but I don't think he's 'destined' for me." She took a deep breath. "I'm confused," she complained plaintively.

She heard her grandmother laugh again. "You're not confused, Angel," she told her soothingly. "Deep down, you know this devil is the one for you; you've just got to let Nature take its course."

"How did you know his name?" Angeline blurted out. A long pause answered her. Just as she became impatient, her grandmother answered, her tones similar to the ones used to explain something simple to a particularly dense child.

"My dear," she began, "Do you *really* need me to answer that question after all these years?" At Angeline's silence, Constance chuckled, and then went on. "All men are like your Devil, looking for just the right woman to make honest men of them. It is the way of things; every woman is destined for one man; some take longer to realize this, while others never do."

Angeline's romantic soul felt her grandmother's words and she felt the familiar wistful tug in her heart; she grew up praying every night that she would find her one true love, that she would recognize him immediately. She had thought Chris was destined to be her lifelong partner until that night almost a year ago. Now she knew better, and she found it easier to deny her grandmother's words in light of her experiences with Chris.

"Grandmother," she began slowly, striving to sound calm and steady, "Devil Damien isn't my destined lover; far from it. He's just someone I've met." A strange anger began a slow smolder in her gut, as she remembered the way he'd kissed her, even when she told him not to, that despite her reservations, he'd managed to make her to want, hell, to *crave* his kiss. Her cheeks heated at the memory of the kisses they had shared, at how her body had yearned for the touch of his. To her annoyance, her grandmother chuckled again. "And he's got you all knotted up," she cackled. "Has he kissed you?"

Angeline's disgruntled answer that in the end *she'd* kissed *him* sent her grandmother into peals of laughter.

"Don't fight it, my dearest," she counseled. She hung up before Angeline could respond, leaving her granddaughter sitting on her bed, more confused and more determined than ever to avoid Devil as much as possible. It was simply too dangerous for her peace of mind to pursue any kind of relationship with him. Besides, not knowing when or if Jessop would show up put a damper on everything. Then, not understanding the need to do so, she crawled between the sheets of her bed and cried herself to sleep, though the sun hadn't yet gone down.

As for Devil, he returned to the beach, his insides knotted, his body tense. Melissa noticed his surly attitude, and mentioned it to Jess; their heads close together, they whispered conspiratorially. They had seen his reaction to Angeline, and hers to him; they had also seen the heated embrace they had shared on the rock and Devil's determined face as he followed Angeline up the trail later.

"Poor thing," Jess sighed, shaking her head in mock sadness.

"He doesn't know what to do with himself," Melissa giggled.

"And I don't think she has any more of a clue than he does!" Jess rejoined.

They put their heads together and plotted various ways to get Devil and Angeline together to stoke the fires more, to give them a gentle *nudge* into each other's arms. When caught by their husbands in the midst of their planning, they simply smiled angelically.

~CHAPTER THREE~

Their first opportunity came two weeks later when Melissa decided to host a dinner party at her house. She made sure to issue an invitation to Angeline, insisting that she join them. She also invited Devil, warning him of dire consequences if he didn't show up.

The night of the dinner party arrived, and Angeline dressed carefully, taking time to finger style her short curls and apply a light touch of blush and lip-gloss. She told herself she was taking her time so she could make a good impression on the assembled guests, but deep down she knew she was doing it in case Devil attended. She hadn't been able to put the kisses they had shared out of her mind, and much to her frustration, had tossed and turned many nights as feverish memories invaded her dreams. She huffed out her breath in annoyance as an errant thought wondered if Devil would be there tonight, and applied a thin coat of brown mascara to her thick eyelashes. Finally, she took a step back and studied herself in the mirror. She wore a pale coral colored sundress with thin straps that tied behind her neck and strappy white sandals. Studying herself critically, she returned to the sink and removed all the makeup, then reapplied a light coat of coral lip gloss to her full mouth. Stepping back, she nodded at herself in approval and after making sure Nico had food and water for the evening, grabbed her small purse and wrap, and left her room.

Michael and Melissa lived a few minutes outside of town, and Angeline found herself pulling into the drive soon after leaving her room. She sat, staring up at the beautiful home, the gardens in full bloom, and warm light shining from the windows. As she stepped from her car, another pulled up, and she immediately recognized Devil. She felt butterflies flutter in her belly as she watched him unfold himself from the vehicles interior. He wore a stark white button down shirt; the cuffs rolled back to his elbows to reveal muscular forearms, and faded jeans that hugged his well muscled thighs snugly. Angeline felt her stomach give up the flutters and completely flip when he smiled at her, his dark eyes warm and appreciative. He crossed the few feet that separated them and took her hands, leaning in to kiss her cheek as he did.

"You look beautiful," he murmured softly.

Angeline swallowed hard and then smiled. "Thank you," she breathed, "you look good yourself." She grimaced to herself at the breathless sound of her voice and struggled to quell the little voice in her head that pointed out just how yummy his backside looked in those jeans and wondered if he would kiss her again tonight. She told that voice firmly to shut the hell up, telling it that she did *not* want him to kiss her again, and she *wasn't* interested in what his backside looked like, and while they were on the subject, she wasn't interested in him in *that* way.

Oh, stop lying, that voice taunted, *you want to jump his bones so badly you can't stand it.*

Angeline scowled to herself, telling the voice to shut up and leave her alone as Devil tucked her hand into the crook of his elbow and led her to the house, casting surreptitious glances at her as they went, wondering why she looked so disgruntled. He leaned closer and whispered in her ear, "Smile; people are going to think that I dragged you here against your will." His words surprised a chuckle from her, and to his relief, her expression cleared into a pleasant mien and she relaxed beside him. He saw Michael smile and shake his head as Melissa sent a satisfied smirk across the room to Jessica as they entered together. He shot a halfhearted glare at the scheming women and groaned inwardly when they both simply grinned widely back at him, mischief shining in their eyes. He forgot to feel put upon when he caught sight of Angeline and himself reflected in a glass door and it struck him how good they looked and moved together; his darkness was balanced by her golden lightness and her petite, almost ethereal presence seemed to offset his own brawn; Angeline's head came just to his shoulder and she carried her petite frame with innate grace, and he basked in the sheer loveliness that seemed to emanate from her.

The coral pink of her dress lent a kiss of color to her lightly tanned cheeks, and her silver eyes glowed with curiosity as they entered the main room of the house, where it appeared everyone in town was gathered. He stood back and watched as she moved away from him to greet those she knew, and was introduced to those she didn't, her manner open and friendly. He listened to her laughter float over the noise of the guests talking, and felt his body react to the sound. He followed her progress through the room and unconsciously edged closer, his hands knotting at his side, as she paused to speak to a young sheriff's deputy and he leaned down to say something in her ear, his eyes delving down the front of her dress. Devil growled low in his throat—there was no need to bend that far down, no matter how petite she was. Angeline heard the rumble of threat Devil made, and her eyes flickered to his in puzzlement as she responded to the comment and moved away, making her excuses. She reached him and smiled up at him, her words hissing from between her teeth. Her small hand came to rest on his forearm, and he felt the not so subtle pressure of her grip. "What are you doing?" She could feel the possessiveness rolling off him in waves, and she followed her natural inclination to exert a little calm over him; almost immediately, he relaxed a small measure, and she did too.

Devil, unaware of what she was doing, but still feeling the lingering effects of his irritation with the sheriff's deputy, swept her with a long look, his dark eyes touching her bare shoulders and the deep décolletage of her dress as surely as his fingers. He felt a possessive knot curl in his gut and his hand clamped down on her arm in a gentle but firm grip, dragging her out to the relative privacy of the patio. He plucked the wrap from her fingers and swept it around her shoulders, knotting the ends together between her breasts. For a long, breathless moment, his knuckles grazed the skin of her sternum, his fingers delving just inside the edge of her neckline, a half-formed thought taking wing through his mind that he needed to mark her in some way, make her permanently his, make it possible to keep her all for himself. Angeline saw the burning intent in his dark eyes and she took a step backwards, breaking the contact.

"I asked you a question," she said in a slightly breathless voice, "I look up, and you're glowering and growling like a bad tempered bear." She took a deep breath to reign in the surge of annoyance she felt rising in her chest. She wasn't going to let this man dictate her actions, nor with whom she would or wouldn't socialize.

She learned her lesson from Chris; the moment she allowed another man to dictate to her was the moment he would have complete control over her, and she didn't want to live like that ever again. Her stubborn determination must have shown on her face because Devil's expression relaxed on its own, without any help from her.

Devil wiped his face with his hand, trying to understand his own reaction to the deputy angling to see down the front of her dress. He had been overcome by such an astoundingly strong feeling of possessiveness at that moment that he could see himself pounding the poacher to a pulp, could see himself dragging her deeper into the shadows and using his mouth to leave his mark on the fragrant, soft as silk skin of her throat, but somehow knew she wouldn't appreciate it if he told her, especially considering that he didn't have any particular claim on her affections or her body as of yet. He glanced at her, taking in the crossed arms, the tapping foot, and the mutinous expression and felt sanity regain a foothold over him.

"Angel," he said softly, reaching out to curl his fingers around the back of her neck. He pulled her unresisting into his embrace. "Forgive me," he murmured, his fingers drawing circles on the nape of her neck, "I don't know what I was doing." The longer he touched her, the easier it became to calm down, to allow the Neanderthal man that had awakened deep inside to go back to sleep, to let the annoyance burn away to make room for the dizzying rush of desire that was steadily growing.

Angeline stood, having lost her train of thought as her body and mind centered on what his fingers were doing. She felt the fingers of his other hand graze the edges of her dress, warm and seeking. She leaned into him, mesmerized by his dark eyes as he watched his fingers touch the bare skin of her collarbone. Her breath came in shallow wisps, fanning his face as she tipped her head back and allowed his touch to travel the long line of her throat. His head dipped and he caught her mouth with his in a kiss of achingly sweet slowness. Angeline sighed against his mouth, giving herself up to the sensations he wrought in her. Without thinking, she allowed herself to let go, to give in to the sweet, fiery sensations awakening in her nerve endings, and it wasn't until she heard Devil's groan that she realized what she had done. That for a small amount of time, she allowed herself to forget that she harbored a secret and allowed herself free rein to experience his kiss on every level possible. Now, it was too late; her need was too entwined with his to safely withdraw without his noticing.

A loud shout of laughter tore them apart, sending an electric jolt of shock through them both. Devil looked up to see Melissa stepping out onto the patio, her eyes peering into the shadows in which they stood.

"Dinner's ready," she called softly.

She turned and cast a look back over her shoulder, then left them, her step complacent and slow, as if she had no idea whatsoever who happened to be in the shadows or what they happened to be doing. She smiled to herself, though, having seen the silent interplay between Angeline and Devil moments before he dragged her outside; it seemed things were progressing at a very satisfying rate. She made a mental note to confer with Jess at the earliest possible moment; if things continued as smoothly as they were, there would be another Bounty Cove wedding in the very near future.

Devil and Angeline took a few moments to gather their wits and calm their breathing and racing hearts; as carefully as she could, Angeline took control of her hunger, doing it quickly but carefully so that Devil wouldn't notice, and telling herself she had nothing to be embarrassed over; she wasn't a teenager who'd been caught making out with her boyfriend on the sly—though a small part of her felt as if she was and had—and reminding herself that there was nothing wrong with stealing a few kisses at a dinner party. Gaining control over that portion of her psyche, Angeline turned her attention to the man beside her, a man who seemed to take great pleasure in turning her world upside down. She watched him closely, alert for any sign that he realized what she'd inadvertently done, but to her relief, he seemed oblivious. He gave her an unabashed grin before dropping another wit scattering kiss on her all too eager mouth. She sighed into him again, and then giggled a moment later when she heard his growl of frustration. The reluctance she read in his expression mirrored her own, causing an odd warming in her chest; it appeared that Devil was just as ensnared as she was. Smiling slightly, she took his hand and sighed in relief to herself as they left the shadows together, neither one speaking. They didn't look at each other, either; for Angeline her emotions were still too new, too raw to examine closely in the light of day. Devil made her want to throw caution to the wind and for a few brief moments in his arms, she had; the memory left her feverish with remembered desire and cold with fear in turns. Devil, on the other hand, felt a righteous swell of smugness; Angeline wanted him, he hadn't been wrong about that. He tightened his fingers around hers a tiny bit, and pulled her closer to his side, vowing to himself to do everything in his power to do whatever it took to keep her there.

They reentered the house and let themselves be seated next to each other at the long table. Devil told Angeline, briefly, how he had designed the house, then had given the plans to his friends, Michael and Melissa, after a crazed old woman had torched their first home.

Angeline willed herself to relax and enjoy the meal, and she felt a rush of gratitude at Devil's efforts to help her do so. Deep in the pit of her stomach, however, she felt a knot that refused to loosen; she knew she wouldn't be able to hold back the flames of desire that seemed to jump to life whenever they were alone together; she wasn't sure she wanted to anymore, and the thought left her shaky and jittery, and more than a little annoyed with herself; where was her determination to keep this man at arm's length? What was it about him that left her breathless and bothered on more than one level whenever he so much as looked at her in a particular way? Memories of the way his eyes had looked moments before he kissed her left her feeling flushed, and grateful to be sitting down; had she been standing, she was certain her weak knees would have refused to support her. She forced her mind from the memories of his touch and concentrated on the meal in front of her. Drawing on the air of friendly conviviality around her, Angeline took herself under control and concentrated on making light conversation with Jessica to her left, trying to ignore Devil's presence beside her, his magnetic pull on her difficult to disregard.

"Do you plan to settle here, then?" Jess asked, curiosity shining from her blue eyes.

Angeline swallowed the food in her mouth, nodding as she did so. "I've been thinking about it," she began. "I'm a veterinarian, and I noticed Bounty Cove doesn't have a vet's office for small animals. I thought it might be worth opening one." She shrugged a little. "I'd just need to find a place large enough to accommodate the office and a home."

She noticed several people were listening to this exchange and lowered her head, a light blush staining her cheeks. Without realizing it, she'd become the center of concentrated attention, and it made her self-conscious.

Out of the corner of her eye, she saw Devil shift toward her, and felt his hand cover hers in her lap. She felt the reassuring squeeze and lifted her eyes to his with a small smile of relief; something about Devil Damien made it easy to be herself in this roomful of new friends, made it easier to be the center of attention without worrying about giving away her secret. She looked down the table as an older man that had been introduced to her as Christian Witcher, Melissa's father, cleared his throat.

"Dev, you should show her the Larsen place," he suggested with a wink and pointing his salad fork in her direction, "It might be just what she's looking for."

Angeline saw Devil nod thoughtfully. "You're right," he said. "I think it might be perfect, actually." He turned to Angeline and explained, "The Larsen house is a split level ranch with an in-law suite situated in the back. It's a rather large cottage, actually, so it might be just what you're thinking of."

Angeline's mind raced over the possibilities; the idea of starting fresh appealed to her, and she grasped at the opportunity eagerly. Excitement sizzled through her nerves as she asked, "When can I see it?" No one except Angeline noticed the lights over the table blink several times in rapid succession. She took a moment to lock down the excess excitement she felt and the lights returned to their steady glowing. She noticed the excited grins on several faces around her and took her emotions under firmer control until she was certain she wasn't leaking every spark of thought and emotion she felt to those around her.

Devil's eyes touched her, taking in the rosy glow of her cheeks and the bright silvery sparkle of her gaze. He felt a rush of deep affection for her in that moment, and didn't bother to quell it, letting it spread through him, allowing it to grow. Angeline seemed so small and vulnerable sitting next to him; just looking at her made him, and he was sure everyone at this table, want to defend and protect her. Yet, there was an innate strength that flowed deep and strong within her, and the more he grew to know her, the more he appreciated that strength; the fact that she was excited about the prospect of creating a life for herself in Bounty Cove, despite the obvious demons still haunting her, made her all the more remarkable. He kept his hand over hers on her lap, enjoying the warmth of her fingers in his palm and squeezed them again, sharing her enthusiasm.

Angeline saw the new look in Devil's eye, and felt a new, deeper spark of—what? Friendship? Camaraderie? Respect?—She didn't know, and wondered at it; there was a subtle shift in the emotional energy she felt emanating from the man beside her and she felt her spirit reaching out to his, yearning to make contact with what it saw as a kindred soul. She looked down at their hands, still resting in her lap, their fingers still entwined. A rush of sweetness flowed through her and she returned her eyes to his face, her lips parted in a silent gasp of surprise as she realized how very close she was to falling completely in love with him. It was happening so very fast, but it felt *right,* and it left her feeling nervous and exhilarated. She searched his face, and saw the fires of want still glowing there, matching her own, but now they were tempered by a newer, gentler emotion. The sounds of the dinner party faded from her hearing as her attention became more centered on the man beside her. It took every shred of concentration to remember what they'd been discussing. "Dev?" She managed to croak, "The house?"

Devil fought down the urge to kiss her lush mouth, to test this strange, new emotion he felt concerning her, remembering just in time where they were. Though he was sure there were a couple of scheming women watching on with interest, he was sure they would be shocked by the kiss he so desperately wanted to plant on Angeline's soft mouth. He saw her waiting expectantly on his answer, and had to search his mind before remembering what she had asked.

He leaned in, his lips brushing her cheek. "Anytime you want, Angel," he said softly in her ear. He didn't miss the answering shiver that sizzled through her small frame. He lifted their entwined fingers and kissed hers, enjoying the way her silver eyes darkened to glowing pewter and the way her breath stilled momentarily. He released her fingers and returned his attention to the guests around him, and finished him meal with hearty gusto. Angeline, he noticed, barely touched her food. Leaning closer again, he murmured, "If I'd known this is how you'd react, I wouldn't have whispered in your ear." He nuzzled her jaw briefly. "Melissa's going to think you aren't enjoying yourself, Angel." He chuckled softly as Angeline's jaw tightened stubbornly, and she picked up her fork. Though she didn't respond to his goading, the look she shot him contained barely concealed promises of dire consequences if he didn't stop distracting her. After all, it would be entirely his fault if she hurt Melissa's feelings in any way; she was certain he knew the effect he had on her, and was using that knowledge to more firmly ensnare her. Taking her riotous emotions more firmly in hand, she made a vow to not allow him to distract her anymore than he already had.

All this while, unseen by either Angeline or Devil, Melissa and Jess were exchanging barely concealed grins of mirth; a few more nudges in the right direction, and their job would be finished. Their husbands each saw the gleeful anticipation in their wives' eyes and simply shook their heads; there was no force known to man or Nature that would prevent these two from playing matchmaker or stop the wheels once Melissa and Jess had set them in motion. To attempt to rein the two friends in was akin to trying control a pair of tornados with a lasso; it simply couldn't be done.

After the desert course had been cleared, the guests returned to the rest of the house. Devil pulled Angeline out onto the patio, and onto the makeshift dance floor. Angeline followed slowly, still trying to sort through her feelings about the man who now pulled her into his arms. He annoyed and tantalized her in turns, left her breathless and scatter brained with a simple look, and could make her angry with yet another look. The havoc his kisses left her senses in was something she couldn't examine too closely without feeling feverish. He was dangerous to her sense of balance, and yet here she was, dancing with him in the warm, intimate dusk of the patio, almost breathless with anticipation of another kiss. She shivered as the tense awareness between them heightened another notch.

"This reminds me of high school," she said quietly with a laugh, trying to keep the mood between them light. "Although back then, I was lucky to be asked to dance by anyone." Devil leaned back and held her at arms' length, skepticism plain on his face.

At his disbelieving look, Angeline elaborated. "I was rather awkward," she admitted with a sheepish smile. "I wore glasses, and had a mouthful of metal, and was very short and chubby." She laughed at the recollection. "Mostly I danced with my sister's boyfriends; I suspect she made them do it." She shrugged lightly. "Cassandra could get men to do whatever she wanted back then; she still can, I expect." She lapsed into thoughtful silence for a moment, and then said, "She meant well, I'm sure."

Devil was having a hard time picturing the petite, willowy woman in his arms as short and chubby with glasses and braces. "I'm not sure I believe you," he told her lightly. "I demand photographic proof."

Her trilling laughter floated over him. "Okay," she said as he twirled her in his arms. "But I warn you, it won't be pretty." She stepped away, and moved into a pool of light, digging through her small clutch purse. After several minutes of searching, she produced a photo of herself and an older, taller, dark haired girl. The two teenagers had their arms around each other's waists, and they were smiling brightly on the deck of a ship, their hair teased by a breeze. Devil took it and scrutinized the photo closely; she hadn't been exaggerating. He could easily see which girl was Angeline; he'd never seen a truer case of the ugly duckling transforming into a swan, and while the rest of her had dramatically changed over the years, those silver eyes of hers hadn't. He returned the photo without comment, and was happy to see she was grinning cheekily.

"I did warn you," she told him, laughing.

She put the photo away and gazed up at him, suddenly realizing just how sexy he really was. His warm brown eyes glowed in the pale light of garden lamps and the wind teased dark hair streaked lighter by the summer sun. His shoulders were broad, his arms muscular. Her eyes drifted to his lips, and she shivered as she recalled just how perfectly made for kissing they were.

As if reading her thoughts, Devil pulled her slowly to him and kissed her, his mouth warm and seeking on hers. She sighed into the embrace and let herself get lost for several moments. She felt so secure, so safe in his arms; it had been longer than she could remember since she'd last felt this way, if she ever had. She sighed into the kiss and gave herself up to it. Several minutes later, the sound of footsteps pulled them apart. She was the only one who noticed the garden lamps flared suddenly brighter for a moment before returning to their normal warm glow. She tamped down on the frustrated surge she felt in her gut at the interruption. She turned to see Melissa and Michael walking hand in hand into the twilit garden, their voices low.

Angeline felt a wash of jealousy at the sight, and she turned away, taking herself out of Devil's embrace; feeling Michael and Melissa so content, so happy, so *in love* reminded her of the emptiness that existed in her own life. Without a word to Devil, she walked back into the house in search of her wine glass. It was sitting on the breakfast bar in the kitchen; exactly where she'd set it when Devil had pulled her outside. Her hand shook as she picked it up and took a large gulp. She drained the glass and poured more, drinking it quickly. She turned as she heard Devil speak her name, and suddenly, she felt brittle, as if she might shatter. Something was wound up tight in her chest, threatening to overwhelm her and shatter her control even as it threatened to suffocate her. She quickly brushed her hand across her eyes to wipe away the tears that had suddenly formed. She set her glass down carefully, and went to him.

"Goodbye," she said quietly, taking his hand and shaking it. "Thank you for a lovely evening. Would you mind making my goodbyes to Michael and Melissa?" She touched her temple lightly. "I feel a headache coming on." It wasn't a lie, but it wasn't exactly the truth, either; she needed to be alone, to sort through her feelings, and a dinner party at her new friends' home wasn't the place to do it. A heavy tension was forming at the base of her skull, and from a lifetime of experience, knew that if she didn't leave, the whole party would soon be feeling irrationally jealous or extremely frustrated in short order. Already she was holding herself together so tightly she was beginning to shake with the effort.

She turned on her heel and made her way out the front of the house to her car, not allowing Devil time to protest, and hoping he would accept her explanation without question; hoping she could get away before the tears truly began. She slid into the driver's seat, and wasn't surprised when Devil was there, holding the door open. Why she thought he'd just let her go with only her feeble explanation, she didn't know.

"What's wrong?" He asked gently, his eyes glowing softly with concern and confusion as he took in her pale and drawn face.

Angeline's mouth turned down. "Nothing," she denied, shaking her head. "Everything," she said, this time contradicting herself. She made an impatient sound and tried again. "I don't know," she shrugged, "I'm just tired, that's all." She pulled the door shut, forcing him to step back and rolled the window down. "I'm sorry," she said as she put the car in gear. She backed down the drive until she could turn around and drove away.

Devil stood, watching her tail lights disappear into the night, his hands shoved deep into his pockets, confusion written across his face. She was lying, and he knew it; he'd felt the way her ardor had cooled when she'd seen their friends in the garden, had heard the barely suppressed tears in her voice, but didn't know what had caused her sudden mood change. With a heavy sigh, and a shake of his head, he returned to the dinner party only to make his farewell an hour later; without Angeline there, he saw no reason to stay.

~CHAPTER FOUR~

A month later, and Devil was ready to pull his hair out; Angeline had spent the last several weeks avoiding him, and everyone else it seemed, like the plague. He was frustrated that he hadn't gotten as much as a glimpse of her since the night of the dinner party. She didn't take his calls, and she changed her habits, going so far as to stop taking her lunch in the park and having her morning and evening meals delivered to her room at the inn. So he buried himself in his work, deciding to give her the time and space she obviously wanted, and took whatever jobs he could, working until he was exhausted at the end of the day so he could come home and sleep without feverish dreams of a slip of a woman with quicksilver eyes, warm and passionate in his arms.

What Devil didn't know was that Angeline simply wasn't ready to face him and attempt to explain her sudden departure, especially since she wasn't entirely sure she understood it herself. Something had happened when she saw Melissa and Michael walking in the twilit garden, and an overwhelming, all encompassing fear and sadness had swamped her. After a month, she still didn't have any answers. So, in an effort to prevent the moment when she would have to figure things out, Angeline did everything in her power to avoid Devil, turning down invitations to dinner or the beach from Melissa and Jessica, worried that Devil would be included. She didn't return his calls, going so far as to ask Miss Blanche to take a message whenever he did call, and becoming irrationally angry when the messages eventually stopped. Yet, perversely, she longed to see him, to hear his voice, to feel his touch again, and it wore against her determination to keep her distance. The worst was late at night when she was alone in her single bed, Nico curled up at her feet; in those long, solitary hours between midnight and dawn, her dreams were haunted by the memory of his dark laughing eyes, his lopsided grin, by the low, soft velvet of his voice, by the heat of his kiss, by the warm silk of his touch. The dreams left her sleepless, distracted, and more determined than ever to keep her distance; Devil Damien simply wasn't good for her peace of mind and he was dangerous to her control. As a result, she isolated herself from one and all and suffered the loneliness in silence and, if she were honest with herself, in pain.

She was so intent on trying to forget Devil and his kisses, that she didn't notice Chris's arrival in town. It wasn't until she came out to her car one morning a week after the dinner party and found all four of her tires slashed that she knew he was a lot closer than she realized; after all, he was the only one she could think of who would vandalize her car. She was a new arrival in town, and she was fairly confident that no one in Bounty Cove knew her well enough to hold a grudge against her, not even Devil, though if she were honest, she had been giving him more than enough reason to do so. And she was just as confident that he wouldn't do anything so malicious, no matter the motivation. She felt paranoia form in the pit of her stomach as she watched the tow truck operator hook her little car to the back of his truck, and she felt jumpy; she was certain Chris was watching form somewhere nearby; her skin crawled as she imagined his eyes roving over her body . And as she sat in the town garage later and watched her tires being replaced, she told herself that if Jessop so much as called her, or she saw his face again, she'd pack everything and disappear.

It felt like a hot, sharp needle of pain had taken roost in her gut whenever she thought of leaving Bounty Cove. She hated the idea of running again, but at this point, she simply didn't know what else to do; if she ran again, there was a small chance she could find someplace that Chris would never find her. Yet, she couldn't bear the thought of leaving Bounty Cove; something about the place called to her at a instinctual level, drew her into its heart, made her feel protected, as if she belonged. And though she was still avoiding him at this point in time, the thought of never, *ever,* seeing Devil again tore at her. That alone should have told her something right there, but she was still too confused to figure out what she was suppose to know. So she packed her belongings in her suitcase and beach bag, and waited, ready to flee at a moments' notice. However, the weeks passed and she didn't see hide or hair of Chris, and she allowed herself to relax again; perhaps the tire slashing had been a random act of an unknown troublemaker, and not her ex-fiancé as she had assumed. She knew she was trying to lie to herself, but still she unpacked her belongings and went back to her routine of secretly longing for Devil, and contrarily avoiding him.

The danger was closer than she realized.

Jessop watched her closely, learning her habits and patterns and knew about her visits to a real estate agent.

He followed her and seeing the large home and its attendant cottage situated on three acres told him all he needed to know: Angeline had no intentions of returning to him. He seethed inwardly as he watched the little blonde bitch through his binoculars as she toured the property. He could see her smiling; looking relaxed and happy, yet noting the circles under her eyes, knowing the mask of ease she wore was just that: a mask. Gloating in the knowledge that he made her wear that mask and knowing that beneath it, she was tense and afraid. She needed to be reminded of her place in the world. Something needed to be done to show her she didn't belong in this little backwater speck on the map. Chris followed her back to town and watched as she went back to her hotel. He hadn't figured out how to get her room number yet, but it was only a matter of time. He glanced at his watch and noted that it was almost lunch time; she would be going to pick up her lunch at the dingy diner across the street any moment.

He smiled to himself as Angeline paused at the front doors and called a greeting to Miss Blanche as she left.

"I'm going to lunch, Miss Blanche; can I bring you anything back?"

Blanche waved her hand and shook her head, saying, "June will bring something over on her lunch break, Dear, but thank you just the same."

Angeline gave the little old woman a smile; she reminded the younger woman forcefully of her grandmother, except this woman wasn't nearly as blatantly nosy.

She stepped out into the noon sun, putting her sunglasses on as she did, and skipped lightly down the steps. As she reached the bottom, she saw a movement out of the corner of her eye; she did a double take and skidded to a stop, fear and disbelief crashing through her when she realized who was walking toward her.

"Hello, Angeline," Chris said in an oily voice as he flashed his predatory smile. "Have you missed me?" He reached her and placed his hands on her upper arms. He leaned close and his mouth slid across hers, making her want to gag. She pulled back as far as she could, and winced as his fingers dug into her arms.

"What are you doing here?" She hissed through her teeth, though she knew what he was going to say, and feared she would start screaming when he did. She clamped her teeth together to keep from shaking.

"I'm taking you home," he said brightly. His friendly tone belied the hard, angry glint in his blue eyes.

Angeline ground her teeth together, pushing the scream down as anger raised its head in her chest, threatening to suffocate her. She wrenched herself out of his grasp, feeling the bite of his nails as she did. "I'm not going anywhere with you," she said tightly. "I'm home here in Bounty Cove; I have no desire to see you or Portland again." She stumbled backwards as he lunged at her, a hand curling around her throat as he slammed her up against her car.

His face was just a breath from hers as he said chillingly, "One way or another, you're coming home with me, Angeline, whether you like it or not."

She struggled against him as his mouth came down on hers, bruising and punishing. She felt her gorge rise and she felt dizzy. She felt the mounting tightness in her chest as the energy produced by her fear and anger grew to monumental proportions. She pushed the growing tide of power down, not wishing to leave a crater of destruction in the middle of Main Street and slammed her heel down on top of his foot, twisting and grinding it with all her might, allowing the energy raging inside her to give her extra strength. Chris howled and abruptly released her. She ducked under his arm and walked away as fast as she could, her head down, her senses tuned to the furious man behind her, ready to run if she needed to, her vision clouded with tears of anger; he'd done it again, shown up and proven to her that there was nowhere in the world that she could go that he wouldn't follow. She almost strangled on the sobs she fought to hold back and didn't see Devil until she plowed right into the solid wall of his chest. His hands came up to hold her steady as she stumbled against him. She almost laughed in relief to see him; she ignored the hot tingle his hands touching her caused as the worst of the pent up power bled away in a rush of relief; suddenly, she no longer felt as if she were in danger. *Devil will make it better,* she thought with a feeling of reprieve. At that moment, she was so glad to see him she felt a dizzy rush of power surge through her and she knelt suddenly, pretending to tie her shoelace. Making sure Devil stood between herself and Jessop, Angeline touched the hot asphalt beneath her feet and released some of the energy seething through her nerves into the earth. She stood again slowly, and tried to smile as she realized there was worry in his expression.

"Is everything all right?" He asked her, concern lacing his tone. "Who is this?" He continued, gesturing to Chris.

Chris stepped forward, his attitude arrogant and his hand out to shake Devil's. "Chris Jessop," he said, introducing himself, "Angie's fiancé."

Angeline hissed and took a step toward him, her small hands clenching into fists, "Don't call me that," she spat with a feral snarl, finding it easy to be a little braver than she would have been if Devil hadn't been there to back her up.

Chris pretended to be puzzled. "I've always called you Angie," he said with a tone of mock hurt. "Why would you want me to stop now, darling?"

"Don't call me your fiancé!" She shrieked, fisting her hands in her hair, "I ended it Chris! Deal with it and get over it! I don't want to marry you!" Once again, the energy began to build as she struggled not to lose her temper. A sudden hot breeze tore down the street, tearing at their clothing and causing the American flag in the town square to snap loudly against its tether with its passing. Giving the bane of her existence a look of pure loathing, she stalked away, her back stiff, doing everything in her power to keep the innocent bystanders on the street from engaging in the acts of murder she felt like committing. She slammed into the diner, patrons giving her a wide berth as she stalked to the back and slid into a booth.

Chris made to go after her, a flash of rage momentarily contorting his features; Devil's hand against his chest stopped him.

"I think she's made herself clear," he said calmly. "Why don't you do as she says and leave her alone from now on?" His dark eyes flicked to meet Chris's cool blue gaze. Jessop dropped his gaze to Devil's hand pushing lightly against his chest.

"If you don't remove your hand," he said coolly, "I will have you charged; I'm a lawyer and I will use every trick in the book to make an assault charge stick."

Devil's hand dropped slowly to his side as he chuckled. "You can try," he told the shorter man insolently. "But I don't think you'll find much help from law enforcement in town. You see," he continued in a cold drawl, nodding to the three men who'd paused in their own activities when they'd heard Angeline scream at the stranger, "We tend to take a dim view of men who accost women in the street, especially when the woman in question doesn't want your attention." He watched as a flicker of panic flared in Chris's eyes as he became aware of how large the bystanders were. “I suggest you go back to wherever you came from, and forget about Angeline, because she’s doing her best to forget about you.” He gave a short, polite nod to Jessop and followed Angeline into the diner where she had taken refuge.

Chris Jessop stood next to his car, speechless, anger surging through his veins. He decided to lay low for a little while and allow Angeline time to relax. Once she had, he would try again, but this time, he would make sure she was alone. As he got into his car and sped away, Michael Kemper, Jamie Andrews, and Pat O’Dell went about their business.

Devil found Angeline huddled in a booth in the back of the diner, her face shielded behind a menu. He slid into the booth across the table from her, and just sat, silent and watching. Angeline tried to ignore the tremors that shook her fingers, and she tightened her grip on the menu as it began to shake. She stared at the words, unseeing and uncomprehending, her ears straining to pick up any clue to what Devil was thinking. Finally unable to put it off any longer, she lowered the menu and looked at him. She was surprised to see a mild look of curiosity on his face; his eyes were a different story. They brimmed with questions and concern. She took a deep breath and let it out slowly.

“Yes,” she said suddenly, “I was engaged to him, and yes, I broke it off.” She laughed bitterly. “He wasn’t who I thought he was.”

Devil leaned in closely and dropped his voice to a husky whisper. “So who was he?” He asked, keeping his voice low, “a woman in disguise?”

Angeline’s lips twitched into a reluctant smile as she shook her head to dispel the shivers that ran riot throughout her body whenever he dropped his voice that low. "He just wasn't right for me," she said. "Let's just leave it at that."

Devil could tell there was something she wasn't telling him, and though it annoyed him that she wouldn't confide in him, he left it alone; he was sure she would enlighten him when she was ready. He was simply glad to finally see her again and to hear her voice; all that was left to make his day perfect was the warmth of her touch. He noticed her fingers were tearing the paper placemat on the table in front of her to shreds; he grinned to himself at the ready-made excuse to touch her and gently laid his fingers on top of hers to still them. She balked at the contact and pulled her hands away quickly.

Sensing, rather than seeing his puzzlement, Angeline tried to smile, but failed miserably. A tear fell to the tabletop. "Please don't," she whispered as silverware quietly rattled against the tabletop and she automatically kicked the table leg beneath her to disguise the vibrations. She scooted out of the booth suddenly and stood, her expression stricken, as the light above the table flickered erratically before burning out with a loud pop. Without a look or word, she fled the diner, ignoring him when he called after her.

~CHAPTER FIVE~

Angeline drove away in her car half-blinded by hot, confused tears. Her thoughts and feelings were a tangled mess, and she needed time to sort herself out before she blew something apart with the force of the emotions roiling in her gut; the rattling silverware and burned out light were harbingers of worse to come if she didn't get herself in hand soon. Before she caused anyone else to feel the uncertainty and doubt that swirled through her thoughts. Her hands shook as residual fear and anger caused by seeing Chris crashed through her and she gagged violently as she relived his unwelcomed kiss. The nausea was so powerful she pulled to the side of the road and opened the car door. Moments later, she was doubled over and heaving, the remains of her midmorning snack onto the gravel. A heartbeat later, as she gasped and wiped her mouth with the back of her hand, giddy relief washed over her as she remembered Devil coming to her rescue, getting between Chris and herself long enough for her to escape, and she found herself laughing in relief. Her stomach calmed and she straightened up and pulled the door shut. Without really thinking about it, she drove out the beach where she had first kissed Devil. She threw the car in park and scrambled out as fast as she could. She practically sprinted down the steep trail, reckless and wild, desperate to reach the water's edge.

As she reach the shore line her pace quickened and she threw herself into the waves, letting them wash over and buffet her. The salty water washed away the brine of her tears and eased the ache of her sobs. She felt the touch of a rip current against her legs and briefly considered letting it take her; after all, to do so would guarantee her that Chris would never bother her again. Reason reasserted itself when she realized that if she allowed herself to be taken by the tide, she'd never see her family or Devil again and she swam parallel to the shore until she broke free of the current's grip. She got her feet underneath herself and stumbled back to the water line and collapsed onto the wet sand, turning over onto her back to lift her face to the sun. The water continued to wash around her body, easing her tension and sweeping away her troubles. She felt the grit of the sand as her fingers flexed deep into the sand, and felt it rub between her clothing and skin, irritating and rubbing her raw, and she sat up to peel her wet clothing off until she was clad in nothing but her bra and panties. She walked higher up the beach and laid out her wet clothing to dry in the hot sun, and draped herself across a flat rock to soak the heat into her bones and blood, allowing the warmth to evaporate the last of her clamoring nerves.

As her turmoil calmed, she relived the fleeting touch of Devil's hand on hers, seeing the concern in the gesture now that she'd calmed enough to think straight. She'd been so relieved to see him, to hear his voice again that the moment his hand touched hers, her brain had misfired, overwhelmed by the sheer sensation of his skin on hers, of the sight of his crooked smile and warm brown eyes, the sound of his low and velvet-smooth voice. It had been a sensory overload, and she'd bolted for the door as fast as she could. Now, with her fright and anger at seeing Chris again evaporated, she was able to think clearly, and she began to assess her reactions and feelings where Devil Damien was concerned.

By the time she flipped onto her belly to warm her back, she'd reached the conclusion that when it came to Devil Damien, she was less than objective; when he was close, when he touched her or kissed her, she forgot everything but the way he made her heart thump hard and fast in her chest and made it difficult to draw a breath. That she simply wanted to lose herself in him and the cravings he stirred in her blood. And while she was at it, it was time to acknowledge her feelings the night of the dinner party at Melissa's; she'd been, for the first time since meeting the Kempers, jealous of the love that her new friend shared with her husband. It had panged in her gut and chest, had strangled her until her throat had closed and tears threatened. Yet at the same time, she'd been frightened. Terrified that, though it felt as if Fate was handing her Devil on a silver platter, that, in the end, it was all just a cosmic joke, and her heart would end up being the punch line. That the moment she let him into her life completely, and he learned about her gift, he would turn his back on her and she'd once again, find herself isolated and alone. On the verge of tossing away her carefully cultivated caution on such a huge gamble, she'd pulled back, had distanced herself from Devil, in order to protect her fragile heart.

It was a difficult pill to swallow when she realized she'd been behaving foolishly for the past month, but eventually, she did. With a sigh to herself, she closed her eyes, and prayed she hadn't been too idiotic to deserve a second chance.

When she grew too warm, she returned to the water to cool her overheated skin, and then walked along the water's edge, in search of shells, sea glass, and pebbles. She sang to herself, a tuneless song without words, and the sound carried on the afternoon breeze to Devil as he watched her from a vantage point half way down the trail. After she'd escaped the diner, he'd followed, worried that in her current state she'd accidently hurt herself. He'd pulled into the space beside her car as she had disappeared down the trail, and had hurried to catch up with her, witnessing her headlong rush down the dirt path and feeling nausea gather in his gut as he imagined her tripping and tumbling to the bottom. He'd followed her down swiftly, reaching the vantage point just as she reached the bottom, ready to recklessly sprint down the trail as she had if it looked like she needed help.

He'd seen her throw herself into the water, had heard the gasping sobs she cried on the wind, and had witnessed that moment of almost-decision to flirt with Fate as the tide pulled against her. He began to breathe again as she made her way back to the beach, and settled in to keep watch as she simply collapsed on the sand, lying still as the water continued to bathe her. His mouth had gone dry when she had pulled her wet clothing from her body and had stretched out on the sun-warmed rocks further up the beach.

Now, he watched her gambol and play in the surf, hearing her trilling laughter as she played tag with the waves as they rushed up the sand. He watched as she danced along the water's edge, her movements carefree and unconsciously sensual. He watched as she suddenly stopped, and dropped to her knees in the sand, and saw the stillness fall over her. Her face lifted to the sky and she didn't move; Devil was struck by how much like a wild pagan woman she looked, half-naked and at one with Nature. Unable to resist, he gave into the gut deep urging he felt to go to her.

Angeline was unaware she was being watched; her attention was turned inward as she knelt in the wet sand. Patiently, she unraveled her thoughts and feelings, carefully laying each one out for examination. She wasn't at all surprised to find that most of the tangle concerned Devil and the feelings he had awakened in her. Slowly, patiently, she held each thought, each feeling, up to the light and studied it, turning it this way and that in her mind, her hands unconsciously moving as they would if she were truly working out a knotted tangle of yarn and letting her heart speak to her when her mind couldn't make heads or tails of something. She organized each strand until they lay ordered and clear in her mind, until she could separate her heart from her thoughts and the confusion fell away. That she had fallen in love with Devil was patently clear, and though the thought sent little tremors of panic through her, she carefully stifled those feelings to think clearly; Devil had truly never given her any reason to be afraid of him; it had been her own senseless panic that had clouded her judgment and had led her to be afraid. Remembering the relief she'd felt at seeing him again in the street told her more than she'd realized at the time, but it was more than time to listen to what her heart had known all along; Devil Damien was a man she could trust. She could hand him her secrets, her heart, and know without a doubt that he would carefully guard them. Calmness fell over her as she reached this conclusion, and she reveled in the hot kiss of the sun and the wet sting of the salt water on her skin; it stirred her senses, tweaking them until she was sensitized to the slightest change in her environment. She knew he was there, standing behind her, before she heard his voice softly call to her. She had come here to clear her mind and find answers; it would seem as if she had gotten at least one: did he feel the same irresistible pull between them that she did? Obviously, he did, otherwise why had he followed her? She remained still, letting his presence fill her. She didn't move as he dropped to the sand behind her and, boneless, leaned against his broad chest as he wrapped his arms around her. She felt the touch of his mouth on her hair and then the nape of her neck. His hands skimmed her belly lightly, and she felt the flutters begin again, leaving her slightly breathless. This time she welcomed the heady feelings his touch awoke in her and allowed herself to simply *feel*. She arched into his touch, wordlessly asking for more.

He shifted until he was sitting and had pulled her into his lap, a broad hand resting lightly across her stomach. She breathed deeply, taking in his scent and the tang of salt and opened her eyes. A small hand caressed his cheek and pulled him closer until she could kiss him slowly and lazily.

Devil held himself still as she explored his mouth tentatively at first, then more boldly as her confidence increased. Against his will, his hand skimmed upward from her belly to cup a small breast; the nipple tightened against his palm, sending a surge of heat through his fingertips and up his arm as she leaned into his touch. A small groan slipped from her mouth as she pulled back, breathing heavily. She glanced down her body at his large hand cupping her so gently, and felt a deep throbbing begin low in her belly. She felt the proof of his want pressing against her hip and she wriggled closer, eliciting a rough growl from him. She gave herself up to his kiss again, finding the waves of pleasure he awoke in her very exciting.

His hand left her breast and travelled downward, steadily stroking her skin, awakening fires in her nerve endings. She gasped and stiffened when his fingers attempted to slip past the elastic band on her panties, and she shoved his hand away.

"No," she gasped.

She heard his groan and wondered if he would get angry. Chris had and so had the one other boyfriend she'd had in the past. She waited, her breath held, for his reaction; waited to see if he would disappoint her as the others had. She watched him, seeing him struggle to rein in his desire and need until he could open his eyes and look at her.

"All right," he said quietly, stunning her. "I've waited this long, I can wait until you want me as much as I want you."

Angeline sat up and scooted off his lap to sit next to him.

"I do want you," she said quietly, her gaze on the sand. "So much it scares me." She took a deep breath, and looked him in the eye as her voice trailed off, her courage wavering.

He waited her out, not pressing her to spit out whatever she was trying to say. Finally, she took a deep breath and blurted:

"I'm a virgin."

~CHAPTER SIX~

Devil sat, pole axed; of all the things he had expected her to say, this wasn't one of them. How could this beautiful, intelligent woman still be untouched? He realized she had started to speak again, and turned his attention to her words.

"You saw my photo; that was actually a good one. My grandmother use to tell my sister and me that someday we would meet the man we were destined for; that he would suddenly appear and we would just *know* he was the one. I held on to that dream for so long, and would pray every night I would meet him soon, and that I would suddenly become pretty because he loved me." She paused, her eyes down as she drew abstract patterns in the sand. "You see, all my life I lived in the shadow of my beautiful older sister; all she had to do was snap her fingers, and there would be a crowd of boys around her, eager to do whatever she wanted. So, if she told them to dance with me, they did. I knew they were doing it only to get on her good side, that none of them was actually interested in me, so I never took their invitations seriously. When other girls were going to the prom, I was at home, studying, because not one single boy thought to ask me without Cassie telling him to do it. Once I was in college, I was too busy to do much dating. The one guy I did date didn't last once he realized I wouldn't sleep with him." She laughed bitterly, remembering how she'd heard the term 'frigid bitch' for the first time; though she couldn't remember the young man's name, the nastiness of his tone when he'd called her that still remained fresh in her memory.

"After school, I came home and opened the animal hospital, and met Chris when he brought his mother's cat in for a broken tail. He paid attention to me, made me feel like I was beautiful, and there was no one telling him to do it; before I knew it, I was imagining myself in love with him. We dated for three years, and I was so happy when he proposed." She grew silent again, her memories causing her stomach to roil sickeningly. She took another deep breath and forged on.

"About a month after I said yes, we went to a dinner party being held by one of the partners from the law firm he worked for, and I ran into an old classmate; Ben and I had spent a lot of time studying in the library together, and I was so happy to see him again. I didn't think anything of it when I gave him a hug and kissed his cheek. Chris did, though, and he beat me up later that night;" she paused as Devil drew in a sharp breath, and continued, determined to finish the story and move on. "He was jealous because I wouldn't sleep with him, but didn't seem to have any reservations around other men; he simply didn't see why I wanted to wait until we were married. It was a sore point between us, and most of our arguments were because I wouldn't sleep with him; that night he became furious. He demanded that I have sex with him; after all, I had accepted his proposal, so what did it matter that we weren't officially married yet?" She glanced at him, the look in her eye bleakly defiant and took a shuddering breath. "I still refused, and he hit me. He didn't stop until I screamed out the truth of my virginity. I must have known, deep down, that he wasn't the one. That night, the blinders came off, and I saw him as he really was."

She turned and drew his attention to a shiny round scar on the inside of her thigh. "That's where he put his cigar out on me; thankfully, I was able to fight back, that all he did was beat me, and that he stopped when he did." She swallowed hard. "I realized after he left that he could have done so much worse if I hadn't been stronger. I broke off the engagement two days later, once I was able to get out of bed. I left Portland to get away from him, but I didn't run far enough away; you met him today. He wants to drag me back to Portland and force me to marry him; he doesn't deal well with disappointment, and he doesn't care that I don't want him anymore." She laughed bitterly. "I think it's now become a matter of my being the one person he couldn't bully and conquer."

She fell silent, her throat dry. She leaned into Devil's side as he put an arm around her shoulders. "So you're a virgin," he began slowly, pushing aside the roar of primal possessiveness he felt and trying to wrap his brain around the idea.

She nodded and she smiled to herself as she felt the emotions swirling through him. "Yes," she answered with a hint of amusement.

Devil shook his head. She was a bundle of contradictions; he thought about the heat of their kisses, her passionate response to his touch, and shook his head again.

Seeming to read his mind, she moved until she was on her knees between his thighs.

She looked him in the eye and said slowly, "No one's ever made me feel like you do, all hot and shivery inside.

It builds up here," she said, placing his hand on her belly, "it builds up until I can't breathe, until it feels like I'm going to explode, and it scares me." She leaned in and kissed him softly. "And it's exciting, too; all these years, I thought I was saving myself for marriage, but," she confessed shyly as she sat back on her heels, "I think I was really saving myself for you. But after spending my whole life praying for you, now that you're here, I don't know what to do."

He felt her uncertainty in the tremble of her fingers on his forearms, heard it in her voice and the hitching of her breath as it fanned across his face, saw it in her wide silver eyes. His hand came up and his fingers pushed through her short golden curls to curve around the back of her head and pull her forward.

"Let me show you," he said huskily.

Gently, carefully, he drew her close, his touch light on her skin. He paused several long moments before kissing her, letting her make the decision, allowing her the chance to put a stop to what was about to happen if she so chose. Testing her resolve and need. Finally, when she didn't offer up any resistance, he kissed her and felt Angeline's sigh as it seemed to start at her toes and spread through her body. Her arms came around him and held him close as she surrendered to the desire coursing through her veins. His lips grazed hers slowly until she started to respond, and then claimed her mouth, driving his tongue past her lips to sweep the damp interior possessively. She let him plunder her mouth without protest until he gentled the kiss and showed her what they both liked. Angeline was gasping when he finally lifted his head to draw in a shuddering breath. His hands were curved around her ribs, his thumbs caressing the bare skin just under the line of her lacy bra. He drew her gaze down to his hands, and ever so slowly, moved them higher until his thumbs just grazed the aching tips of her breasts. She groaned in need and leaned into the touch, her body begging for more. Devil shifted until he was lying on his back in the warm sand, Angeline sprawled across his chest and held her still while he kissed her again, his tongue teasing and beguiling her with each touch, his hands setting her body on fire wherever they touched.

Angeline squirmed to be as close as she could to his heat and heard his growl as her belly pressed against the rigid proof of his desire. She sat up, her thighs straddling his and wiggled against his groin, feeling more of that molten fire that pooled and throbbed between her thighs. Devil reached up behind her back and undid the clasp that secured her bra, slowly sliding it down her arms and tossing it aside before dragging her back down against him. She gasped at the feel of his shirt against her bare, sensitized flesh, at the searing stab of heat that shot through her. She almost sobbed in delirium as his mouth left hers to taste the gentle slope of her shoulder. Almost too late, she remembered to lock down her control in order to allow them both to feed their passions naturally.

Devil groaned as he felt a part of Angeline pull back, even when she was so close to surrender. His body ached and felt tight, his skin feeling too small for his body. Everywhere his fingers explored he encountered the hot silk of her skin. He groaned when he felt her heat through her cotton panties and remembering she was a virgin, he dragged his mouth away from hers reluctantly.

"Ah god, Angel," he ground out, as he stilled her hands. "We've got to stop." He was certain she was holding a portion of herself back out of trepidation, and struggled to reign himself in so that he didn't scare her.

His words were slow to penetrate her brain, and when they did, she discounted them; she had saved herself for this moment, and she didn't want it to end. She wanted him to make love to her here, on the beach, the ocean washing around them; this is where she felt in tune with the world around her, where she felt she belonged most of all.

"No," she whispered brokenly against his throat, "we don't." She opened her eyes to stare into his, and saw him licked his lips slowly. "Make love to me, Devil," she whispered against his mouth, begging. "Please."

She felt a thrill of fear tinged excitement as he grabbed her hips and ground himself against her. He felt so hard and big against her soft flesh and she mewed in her throat at the sensation. His big hands squeezed her breasts and his mouth tormented her nipples. She gasped as he turned suddenly and she was beneath him, his hips cradled between her thighs. He rocked against her in a slow, long stroke, and watched as she gasped in surprise then purred. Repeatedly he did this until she caught the rhythm. His hand slipped between their bodies to stroke her dewy, swollen flesh. Small whimpers and gasps of pleasure erupted from between her lips as he tormented the very core of her need. He wrought an almost painful frenzy of need in her that begged for something she couldn't quite name. Her back arched deeply as she pressed against him. He jerked his shirt over his head and gathered her against his chest, the electric contact of skin on skin shaking him. Unable to hold himself back, he left her warm body, noting her cry of disappointment, and yanked his damp jeans off.

Angeline almost purred when he returned, his body hovering over hers, his thighs pushing hers wide. She reached down and touched him, her curiosity burning deep. Eyes closed, she felt the hard, hot silk of his member, and her throat went dry as fierce need clawed through her. She lifted her hips, and gasped as the tip brushed against her sensitive flesh. She felt him tug her panties, hearing the small sound of material ripping, and cried out as he touched her finally, her body unconsciously tensing.

"Relax," he growled, doing his best to rein in his own drive.

He pulled her close and she surrendered to his slow, drugging kisses until she was once again mindless to all but the hot passion riding through her blood. Slowly, steadily, he pushed into her tight passage, shaking with the effort to go slow.

Angeline's eyes widened and she winced a little; she didn't feel pain, exactly. Rather she felt a fullness that became more and more pleasant as he continued.

"It might hurt," he warned her as he stopped; her thin barrier prevented him from going any further.

Angeline nodded her eyes wide and trusting. Taking a deep breath, he cupped her bottom in his large hands and lifted her hips high to receive his quick, deep thrust. He held himself still, trembling as her tightness cradled him.

She felt no discomfort. Rather, there had been a twinge, a pinching sensation that faded almost before she could take note of it. She felt him, deep in her body, throbbing, and the sensation caused her blood to erupt into flame; all these years, she'd waited for him, and she was deliriously happy that she had. From this moment on, she belonged to him, heart, body, and soul. She breathed deeply, each breath feeling like liquid flame in her throat as tears of joy clouded her vision. Her hips rose on their own accord to meet his next thrust, and instinct took over.

Her head thrashed side to side as she rode the rising tide of passion, her cries coming high and breathless. He drove her slowly and steadily, higher and higher, his fingers stroking her sensitive flesh all the while holding his own need in check until she threw her head back and cried out to the sky above as she came undone around him. He thrust quickly and deeply then even as her body trembled and to his surprise, he felt her tighten again, her cries mingling with his as his world imploded. They lay clasped in each other's arms in the sand, unaware someone was watching them from the cliff above with furious eyes and deadly intentions.

Chris Jessop drove away, rage seething through his body; his hands so tight on the wheel, his knuckles were white. His fist pounded the steering wheel but it didn't do anything to alleviate the sense of betrayal he felt. The little whore had given away what was rightfully his and he made plans to make her pay. Painfully, shamefully pay.

The lovers were unaware of their audience as they slowly disengaged their tangled limbs. Angeline felt light, as if she would float away without the anchor his body provided. Devil was still stunned; still unable to believe the gift she had given him, and though he was still certain he hadn't experienced the full depth of her passion, he felt humbled that she'd trusted him so much. He felt his heart lurch in his chest as an unfamiliar feeling rose up around it; a feeling that he wasn't ready to hold up to the light and examine. But it was a feeling that was possessive, tender, protective and uplifting all in the same breath; it left him feeling heroic and powerful. It left him feeling small and humbled. His arms tightened around her as the light breeze touched her skin and she shivered. When that same breeze kissed his own cooling skin, he suggested in a low voice that it might be better to find somewhere warmer. Together they rose, searching the sand for their clothing. She dangled her ruined panties from a fingertip, laughing at his abashed expression.

"It's all right," she crooned standing on her toes to kiss him. "I have more."

Devil pulled her against him and tipped her head up, a long finger caressing her smooth cheek. Her silver eyes glinted in the fading light of dusk and he watched her dark gold lashes flutter shut as he claimed her mouth in a kiss that was possessive, tender, and promising. They broke apart slowly, reluctantly and continued searching for clothes until they were dressed.

They climbed the trail hand in hand, and he pinned her against his car to kiss her again.

"Come home with me," he suggested in a low voice.

He felt rather than saw her nod. He handed her into her car, then went to his own. As he led the way back to his place, he found himself watching her in the rearview mirror, his body and heart already missing her.

~CHAPTER SEVEN~

Angeline awoke the next morning, nestled under a feather comforter, Devil's arms around her. She lay there, warm and content, her bones feeling like marshmallows as memories of the evening before and the way she'd begged for his touch caused her cheeks to pinken and her blood to turn molten. She considered slowly awakening him for a reprise, but other needs brought themselves to her attention and with a smothered sigh, she carefully slipped from his bed, and finding his robe, wrapped the voluminous folds around her body, giggling at the way the ends pooled at her feet. She padded quietly out of the room and down the hall to the bathroom. She took care of her needs, and stomach rumbling slightly, sought out the kitchen, and yawning, perused the refrigerator for a snack. Careful not to trip on the robe, she nibbled on a slice of cheese as she crossed the large room to make coffee. Once the machine was happily chugging away, she stretched long and slowly, feeling twinges in muscles she didn't realize she had had before last night. She leaned a hip against the counter while the coffee brewed and looked out the window over the sink. She found herself looking out onto a large backyard that sloped down to a small creek that ran through a small stand of trees. As she watched, she saw a doe and her fawn step delicately into the sunlight and drink from the creek. She smiled at the sight, feeling calm and at peace with her world. She knew Chris was still out there, somewhere, plotting and planning, but at this moment, he seemed very far away.

Once the coffee was brewed, she poured it into two mugs and searched the cupboards for cream and sugar. She shrugged when she didn't find any and decided to drink hers black like Devil apparently did. She carried the coffee back to his bedroom and found him just beginning to stir. She set the mugs on the nightstand and leaned over to kiss him fully awake, his robe gaping wide at the front.

Devil decided there wasn't anything better to awaken to than the sight of naked breasts. He buried his faced between her breasts and pulled her down on top of him. He continued to nuzzle her until his mouth settled over a pouty peak and drew on it deeply. Angeline purred as a wash of heat flowed over her. She sat up and watched, a little breathless as Devil untied the sash of the robe, allowing it to fall open. He rolled with her until she was beneath him, urgent and pleading. He entered her slowly, finding her ready, and let his mind go blank.

They showered together later, their slick, lathered bodies sliding sensually against one another. Devil found it hard to believe the little wanton he held in his arms had been a virgin less than twenty-four hours before. Angeline was a sensual creature, eager for each new lesson in passion he could teach her, and was proving herself a quick learner. Devil was finding it harder to hold himself back where she was concerned, and worried that he would hurt her when he did, inevitably, lose his tight control;

though they fit together perfectly, she was still a very small woman. They eventually ate breakfast, and Devil drove her back to her hotel room so she could change clothes and replace her ruined panties.

They didn't see Chris watching them from across the street. The engagement ring Angeline had returned to him sat in his clenched hand, his grip on it so tight the solitaire bit into his palm and drew blood. He was willing to wait until he could get her alone; and when he did, he would make her pay, oh yes. She was *his,* and he didn't like to share what belonged to him.

Devil and Angeline spent the day together in her room, ordering food to be delivered when other appetites intruded on their play, Devil doing his level best to snap the tight control Angeline still seemed to hold over herself. Angeline felt her command of herself being chipped away at, but was unable to do anything to shore it up as Devil drove her closer and closer to complete surrender; each touch, each kiss, each slide of his skin against hers eroded her control, and she wondered if either of them would be left standing when the inevitable end came. Over and over, he drove her, each pinnacle higher and keener than the last, and she truly began to wonder if it were possible to die from so much pleasure. By the time he let her sleep Angeline was exhausted, her body lethargic, her mind a blissful blank. She slept deeply in the shelter of his arms, content and unworried.

~CHAPTER EIGHT~

It was several days later when Angeline received the call that her offer on the Larsen home had been accepted. Devil sat back and watched her dance around his kitchen joyfully, her bright eyes shining, her cheeks flushed with excitement.

"Oh Dev," she breathed when she started to settle down, "It's starting to come together; it's actually starting to happen!" She plopped herself down onto his lap and wrapped her arms about his neck. She kissed him soundly and hugged him tight. "Let's go out there," she suggested on a whim. "Let me show you what I want to do." She jumped up and tugged his hand, leading him to his truck. She bounded up into the passenger seat and snapped the buckle around her slim hips. Devil slid in next to her, and drove her out to her soon to be home. The drive took only a handful of minutes; he lived about ten miles from the property.

Angeline hopped out of the truck when they pulled into the driveway and waited with barely suppressed excitement for him to join her. With a grin, she led him around the property, holding his hand, and occasionally pulling him quickly here or there.

"The house and cottage are in good condition," she was saying, "I'm going to have the cottage completely stripped and rebuilt to accommodate treatment rooms, a surgical room, and of course, radiology." She pulled him around the backside of the cottage, and pointed out the rather large paved patio. "I'm going to have this enclosed and have dog kennels built, with drains in the slab for easy cleaning." She continued, ticking each point off on her fingers.

"Will you treat larger animals, like horses?" Devil asked her enthusiasm contagious.

Angeline shook her head. "No," she said earnestly, "I've checked, and there's already a vet the horse and cattlemen use. I'm more interested in treating small house pets." She took his hand again and pulled him behind her. "Come on," she said, laughing, "let me show you the house!" They toured the front, Angeline pointing out where she wanted flowerbeds put in and trees planted. "Melissa gave me Pat Dell's name, and said he was the best man for the job. I plan to hire him and his crew the day I get the keys." They strolled around to the back, and walked up the steps to a large wooden deck. "I'll have this screened in," she said musingly. "That way Nico can have an outdoor place; he's always trying to get outside," she added. She threw her arms wide. "The whole yard will have flower beds and paths and maybe a gazebo, like Melissa's, and I'll put benches under those weeping willow trees that hug along the bank of the creek." She hugged herself tightly. "It'll be perfect," she said, laughing happily.

Devil could see her plans in his mind's eye, and he had to admit it looked wonderful. He felt a sudden tug against his heart, and a little voice whispered in his head.

It is perfect for her, it said, *but what about you? Where do you fit in?*

He stifled that voice as she turned to him, her silver eyes shining brightly. He pulled her into his arms and kissed her lightly. "It sounds great," he told her. He pushed lingering doubts ruthlessly away, determined not to worry about anything unless he needed to; after all, it wasn't as if they'd pledged themselves to each other for all of eternity. They spent another half hour at the house, Devil doing his best to ignore the small voice in his heart that had already sworn itself to Angeline.

The next day, Angeline fell from her lighter than air happiness to the pit of devastation; the realtor called to say someone had made a better offer on the Larsen property. When she heard the bid, tears welled in her eyes; there was no way she could make a counter offer without using every cent she had. If she did so, she would have nothing left over to set up her practice. She tearfully withdrew her bid and hung up. When she told Devil the news, he consoled her as best he could, but that little voice had returned, and it was laughing gleefully. She huddled in Devil's embrace, sobs shaking her petite frame as if her heart was breaking. He soothed and comforted her as best he could, but wasn't sure it was enough. A moment later he had his suspicion confirmed when she suddenly pulled out of his arms and grabbed her bag. "I need to be alone," she told him tearfully. "I'll see you tonight at Jessica's."

Chris Jessop watched as Angeline drove away from town, headed for her place of solace on the beach. He followed her, keeping his distance so she wouldn't notice him, and once he saw her disappear over the sandy rise, pulled into the lot to watch her. He'd known her for three years, and had learned of her need to be on her own in the beginning of their relationship. The first time he became truly aware of it was the day one of her patients at the clinic had died, despite her best efforts to save the animal. Jessop himself had never seen much use in having pets, but seeing Angeline's upset over the loss had him scrambling to comfort her, to show her he was just as sensitive and sappy as the next guy was. It hadn't been enough

Sobbing, Angeline had begged him to cancel their weekend plans to drive to Seattle so she could stay home; she had said she needed to be alone for a day or two. Jessop, grinding his teeth in annoyance, had reluctantly agreed, and later followed her small car as she drove northwest of Portland to the coast. He watched her as she checked in to a small bed and breakfast in Astoria, her overnight bag slung over her shoulder. She seemed to be well known by the man at the check in desk; he greeted Angeline as if she were an old friend, and in a shorter amount of time than Chris expected, Angeline was securely ensconced in a bungalow on the beach.

Later that night, he watched her as she walked the beach in the moonlight, clad in shorts and a tee shirt, her arms wrapped tight around her body as she slowly made her way to the waterline. At first, Jessop had worried that she would simply continue to walk into the water until it covered her head and allow the tide to take her. Prepared to stop her if he needed to, Jessop watched, tense, until it became apparent the Angeline was simply taking a moonlight swim. She was alone on her stretch of beach and the solitude seemed to give rise to a side of Angeline Jessop hadn't suspected existed; her demeanor altered with each passing moment until he realized that he was seeing her as she truly was; free, uninhibited, natural. As she emerged from the water, the moonlight glinting off her wet skin, her tee shirt plastered to her lithe body, Jessop was suddenly aware that if this side of Angeline ever got out, it could be very embarrassing for him; she was a tree *hugger, a wild child;* this was her true nature, not the polished, accomplished, sophisticated woman that he and his friends saw. He felt lied to, betrayed.

He watched her flop boneless onto the sand, her delectable body limned in silver moonlight; her wet shirt clung to her body, and even from his vantage point, he could tell she didn't wear anything beneath it; there were no bra or bikini lines to interrupt the smooth blending of line and curve of her body. The same body that had tempted and teased him all this time, and yet she'd kept from him. The urge to go to her then was almost too powerful to resist; he imagined peeling that wet shirt from her, could almost taste the salty satin of her skin beneath his tongue. Yet he held himself in place, knowing she wouldn't appreciate the intrusion, or the fact that he'd followed her. So, he'd watched, noticing the serenity that fell over her, noticing and taking note of it as if this behavior of hers was something that needed to be corrected. He made a vow as he watched her roll over and climb to her feet then head back to her bungalow that he would change this flaw in her character.

Now, he would use her predictability to trap her, to put her right where he wanted her. He had followed Angeline and her lover for a week, learning where Devil Damien lived, and when he had realized she was planning to reopen her business, he had acted. Using contacts he had back in Portland, he had learned how much cash Angeline had, then gone to the real estate agent and made a higher offer on the property she wanted, knowing she would never be able to top it without using all of her funds. Seeing her head bowed and her shoulders slumped sent a vindictive thrill through him. He left her to her thoughts and drove away, knowing it was too early to take her; he needed her alone and isolated from the small group of friends she had surrounded herself with, unable to trust them. In short, he would destroy the little life she was so carefully building, then he would destroy her.

A dark, frightening smile lit his features as he continued to make his plans.

~CHAPTER NINE~

Devil paced his living room, glancing impatiently at the clock as he waited for Angeline to arrive. They were due at Jamie and Jessica's place for dinner, and he had expected her back before this. He still didn't quite understand her need to be near the water when she was feeling wrong footed or upset, but he was willing to accept it; he was so taken with her now that he couldn't imagine Angeline reacting any other way. He glanced at his watch again and felt a prickle of worry as he remembered her reckless, headlong flight down the steep path the last time she needed time alone. Maybe she had fallen on the trail and been hurt somehow…

Stomach clenching at the thought, he strode over to a side table, picked up the phone, and dialed Jamie's house. He waited impatiently for someone to pick up, and when Jessica did, he wasted no words. "Jess," he said quickly. "We're going to be late. Angeline hasn't come back from the beach yet, and I'm getting worried; I'm going to head out there and make sure she's all right."

"Dev, she's here already," Jessica told him, sounding confused. "She just walked in. Here, I'll put her on."

When he heard her voice, a wave of relief washed over him that was so strong he felt his knees go weak. "What are you doing there?" He demanded irrationally.

Angeline stammered a moment. "I got your note," she said, her tone cautious. "The one you left on my door."

Questions crowded his mind, and he shoved them aside. "I'll be there in a few minutes," he said. "Be waiting for me out front." He disconnected the line and grabbed his keys.

Angeline stood, shocked, the phone still held to her ear, the dial tone loud. Devil's brusque tone startled her; it was so different from the voice she heard in her head when she thought of him. She squared her shoulders, replaced the phone on its base, and made for the front door. She was slowly breaking her old habit of hiding behind her timidity, and her true nature was beginning to reassert itself; there was no way she was about to let him think he could boss her around and she would obey meekly. Yes, she would be waiting out front as he requested, but if he wanted a fight, a fight was what she would give him. She swiftly wiped her sweaty palms on her dress, straightened her spine and opened the front door to step outside. Jess and Melissa watched her mental preparations with glee; Devil had certainly met his match.

Devil arrived a few minutes later, and when he saw her standing on the footpath between the drive and the door, he felt another surge of relief that was quickly followed up by a shock of annoyance. He got out, slamming the door shut, and in a few long strides, he was in front of her, his hands on her shoulders, shaking her lightly. "Do you know how worried I've been?" He ground out before his mouth crashed down on hers in a frantic, bruising kiss.

Angeline pressed her hands against his chest and pushed as hard as she could. She suddenly felt overwhelmed and claustrophobic and not a little perturbed. She wrenched her mouth away from his and pushed again. "Devil!' She said loudly, sharply, pulling herself out of his arms, "Devil, stop!" She stepped away as he reached for her again, unconsciously pushing him away with a small surge of energy. "What is wrong with you?" She demanded, "I came here like your note said to!" She watched him pause a moment as the surge halted his advance briefly. She held her breath as puzzlement temporarily flashed across his face before he continued his moving towards her. She backed away from him, not frightened, but certainly annoyed. She kept several feet between them, trying in vain not to feel the jump in her pulse at the almost predatory gleam in his eye as he stalked her, silent and seemingly dangerous. A shiver went up her spine as she wondered if he would gobble her up whole if he caught her. Her slightly hysterical giggle turned to a gasp as her heel caught on the edge of the walkway, and she stumbled backwards, her arms wheeling to keep her balance. Devil's hand shot out and grabbed her wrist, pulling her back so fast her head spun. She found herself pressed tight against his chest and took a moment to calm her racing heart.

"Where were you?" He finally asked in a more even tone, his face tucked against the side of her neck, nuzzling.

Angeline sighed heavily, striving to inject a little serenity between them. As she calmed her breathing and heart rate, she felt Devil's arms tighten around her, and in an attempt to quell the maddening, bone melting effects of his lips and tongue on her neck, she became defensive. "I met a good looking guy and went to a bar for a few drinks; then once he was nice and drunk, I went back to his hotel room and had wild, hot sex with him," she said with a trace of sarcasm, her face pressed against his chest. It was, perhaps, the wrong thing to say, and she knew it would only goad his prickly temper if she kept it up, but she was so annoyed with his bad mood that she didn't care; without thinking, she fed a little of her own temper to him. Almost too late, she realized what she was doing and tamped down on her annoyance and struggled to regain a modicum of calm. She held her breath, waiting for an explosion.

He surprised her by chuckling. "As long as you had a good time," he finally said allowing the feel of her in his arms, the taste of her on his tongue, and the smell of her light perfume in his nose to calm him. He realized how surly and unreasonable he'd sounded and knew he deserved worse than her mild sarcasm; he deserved a tongue-lashing. He deserved to be told to take a long walk off a short pier, but he'd grown so worried and had imagined all sorts of horrible things happening to her that he had let his better judgment take that walk. Sighing heavily and allowing himself relax, he took her hand and guided her to a garden bench; he sat and pulled her down onto his lap, smoothing his fingers along the soft curve of her cheek.

"I'm sorry, Angel," he said softly, letting go of his worry and ire. "Tell me about the note you found."

Angeline leaned into his touch with a sigh; she loved how his touch made her feel. "It was taped to my door," she told him, breathing easier now that she knew there would be no explosion. "I was running late, and it said to meet you here instead of coming out to your place first; I was relieved that I'd have a few more minutes." She sighed as his lips traced a path along her jaw. "I fed Nico, showered, got dressed and came here," she continued, her voice growing more and more breathless. "I was a little put out that you weren't waiting for me." This time when she sighed, it was a sound of pleasure; Devil's wandering lips had found the sensitive spot below her ear.

"I didn't leave that note," he murmured. His mouth stopped its explorations as a thought struck him. "Did anybody follow you here?" He asked his voice suddenly serious.

Angeline shook her head, hating the abrupt distance between them. "I don't think so," she said, thinking hard. "I didn't notice anyone," she continued, frowning. "Why? Do you think someone else left that note?" Her eyes widened, panic already crowding the edges of her expression. "Do you think Chris had anything to do with it?" Her voice took on an alarmed and pitchy tone.

Devil shook his head as he set her on her feet. "I doubt it," he hurried to reassure her, "No one's seen him around since that first day he was here." He stood and took her hand. "Come on, Angel," he said, "I'm hungry." He heard the shaky, frightened sound of her laugh and he put his arm around her and squeezed her gently. "Don't worry," he said quietly, kissing the top of her head, "I won't let anything happen to you." Angeline nodded silently, feeling safer with his large body next to her, with his strong arms around her.

But he's not always by your side, is he?

That worried voice whispered in the back of her mind. She pushed the thought aside, determined not to live in fear or give in to the temptation to run again.

Later that night they lay in the dark, wrapped in each other's arms, their hot skin slowly cooling in the breeze that drifted through the open windows of Devil's bedroom. Though he hadn't said anything to Angeline, the mysterious note that had been left on her door concerned him. He had quietly made inquiries among his friends at the party that evening, and none had known anything about the note. In the morning, he would call Blanche and see if she knew anything.

Angeline snuggled closer against him in her sleep and he tightened his arm around her. Sleep was slow in coming, but eventually it claimed him and he fell gratefully into its embrace.

She ran from someone in the dark; cold sweat trickled down between her shoulder blades, soaking through her shirt and making it feel clammy against her skin. Her breath burned in her throat and her heart threatened to burst from her chest as hot exhaustion surged down her legs. She had a stitch in her side, and though she wanted to stop, she knew she couldn't; if she stopped running he would catch up to her and she would die painfully and screaming. The knowledge kept her moving, fear nipping her heels like a pack of rabid dogs.

Suddenly, she couldn't lift her feet anymore; they seemed mired in thick, foul smelling mud. Frantically she lurched forward, dragging her feet through the morass. Whimpers tore from her throat as she struggled not to scream. She struggled with all her might to break free of the mud's grasp, and with a huge lunge, she broke the grip the quagmire had on her. She stumbled to her knees, and fought to stand again, but fear and exhaustion defeated her. She could sense him behind her, and covered her head with her arms, too tired to fight, too alone to try. His presence suffocated her, pulling her down into blackness...

Angeline awoke screaming. The fear rushed through her, suffocating and hot, searing her nerve endings and slamming through the foundation of the house. She didn't feel the tremors in the bed beneath her as she fought with the covers that tangled around her sweat-drenched body, her hands flailing and her feet kicking. She struggled so hard she fell out of bed and landed hard on her side. The impact knocked the wind out of her and she crawled, sobbing and frightened for the door, the floor lurching beneath her. She cried out as arms pulled her back and held her tightly, imprisoning her hands between her body and something warm and hard. She was so cold the heat was almost painful. She begged for her life, pleading in a hoarse voice, "Please, I don't want to die!"

"Angeline!" A loud, deep voice said in her ear. "Angel, it's me, Devil. Come back, baby, come back to me." It was a voice she knew, even in her nightmares; a voice she was willing to crawl on hands and knees across broken glass for. It was a voice that guided her home. Devil's voice penetrated her night terror and her struggles grew weaker as the nightmare's grip loosened.

Devil sat on the edge of the bed, holding her close as she sobbed brokenly into his shoulder, her small body curled in his arms like a child's. He could feel her heart racing under his palm as he touched her with calming and comforting fingers, lending his warmth to her chilled skin. "It's all right," he murmured. "I'm here. Nothing's going to happen to you," he whispered against her golden curls. "Don't cry, Angel," he told her. "You're safe; I won't let anything happen to you." Her tears slowed, and then finally stopped, though she still clung to him as if her life depended on it. Devil shifted until they were lying side by side, Angeline tucked close. "Do you want to tell me?" He asked in a quiet voice. He felt her nod just before she shifted away from him to turn onto her side, her back to him.

Slowly, haltingly, she told him about her dream, hating how silly it sounded spoken out loud. Devil's fingers traced a path along her back, and she allowed herself to sink into a relaxed state as he pulled her back against his side. Devil's voice rumbled beneath her ear.

"It was a nightmare," he told her, his voice low and soothing. "Seeing Jessop again after everything he's done to you probably caused it; I'm surprised you haven't had one sooner.

Angeline wanted to believe him, but knew the dream had been more than the product of an overactive imagination. It had been a warning. "I have these dreams, sometimes," she began slowly, her voice slightly muffled. "Not all the time, just when I need to be warned about something." She fell quiet for a moment, waiting for Devil to tell her she was being irrational. When he didn't, she went on. "They usually come true." She waited, tense. She didn't know what she would do if he laughed at her or called her crazy. "I've never told anyone," she said softly. She ignored the voice in her head that clamored for her to tell him the entire truth, to tell him what she could do.

Devil didn't laugh or call her crazy. Instead, he pulled her even tighter to his side, tucked her head into his shoulder, and kissed the top of her head. "Nothing will happen to you while I'm around," he growled with finality. Though he hadn't been expecting her confession, it made an odd kind of sense to him; somehow it fit that she dreamed about things that later came true. There was simply something about Angeline that made such things possible, made them believable.

His arms tightened around her small body as he stifled a shudder of residual fear. Something had happened deep inside his soul when he had heard her screams; something that slammed into his gut and made him face what he had been trying to deny these last several weeks:

Angeline was his and his alone; he would die to protect her.

He would kill to keep her safe.

He loved her.

It seemed as if the world suddenly rocked beneath him as this last thought hammered itself home; it tattooed itself indelibly on his heart and brain and he suddenly felt lighter because of the soul deep acknowledgement of the fact. Angeline's body relaxed as sleep overcame her again, and closing his eyes, he did the same, vowing to do everything in his power to keep her safe. And wondering if the earth *really* had moved in his moment of epiphany, or if it had been his imagination.

~CHAPTER TEN~

The summer days passed into fall, bringing cool rains and foggy mornings, and the trees traded in their summer green frocks for dresses of red and gold. Angeline's dream hadn't returned, and Devil had been unable to track down the source of the note left on Angeline's door. No one seemed to know anything about it, and though Aunt Blanche admitted to writing it, she had only taken a phone message.

"My hearing isn't as sharp as it once was," she was overheard saying to her sister, June, "it sounded like Devil." She had taken the message and taped it on Angeline's door. The more he thought about it, the more certain Devil was that someone had been following Angeline that evening as she drove to Jamie and Jess' house, and that someone had been Chris Jessop.

"No one followed me, Nick!" She said, throwing her hands up in exasperation. She flopped down into an overstuffed chair, her leg dangling over the arm, and folded her arms over her chest. The tableside lamp flickered weakly. She set her jaw stubbornly and refused to listen to anymore of Devil's conspiracy theories. The lamp stopped flickering as soon as Devil changed the subject.

In truth, Jessop *had* planned to follow Angeline to the dinner party that night, but his car had developed engine problems and he had ended up returning it to the rental agency and trading it for another car. No one but he knew how close he'd come to grabbing Angeline and running. Far from letting himself grow impatient, he revised his plans. *Soon*, he told himself. *She will be mine soon.*

Meanwhile, Angeline had begun a new search for home and office space; so far, she had been shown three other properties, but none of them had been as perfect as the Larsen home had been. "Maybe I'm being too picky," she admitted grudgingly one crisp, cool afternoon. She and Devil walked hand in hand along the trail that meandered alongside the creek that ran behind his house. "I really had my heart set on that property," she confessed with a sigh. "I could see it in my mind crystal clear; it was perfect." She laid her head against his shoulder as his arm came around her. "It was already becoming home in my..." Her voice trailed off as she saw Melissa hurrying down the trail toward them, her steps quick and determined. She had something clenched tightly in her hand. She came to a sudden stop in front of them.

"There you are!" She exclaimed. "Do you know how long I've been looking for you?" She asked, throwing her hands up. She accidentally flung a crumpled piece of paper at Angeline. "Sorry," she said, chagrined as it bounced off Angeline's shoulder and fell to the ground. She pointed to the paper at their feet. "That was left on my windshield this morning."

Devil picked it up and smoothed it out; the note was typewritten, the lettering streaked and smudged. He read it aloud:

"Don't let the spooks get you."

He looked at Melissa and smirked. "Someone's yanking your chain," he told her with a touch of boredom in his drawl. Melissa took back her note with a grin.

"That's what I thought at first," she said, handing him another piece of paper, this one folded neatly into a square. "Jess found this one tucked *inside* her newspaper this morning."

Devil unfolded the note and read:

"Is Daddy really Daddy, or is someone telling lies?"

It, too, was typed, the lettering smudged. "So," he said slowly, handing the note back to Melissa, "someone thinks if people knew about your little ghost problem they'd call you crazy and never speak to you again." He tapped Jess' note. "And here they think if it ever got out that Jamie isn't the father of Jess' first baby, she'll be ostracized by the community, or that Jamie will leave her." He snorted as Melissa giggled.

"Whoever it is doesn't know the people of Bounty Cove very well, do they?" She said, laughingly. She sobered a little, though her lips still twitched with humor. "You said to let you know if anymore notes showed up."

"Like mine?" A deep voice asked. Angeline turned to see Michael and Jamie walking toward them. Michael handed Devil a small note, quoting as he did: *"Does she know you married the money?"* It looked just like the other two. All eyes turned to Jamie who spread his hands out in front of his body as he shrugged. "I feel *so* left out," he said, mockingly rolling his eyes. "They must not have anything on me yet."

Angeline had been standing aside, quietly reading each note and listening to the conversation. She had felt a tiny spark of anger light in her belly as she read the words on each paper. Now it was threatening to blow up into a full out inferno of rage. She had to get away before someone got hurt, before she infected her friends and they turned on each other. She could feel the pressure already building around her as the wind began to pick up. She slowly backed away from the group. She glanced at the notes held in Devil's hand. "He hasn't gotten that printer fixed," she said before she could stop the words. All eyes turned to her as she clapped her hands over her mouth, her eyes wide, as if she had just said something obscene. Devil's dark gaze fixed on her pale face, rooting her to the spot against her will.

"Angel," he said in a quiet, still voice, "do you know who's sending these notes?"

Angeline shook her head as she began to back away again, the look in her eyes telling a different story. Devil stepped toward her and held her still, his hands on her shoulders. "Tell me." It wasn't a request.

Angeline shook her head again, her hands still over her mouth. She pulled out of Devil's grasp and backed away quickly, her hands dropping to her sides. "I'm sorry," she told him and the others, her eyes solely on Devil, her expression one of angered anguish. "I have to go away." Fear, pain, and sadness shone from her silver eyes. "I have to go," she said again. "It's the only way you'll be safe." She began to tremble as she fought the need to release some of the turmoil rolling through her.

Devil stepped toward her again. "Angel," he said soothingly, "there's nothing to worry about. We can handle whatever it is."

However, Angeline just shook her head, the pressure in her belly growing quickly now as perspiration rose on her skin. She had to leave them, to get away, before anyone got hurt. The knowledge she would never see any of them again pierced her heart as tears slipped down her cheeks.

"I have to go," she whispered.

She turned quickly on her heel, and ran right into Michael and Jamie as they inadvertently blocked her path. She felt Devil come up behind her, his hands wrapping around her upper arms in a gentle grip. She struggled against him, but he wouldn't release her. Her struggles became more frenzied as the wind around them picked up and the tightness in her gut and chest became unbearable.

"Let me go," she moaned, pleading, "Before it's too late."

However, even as she said the words, she already knew it was far too late; she felt the surge through her body as her shaky control dissolved. She let out a low moan at the impact and went limp in Devil's grasp even as she felt unbearable relief that the impending break had finally come; the only hope she had now was that the storm would pass quickly and she'd be able to escape before the others had time to recover themselves.

That and pray she didn't kill someone.

Devil turned her in his hold and pulled her close. His hands framed her pale face, his thumbs brushing away her tears. Her eyes opened and he felt himself swamped by the pain and sadness in her gaze.

"I'm sorry," she whispered, hanging limp in his grasp, "I meant to tell you." She reached for the ragged remnants of her control and cut off the flow of emotion between them.

Devil blinked as he became aware of a sudden *absence* in his heart and mind; it left him feeling cold and oddly bereft. He stared down at Angeline and felt a glimmer of realization that she was the cause of the void, that she'd somehow removed herself from him. Shaking his head, he shoved all other thoughts to concentrate on protecting Angeline; he could feel the wind picking up more, whipping the tree limbs above their heads and pulling at his clothes and hair. He flinched as thunder rumbled overhead and he ducked as a small branch sailed past, his body automatically shielding Angeline.

"Let me go, Devil."

Her voice drifted to him over the sound of the whistling wind. His attention shifted back to the small woman in his arms and he was suddenly aware of a growing heat that seemed to emanate from her; beads of sweat dotted her forehead and face. The temperature of her skin rose dramatically as the air around them began to chill.

"Nick, please," she whispered, "Let me go; I love you too much to hurt you," she said brokenly as she became too hot to hold.

Devil dropped his hands from her body, watching as she stumbled away from him the moment he did, vaguely aware that she'd used his given name, but more importantly, she'd told him she loved him. The fact that she chose now to do both cemented in his gut the realization of just how much danger they were in. He backed away from her slowly until he bumped into his friends. The four of them huddled together, their eyes narrowed against the dust that had been kicked up by the suddenly fierce wind. And yet, while his friends shielded their faces, Devil didn't; he kept his gaze on Angeline, determined to protect her if he could, afraid that he couldn't.

"Don't follow," she gasped as she moved slowly away, her heartbreak ravaging her expression. She read the fear in his squint-eyed gaze, and it tore at her as nothing else ever had, not realizing it was fear for her safety, *not* fear of her that she saw in his expression. She took another step then gasped again. "Stay away," she said, stiff and trembling, her quicksilver eyes glowing with blue fire, "it isn't safe." She forced herself to stumble as far as she could away from the people who, for a brief time, had been her friends and had made up her small world.

The small group huddled together, shivering, as the temperature continued to drop; the wind continued to rush toward the small woman standing apart from them, her small frame seemingly encased by the whirlwind around them. They blinked as blue lightening sparkled around her body as she withstood the tempest, her arms outstretched and her head thrown back, her face pointed to the sky. The wind became a living entity, seething and churning around her, seemingly awaiting her command or the moment to tear her apart.

She screamed, the sound knifing through Devil; it was a sound of pain that reverberated through his soul. He wanted so badly to reach out to her, to help her, but there was no way he could get to her now; the wind had engulfed her in a wild, churning cocoon, whipping the dirt and debris at her feet into a scouring cyclone. He heard her scream again as the pressure tightened ever more, causing their ears to pop painfully. Devil closed his eyes against the sound and the pain. When he opened them again, he saw that Angeline had risen a foot in the air, hanging limply like a rag doll. Lightening flared constantly now, licking and tasting her skin, eager to devour her body and soul. He watched as she shrank into herself, pulling her arms tight against her body, the lines of her frame tense, her face a mask of pain and concentration. He held his breath as he watched this small woman struggle to contain and withstand the power that seethed around her in a violent storm. She screamed again, this time her voice ringing with defiance as well as fear and pain. She suddenly thrust her arms out, palms up, fingers outstretched.

It was difficult to keep her thoughts focused on the task of grounding the energy around her; seething, piercing pain flickered at each spot on her body where the blue energy surges touched her, making it difficult to keep herself on task. The pain and fury swirled in her gut, and she struggled to reign in her temper before it broke free and hurt someone. For herself, she spared no thought; as long as no one else was hurt, it didn't matter what happened to her.

The seething energy suddenly pulled suffocatingly tight, and then rushed through her, causing her body to stiffen suddenly, and making her muscles and joints scream in protest as her nerve endings burned. Gasping and gulping in great lungfulls of air, Angeline clenched her jaw and focused her thoughts into a point, concentrating on getting herself back to earth. Carefully, she took a step forward, bracing herself for the thudding impact she would feel in her feet and knees. Still, her joints protested as she crashed to the ground, pitching forward to land hard on her hands and knees. The tempest rushed through her as she grounded herself to the earth, and wave upon wave of power rippled through the ground, knocking Devil and his friends off their feet.

The wind howled, long and loud then was cut off, almost as if the sound had been sucked away. It was over so suddenly, the absence of the wind was like a shock.

A still and stunned silence hung over the creek as her four friends picked themselves slowly up off the ground.

~CHAPTER ELEVEN~

Angeline collapsed onto her belly, her face pressed into the dirt, her fingers clutching at the moss covered ground. She cried hard as her heart broke, and the tears extinguished the blue flames that had lit her pale eyes. Slowly, she dragged herself to her feet, her face averted; she was afraid to see the fear and loathing she knew would be in their eyes. "It's better this way," she told herself, unaware she had spoken aloud, "just leave."

Her silver eyes flickered to the huddled group long enough to make sure no one was injured, then she shoved her hands into the pockets of her jacket and head down, she walked away, defeat riding her shoulders. She shivered violently as she dealt with the aftershock of so much power slamming through her system but kept going; knowing the ice in her blood and skin would eventually melt, that sooner or later, she'd be warm again.

She moved as quickly as her sore and stiff body would allow across the backyard and through the back door of Devil's house, pausing to snag her purse off the breakfast bar as the lights flickered around her and the television and radio both squealed with static. She felt so raw, so unsteady. She took a deep breath and held it, struggling to contain the residual emotion and power that strained to flood out. She felt as if she was trying to hold back a tidal wave with tissue paper; she needed to be alone, to allow herself the time to give in to the pain and misery that was threatening to eat her alive; she needed time to grieve for what could have been and for what she had lost. She wanted to cry, to scream, but was afraid to, afraid that if she weakened now, there would be nothing left standing in the aftermath. Hurrying to the bedroom, she paused long enough to snatch her hairbrush off the bathroom vanity.

Devil caught up with her as she rushed around the bedroom searching for clothing and other belongings, a small sliver of her brain marveling that so many of her belongings had managed to migrate from her room in town to Devil's house. Each item she found was stuffed unceremoniously into her beach bag. "I'll be done in a minute," she muttered as she passed him, not looking at him, afraid to see the loathing in his eyes. She ignored the trembling in her hands as she packed, her attention so diverted that she didn't notice how scraped and raw her palms were.

Devil stood in the doorway, watching in silence, unsure what, if anything, he could say. He watched her brush more tears from her cheeks and the overhead light began to flicker erratically. He watched as she sighed heavily and held her breath a few moments, her chin and lower lip trembling; she closed her eyes tightly and the light settled down.

"I didn't want you to find out like this," she whispered finally, defeat bowing her shoulders and pulling her head down. Her gaze touched his for a brief moment, then she turned away to resume her haphazard packing. Her feet became tangled in the bedspread that spilled onto the floor and she fell heavily, a sharp cry bursting from her pale lips.

Devil was beside her in half a heartbeat, helping her to stand and guiding her to sit on the bed. He continued to stand, but held onto her cold and trembling hand as he wiped more tears from her chapped and wind burned cheeks. He watched as she began to fidget under his gaze and he dropped to his knees in front of her, holding both hands in his. He frowned at the bloody scrapes on her palms. Without a word, he stood and left the room. Vaguely, Angeline was aware of the sound of water running in the bathroom sink, but didn't pay any attention. She'd just gotten to her feet to resume packing when Devil returned. Without a word, he sat on the foot of the bed and gently pulled her down beside him.

"What was that?" He asked, his voice holding none of the fear and accusation she was so accustomed to hearing; instead, she heard nothing but cautious curiosity. "Are you all right?" He asked, this time in a concerned voice as he began gently cleaning the sluggishly oozing blood from her hands. He looked up as he felt a sudden stab of shock in his gut; the sensation felt like a fist.

Angeline's eyes widened in shock; no one had *ever* worried about her after an episode except her grandmother; Cassandra, her sister, had told her why: *Who cares if the freak is hurt as long as no one else is?* Tears shimmered in her eyes again and Devil felt warmth infuse the cold fingers he still held. He watched as the lights in the room flared and dimmed in a steady rhythm, almost as if they were in concert with the beating of her heart. The gut-punch sensation faded away, leaving him wondering if he'd actually felt it.

“Are you doing that?” He asked as she took a deep breath and the lights steadied.

She nodded in answer to his question. Not knowing why she did it, Angeline decided to take a chance. “Kiss me,” she whispered as she stood and pulled him to his feet. “Please kiss me, Dev.” He almost didn’t hear her plea; her voice was the thinnest of threads.

Devil was more than happy to oblige her, though he wasn’t sure what it had to do with anything that had happened down at the creek. He dipped his head and brushed her mouth with his.

“I won’t bite,” she whispered as he lifted his head, “unless you want me to.” Her attempt at humor was weak, but he took comfort in it.

She took his hands, placed them on her hips, and then pulled him into a kiss that stunned and tantalized them both with its carnality. He hauled her roughly against his body, the hard line of his need rising instantly to press into her soft belly.

Angeline let the power of the kiss flow through her, fill her. She tried to get as close as she could to him, letting the feel, taste, and smell of him fill her senses, tangling her own need with his. She opened herself and let the force of their need flow through her and around them, holding them in a warm, golden glow, feeding it back to him through the connection of their lips. She let him gentle the kiss eventually; he pulled back and rested his forehead against hers, his breathing ragged. Angeline opened her eyes and smiled.

“Look,” she whispered.

Devil opened his eyes and glanced around. He gave a sudden shout of surprised laughter; they hovered about three inches off the floor. He grinned down at her as his hands instinctively tightened around her.

"How do we get down?" He asked an amazed grin on his face.

She held still and turned him until his back was to her, saying lightly,

"Carefully step down, like you're going down a stair." She stopped him as he started to follow her instructions. "But don't let go of my hand, otherwise you'll crash." She held his hand tightly as he stepped carefully downward, first one foot then the other. He turned and watched as she did the same. She was pale and a little shaky as they sat together on the foot of their bed. He put an arm around her shoulder and pulled her close.

"How long have you been able to do that?" He finally asked in an awed voice.

Angeline shrugged. "All my life," she replied. "I can channel my emotions into energy, and in a pinch, can borrow the energy other people create with their emotions. My grandmother was the first to realize, and she taught me how to control it, taught me how to not drain the energy from the people around me." She shrugged again. "I saw a doctor once; he said I was 'hyper-empathic'," she sighed heavily, shaking her head and rolling her eyes; "whatever that means." She leaned against him, her body limp. "I can actually *feel* the energy generated whenever someone experiences fear, anger, joy, sadness, or loneliness, and I can use it if I need too. Usually, though, my own emotional energy is enough." She grimaced. "Sometimes too much," she added ruefully. She darted a nervous look at him. "And I can influence the emotions of people around me; calm them down if they need it, and if I'm not careful, I can make them feel what I'm feeling. That's what just happened; I was on the verge of losing control, and everything I was feeling would have spilled out and infected you and the others. I couldn't let that happen." She swallowed hard, feeling the need to defend herself, though he hadn't said a word and his expression hadn't changed. "I usually don't have any trouble controlling it, but lately it's been a different story; I'm not attacking you, I promise," she hurried to reassure him, her now warm hand caressing his cheek, "But you are very bad for my control." Her smile was hesitant, but something warm and pleading shone from her eyes. "You make me want to just let go and hope for the best." She shivered and shook her head. "I don't know what would happen if I ever did, and I've been too afraid to find out." She took a deep breath as the lights began their lightshow again. When they steadied, she continued. "Today, I got so mad when I realized Chris was playing his games with you and the others, and it blew up inside and around me before I had a chance to rein it in." She jumped to her feet and began to pace. "I'm not sure exactly what happened," she muttered half to herself, "I don't know why it built up so fast." When she looked at him, he saw the untruth lurking in her eyes; she knew *exactly* what had happened, but didn't want to say. He decided then and there to pry the truth from her one way or another.

"I didn't mean to lose it so badly," she continued, her tone earnest as she tried to make him understand. "I tried to get away so I could bleed the excess off, but I couldn't." She saw when he put two and two together.

"The cove," he exclaimed, looking up at her, understanding lighting his expression, "you go to the cove whenever you're upset."

Angeline nodded in relief. "Being near the ocean calms me, helps me find my center so I can keep from melting down like I did today. I knew almost immediately that my control was blown away; I was so angry and when I couldn't get away, I started getting scared, too; I was afraid I could never face you or the others again once you knew what I can do, and I didn't want any of you to get hurt." She sighed at his questioning look. "It's happened one other time, my losing control like that, and a boy got hurt. It was an accident, but pcople who once called me their friend suddenly treated me like a leper, and I didn't want to go through that again." She saw him shaking his head. "Even if you don't have a problem with it, your friends might," she argued, defensive again, "I won't make you choose between a your friends and me." She stopped in front of him, her expression grave. "I'll tell you everything I know about Chris and the notes, and then I'm leaving." Her voice broke and she turned away, trying to hide the tears that had begun to spill down her cheeks. Just then, Michael, Melissa, and Jamie burst noisily into the room, having been eavesdropping in the hallway outside the room.

"You can't leave!" Melissa said shrilly. "I'm your friend, too; don't I get a say?" She looked so fierce that Angeline was afraid to tell her she didn't.

Michael pulled Melissa back. "Down girl," he muttered to her, earning a scathing look. "What my sweet wife is trying to say is we want you to stay."

Angeline took a deep breath, looking from face to face, unconvinced and afraid to be hopeful. "It's my ex fiancé," she told them. "I told him a year ago to get that portable printer of his cleaned and serviced; obviously he hasn't, and doesn't think I will remember what a mess that printer made of everything."

She grabbed her beach bag and looped the straps over her shoulder. "Chris thinks he's smarter than everyone else, but he isn't one for really thinking things out; he acts like a spoiled bully when he doesn't get his way, and will stoop to just about anything to get what he wants." She took a step toward the door. "He's in Bounty Cove, trying to make things miserable for me. Once he realizes I'm gone, he'll follow me; he'll move on and leave you alone."

She took another step. “I should go now, before this gets any harder.” The words came out tear-laden and choked.

“Not until you explain what happened at the creek,” Devil said in a deceptively mild voice. There was no way in Hell he was allowing her to just walk away; no way would he be able to live with himself if she did.

Angeline rolled her eyes. “What’s to explain?” She asked in exasperation, and impatient to make a clean break. “I got angry and lost control.” She took another step, and tried not to call attention to the bedside lamp as it flickered.

Devil slowly shook his head. “There’s something you’re not telling me,” he told her, remembering her confession of love. Before she could reply, he pointed to the light above their heads; it was flickering madly, the glow bright and intense. He quirked a dark eyebrow at her; “Tell me,” he persisted, “because whatever really sent you around the bend earlier is still bugging you now.” He pushed a little more. “You weren’t just angry; there was something more; I could hear it in your voice when you screamed.”

Angeline’s head dropped and her shoulders drooped. “I have to leave you, and I don’t want too,” she whispered, and Devil felt a wave of sadness ebb and flow between them; he realized suddenly that the alien emotion was coming from Angeline and in that moment, understood just how lonely she really was; the emotion flattened him. He crooked his finger at her, beckoning her to his side; he frowned when she shook her head.

“I have to go now,” she whispered. “It’ll be better once I’m gone.”

Michael stepped in front of her, blocking the exit. “You mean the mere thought of leaving this miserable bastard caused you to create your own personal tornado?” He shook his head in wonder as Angeline nodded, grateful someone was trying to understand what had happened without her having to spell it out; she was ashamed that she'd allowed herself to lose control so completely.

"Anger is a clean emotion," she said flatly. "It flares and dies pretty fast. It hurts to think about leaving," she added, "and pain muddies things up a lot, because there are so many different kinds of pain, so many different layers to it."

"Where will you go?" Jamie asked worriedly. "I hope you don't plan to go too far away," he continued. "Devil won't be easy to be around if you do." He shuddered for effect then gave Angeline a grin that she answered with a weak smile of her own, showing that she appreciated Jamie's attempt to lighten her mood.

Angeline jumped as she felt Devil's arms come around her. He kissed the top of her hair softly and gave her a gentle squeeze. "You can't leave," he murmured against her hair, "You know it's already too late." Angeline felt her resolve weakening as she unconsciously relaxed against his body.

It would be so easy to stay, she thought to herself wistfully, *how nice it would be to stop running once and for all.* Chris Jessop's face floated before her mind's eye, turning her stomach and causing a clammy sweat to break out on her palms and down her back.

"No!" She cried, pulling out of Devil's embrace, denying the truth of his words. All the light bulbs in the room blew out loudly, showering them with glass. She began to pace in agitation. "Don't you understand how dangerous I am?" She pointed to the overhead light fixture as it smoked slightly. She glared at Devil; she could tell he had felt the shock of energy as it rushed out of her and through him into the room. She watched as he sank onto the foot of the bed again, his expression shocked. "I could hurt you without meaning to; don't you know how much of a danger I am to you?" Her eyes pleaded with him. *Please*, her heart whispered, *I don't want to hurt you; I love you.* She watched him nod slowly and felt her heart clench.

Melissa stepped in front of her, her arms folded across her chest. "Yes, we do," she said in a lazy drawl. "At the rate you're going, you'll bankrupt Devil, replacing light bulbs and lamps." She saw Angeline's lips twitch. Melissa's voice dropped, pleading in her tone. "If you leave you'll hurt us worse than you can imagine." She hugged Angeline tightly. "You'll break our hearts," she whispered, "especially Devil's"

Indecision bowed Angeline's head until it lay on Melissa's shoulder. "You're not afraid of me?" She whispered, the words catching in her throat.

Jamie pushed Melissa aside and wrapped Angeline in a rib-cracking hug. "Frankly," he told her as he released her, "I'm more afraid of what Devil will do if you go."

Angeline moved away, her eyes on the backyard beyond the deck outside Devil's room. "If anyone knew," she began, chewing her bottom lip. "I don't want any of you to be embarrassed; I don't want to cause you any trouble. I embarrassed Chris," she added, almost to herself, as if it was explanation enough for her leaving them.

Michael chuckled. "This is Bounty Cove, darlin'," he drawled, "And let me tell you, this little town attracts more than its fair share of weirdness. No one's going to look twice at you or be embarrassed by you." He shrugged. "Hell, most people won't even notice a few flickering lights, or the occasional light bulb blow out. Those things happen all the time naturally."

She turned and looked at them, her arms akimbo. "Fine," she said. "So no one's worried I'll accidentally blow them up, but what about Chris? He's still out there and he can cause more trouble for you than for me; he's a lawyer who has no problem with playing dirty. He'll dig around until he finds something serious that he can actually use against each of you, simply because you're my friends, just because you're trying to protect me from him." She took a deep breath, steadying her resolve. "I don't want any of you hurt by him or myself; that's why I'm leaving."

Devil jumped to his feet with a roar. "Like hell!" He grabbed Angeline by the shoulders and shook her. Angeline ground her teeth together tightly to prevent herself from accidently flattening Devil where he stood; pain radiated throughout her system and it was becoming harder and harder to keep it reined in. She was afraid of what might happen if she didn't leave soon; the pain was simply too much to bear anymore. The clock radio beside the bed began to smoke and sparks escaped from the speaker vents in the top.

"You're not going anywhere," he ground out between his teeth. The bedroom door shut as the other three beat a hasty retreat. Devil's hands gentled. "No more running, Angel," he said gently. "It's time to stand and fight for what you want." He kissed the tears from her cheek before kissing her trembling mouth. "Don't go," he whispered. "I can't live without you."

Angeline's heart responded to the naked need in his voice; not just the physical need that was always between them, but the emotional and spiritual need as well. She kissed him and felt her uncertainties melt away under the warmth of his touch. A seed of hope blossomed in her heart, gently replacing the sorrow and loneliness that had resided there, nurtured by the love she felt emanating from the man who held her so securely in his heart and arms. "We should get outside before you don't have any electronics left," she murmured, trying to keep her voice light.

They stepped out to the deck off the bedroom and waved goodbye to their friends; when the trio was gone, she and Devil resumed their creek side ramble, stealing kisses and caresses every few steps. They came to a small footbridge that spanned the creek and led to the far side of the gurgling waterway. Angeline spied a small stone structure on the other side; she and Devil headed for it quickly as a light rain began to fall. They ducked inside as the rain and wind intensified.

Angeline sat in a stone bench, pulling Devil down with her. She sighed as he hauled her against his chest and her hands sought to touch him wherever they could as she returned kiss for fiery kiss. She needed his touch, the feel and heat of him as she needed to breathe. She sighed against his mouth and snuggled against his hard chest.

"I wish we could stay here forever," she said wistfully as she listened to the patter of the rain on the leaves of the trees and the steady beat of his heart. The air around them grew warm as she let the residual energy bleed off. She relaxed as she felt the tension leave her mind and body; she was safe here with Devil; she trusted him with her life.

"This is the Kissing Temple," he told her, his quiet, deep voice shaking her out of her reverie. "My great-grandfather built a similar one for his wife." He dropped a kiss on her damp mouth. "The story goes that he took a walk with her one evening during a party his parents were hosting and they fell in love; he later had a similar temple built on the spot where they kissed for the first time for their first wedding anniversary." He dipped his head and kissed her slowly, the heat of it leaving her yearning for more. He pulled away and resumed his tale. "Even after he died, she would go out to the temple every year on their anniversary. The original temple is at my grandmother's house, and legend has it you can go out to it on the night of their anniversary, and see them kissing in the moonlight." He paused to kiss her upturned nose. "I had this one built in the hopes of having someone to share it with someday."

Angeline sighed dreamily. "How romantic," she said, leaning up to kiss his chin and tucking her hands against his body to warm them.

Devil chuckled softly as her fingers accidently tickled as they skimmed his ribs. He captured her mouth with his own and kissed her slowly, stealing her senses away. He slid his mouth along her cheek to her jaw, his lips tracing a path to her ear. "Don't go, Angel," he murmured softly. His mouth slid to her throat as he lifted her high against his chest. "Lie to me if you have to," he said roughly, "just say you'll never leave." He claimed her mouth in a kiss that seared her soul and made her toes curl.

"God, I love you," he said hoarsely, clutching a handful of curls. He tugged lightly, pulling her head back so he could see her eyes. "I love you," he repeated, savoring the taste of the words on his tongue; he suddenly felt lighter, as if a weight had been lifted from his chest. He felt the warm air around them pulse as if it was in tune to the rhythm of her heartbeat. He felt a surge of something from her that sank into his body and warmed him quickly. He watched her eyes flutter open and saw her silver eyes turn the color of charcoal and felt her breath fan across his cheek. Her tongue darted out to moisten her lower lip and he swallowed a groan.

Angeline was happily stunned; she felt that small seed of hope sprout shyly in her chest, unfurling tender tendrils that sought the warmth he offered. Her heart thumped in her chest, as her soul sang to the heavens; he loved her! All her life she had waited for him; had hoped and prayed she would finally find him. She had been so terrified of losing him so soon after finally finding him that she'd almost incinerated herself and everything around her out of sheer misery and the need to rail against the unfairness of it all. Now he had declared his love for her, and while she was deliriously happy, a tiny part of her heart and mind held back. Her small hand lifted and fluttered in the air near the side of her head.

"What about...?" Her hand fell to her lap.

Devil smiled softly. "What about it?" He asked with a shrug. "It's part of you; it makes you who you are, and I love you—*all* of you; I can't love just bits and pieces, Angel." He held his breath, praying she would hear the truth and believe it.

Angeline worried her bottom lip between her teeth. She gazed at him for several long heartbeats and felt the honesty of his words radiating from him. She felt her soul silently answering him, reaching for him, yearning for what he offered. She dropped all her defenses and threw herself into his arms, laughing as tears ran down her cheeks.

"I love you," she whispered repeatedly between kisses. "I'll never leave."

Devil heard the honesty in her words and felt it in her kiss and touch. He was startled by something out of the corner of his eye and chuckled when he realized what it was: the fallen leaves that littered the floor of the stone temple now flittered around them like butterflies as a golden light bathed them in a warm glow. He returned his attention to Angeline and deepened the kiss until he lost his wits. His hands molded themselves to her breasts, stroking and squeezing gently. Sweet little sighs escaped her lips as she arched deeper into his touch. She felt herself melting under his kiss, glowing under his touch.

His lips traced her jaw to the long line of her throat, then on to the gentle slope of her shoulder. He lifted her to straddle his lap and pulled her shirt over her head. She leaned back against the arm he had wrapped around her back and tipped her head back as he pressed hot wet kisses across her shoulder and chest. She gasped his name as his mouth grazed a tight nipple, the lace of her bra adding a sweet friction. Her fingers clenched in his dark hair, holding him close, her body pleading for more.

Fire exploded through her blood as his warm fingers brushed the skin of her belly, and skimmed over her ribs, tracing slow, tantalizing circles just below her breasts causing a heavy throbbing deep in her belly. She whimpered deep in her throat as his clever fingers undid her bra. She sighed into his touch.

"Your shirt," she panted and pulled the hem of his shirt out of his waistband. She waited impatiently as he pulled it over his head and tossed it aside. He grasped her bottom and stood suddenly, turning to lay her across the stone bench on which he had been seated. The stone was slightly warmed from his body heat, but she still gasped as the cold of the stone touched her feverish body. The contradictory sensations of warmth and cold collided within her, causing her blood to pound just a little harder through her body. She whimpered in need as her nipples hardened more.

He knelt next to her, his lips and tongue tasting the soft skin of her inner wrist. "Close your eyes," he said in a husky voice. When she complied, he lowered his head to kiss her damp and swollen mouth. She jumped slightly and tried to wrap her arms around him. Devil pushed her hands down and away, determined to snap her control once and for all.

"Relax," he told her. "I want to drive you crazy."

"You already are," she complained. His response was a chuckle that sounded heartless to her ears. She would have pouted if he hadn't chosen that moment to kiss her again.

He held her hands loosely in his as he continued to kiss her. He felt her relax little by little, as the heat rose between them. He let go of her hands, stroked, and kneaded her muscles until she felt as if she had been reduced to a puddle of quivering, hypersensitive flesh. She floated on the pleasure his touch gave her and when his mouth closed over her nipple she gasped, the pleasure as sharp a contrast that it was almost painful. She tried to touch him, to twine her fingers through his hair as he continued to lavish hot, wet kisses across her chest and to pull deeply on her nipples, but once again, he held her hands away.

"Not yet," he growled, his dark eyes glimmering wickedly, "I want to watch you shatter."

He shifted, his fingers continuing their exploration of her ribs as his tongue laved wet trails across her belly. He could feel the heat of her blood as it flushed her skin a delicate pink. His fingers roamed past the waistband of her jeans, delving until he touched her damp and swollen flesh. The breath rushed from her body as a cry erupted from her lips, her hips lifting against his hand to seek relief. Yet it wasn't enough; not nearly enough to satisfy him.

Devil stroked the damp curls, teasing and tormenting the sensitive nubbin of flesh hidden in her soft folds. She sobbed his name, her head tossing side to side, her hands clenching and unclenching. She moved restlessly against him, shivers of pleasure darting through her legs and arms.

"Devil, please," she cried. He rose quickly and pulled the rest of his clothing off as she shimmied out of her jeans.

Within moments, he was holding her close, his large hands cradling her body as he shifted her easily until she was seated on his lap facing him. He had to grit his teeth as she wiggled against him, teasing and seeking to drive him mad. Desperate to gain the upper hand again, he suddenly stood and turned, laying her gently across the stone bench.

"Not yet," he told her again, his voice a low growl as she reached out to pull him to her. He caught her small hands in his and stretched them above her head as he slid slowly into her. Angeline groaned low in her throat as she arched her back, bringing her full, pouty breasts to his attention. He caught a nipple between his teeth gently and sucked hard as he thrust deeper. He teased her, his body moving slowly upon hers as he held himself back, resisting her urging pleas. He meant to break her control completely, to drive her beyond frenzy, even if it killed him. Resolutely, he grit his teeth and resisted the siren call of her writhing body and pleading cries.

The soft golden light pulsed around them in time with the throbbing of her heart; the air grew warmer, moister as the heat of her body grew. A sheen of perspiration dampened her skin and she glowed. He sank slowly into her and withdrew just as slowly as she writhed beneath him, testing the limits of his own control. She managed to free her hands and she reached up to plunge her fingers into his hair, pulling him down to her for a soul searing kiss. Her tongue rubbed against his in the same rhythm her body created beneath his; she pressed her hot aching body against him, feeling him throb and pulse heavily deep within her body, seeking relief that only he could give her. Devil felt himself slipping away, his body switching to autopilot and he shook himself. He grasped her backside and lifted her hips high against him.

"Look at me," he ground out between his teeth, his voice tight.

Angeline struggled to open her eyes as he pulled back to the very edge of her body. Her silver eyes, now charcoal dark, glowed like starlight on a soft summer night.

"Let go," she heard him say just before he thrust deep.

She shattered.

She burned.

The world imploded around her.

She came undone hard and fast in a firestorm of pure sensation; her back arched as she cried out, every fiber of her being incandescent. She lost herself to the inferno he unleashed in her blood; flames and sparks licked her nerve endings as heat blossomed from the point where their bodies joined. In an instant, she felt her soul fly apart in a breathless rush of phoenix wings.

Devil held himself motionless above her as he witnessed her complete surrender to exquisite pleasure; her eyes wide, her voice urgent, her nails leaving red welts in their wake as she clutched him for anchorage. He felt the surge of power explode through her nerve endings into his body, causing fire to ignite in his blood, infecting him with the soul deep bliss she was experiencing. He felt as if his skin was seared by her heat; his blood boiled in his veins and he felt the air rush from his lungs. The golden light flared as the fallen leaves fluttering around them each burst into flames, one by one by one. She moved beneath him, her body seeking more, her hips moving in a frenzied, sensual invitation. She pulled him down to kiss him, her tongue hot against his. The embers of her passion flared anew, hot and searing, and she drew her knees higher, allowing her thighs to fall open wider, her hips lifting high to meet his downward thrust, a burning ache spreading from the junction of their bodies. She gasped at the power of the sensations that flowed through her nerve endings—more intense and immediate this time than before. She rose up, her arms clasping around him as her teeth bit into his shoulder, inadvertently drawing blood. Devil let loose, his control gone, and drove them both hard and relentlessly until they both cried out as the conflagration incinerated them both. Devil felt his mind go blank as he emptied his essence deep into her body, happily following her into the inferno.

~CHAPTER TWELVE~

Angeline was limp; the mere thought of moving so much as an eyelash seemed an impossible task. She felt a heavy, heavenly lethargy steal through her limbs and she sighed at the feel of Devil's weight upon her, pressing her against the stone bench. She wasn't uncomfortable; quite the contrary—she welcomed the feel of him covering her, warming her. Gradually she felt the energy returning to her limbs, and was startled to realize it was fed to her by the man slumped over her. She tasted that energy, tested it, drew it deep within herself and made it part of her own swiftly regenerating reserves. He had broken her control, left her unable to shield him from her own feelings, and leaving her open to his in return. She felt stripped, exposed, and she instinctively feared that vulnerability she now felt as she lay beneath him. She became aware of the chilling rain that blew into the temple on a cold wind and she shivered and tried to burrow closer into Devil's warmth.

Devil, meanwhile, was finding it difficult to breathe or think; the overwhelming power of their mutual climax had robbed him of his breath and what few wits he had left. However, he too, was becoming aware of his surroundings, and felt the cold rain on his overheated body. He felt shivers radiating from Angeline as she huddled beneath him, and he shifted, pulling them both into a sitting position. He held her loosely, still stunned by the absolute glory of her shattered control; he had witnessed the jaw dropping power of Angeline's ability in all its terrifying splendor, had realized that the tiny woman in his arms was much stronger and braver than he'd ever imagined, and it profoundly humbled him. He felt her shiver, and he nuzzled her ear.

"Are you cold?" He asked, feeling the goosebumps rise on her skin. Mutely, she shook her head and tucked her face closer to his body. It was then that he became aware of how still she was. "Did I hurt you?"

Again, he felt her head shake. Again, she pressed in closer. Alarmed, he tightened his hold, and was dismayed at the warm dampness he felt against his skin. He gently forced her head up to peer into her silver eyes. "What is it?" He asked, afraid he had hurt her and she was trying to spare him the truth.

Angeline sniffled, and tried to smile. How sweet and earnest he looked in that moment! She tried to reassure him. "It's nothing," she soothed, touching his cheek, "I've never lost control when I was happy before." This time when she smiled, it was easier. "It's a very odd feeling, that's all." At his quizzical look, she tried to explain. "I told you that anger is clean, and pain makes things harder to control, because there are so many degrees of it." He nodded and she furrowed her brow, searching for the right words. Finally, she asked, "How do you feel?"

Devil frowned, but said the first thing that came to mind: "Light."

Angeline seemed to deflate in his arms. "That's exactly how I'm feeling, too," she told him, her gaze steady on his. "Joy, no matter the reason, is one of the purest emotions a human can experience; it lifts you, makes your soul take wing. Everything I'm feeling, you are too, and I think I might be feeling things from you in return." When he looked confused, she sighed. "You made me lose complete control," she told him, and then swiftly covered his mouth with her hand when he started to protest, "It's all right." She closed her eyes, looking deep inside herself for a moment. She smiled as she opened her eyes again. "The energy it takes for me to maintain control, to shield myself and others around me is quickly rebuilding, thanks to you." She couldn't actually show him what was happening, so she let him feel it instead.

Devil's eyes widened as she laid a small hand over his heart and kissed him; he felt a thread of his own energy filtering into her, feeding her, strengthening her. She in turn took his energy and made it her own before feeding it back to him in a continuous cycle. And he suddenly understood that that single, tenuous strand of energy was slowing knitting itself into an unbreakable bond between them.

"I'm the happiest right now that I've ever been in my life," he heard her murmur, "Because of you, I feel lighter than air; and because of what you did to me, you feel it too."

He opened his eyes wide and stared at her, noticing for the first time that the golden glow that had bathed them while they made love had not diminished; instead, it seemed to be growing steadily brighter, warmer, in time to their synchronized heartbeats. It was mystical, mythical, this connection between them, and he didn't want it to end.

Angeline had braced herself for rejection once he came to grips with what was happening between them, and though the thought of severing the connection between them burned like acid in her gut, she prepared herself to do just that as quickly and as cleanly as she could if that's what he wanted. So when he suddenly smiled and kissed her, she was all the more surprised and confused. She pushed herself back, out of his kiss, and stared at him in shock. "You're not disgusted?" She asked, trying to keep the hope blossoming in her chest under careful control.

"I love you," he told her simply. "You are the most courageous, strongest, most beautiful woman I've ever known. If I had any idea that breaking your control like that would tie you to me like this, I would have done it sooner."

Angeline stared at him wordlessly, the absolute truth of his feelings and words ringing crystal clear in her heart and ears. With a little cry, she threw her arms around him and kissed him soundly, joyously.

They eventually dragged their clothes on a long while later, their movements slow, and he helped her with the clasp of her bra when he realized her fingers were still too clumsy to complete the task. They ran through the raindrops and back up the gentle slope of the backyard. The thin linen shirt Angeline had worn was soaked through, and he could see her nipples, pink and hard, through her top and bra. He felt a stirring in his body, and shoved it aside for the time being.

Once they reached the house, Devil took extreme pleasure in undressing Angeline in order to get her into a hot shower. He joined her within moments and shampooed her hair before lazily running soapy hands over her curves. She arched into his touch like a cat as his long fingers stroked through the thatch of curls at the apex of her thighs. She clung to him weakly as he stroked and probed, her knees unable to support her weight. He lifted her and wrapped her slender legs about his hips before turning off the water and stepping out of the shower. He kissed her slowly, drugging her senses as he carried her to the bedroom. He lowered her to the bed, following her down. This time they took their time, stretching each touch, each sigh, each moment as far as they could, prolonging their union as much as possible. Devil wanted her to feel nothing but passion and pleasure. Her keening cry of release as she reached her moment told him he had accomplished that goal. He joined her in sweet oblivion moments later.

Angeline awoke much later, the sky outside the windows dark and stormy. Devil was curled around her, his front to her back, his arm draped across her hip. His hand pressed against her belly, his fingers stroking the skin even as he slept. Her stomach growled impatiently and she needed to use the bathroom. She squirmed out from under his arm and rose from bed. She rummaged through her beach bag until she found her long nightshirt. She pulled it over her head and padded on bare feet to the door.

"Where are you going?" Devil asked sleepily. Angeline went to him and bent to kiss him.

"I'm hungry," she told him. "I'll be back in a few minutes."

She turned and left the room. By the time she was finished in the bathroom Devil was awake and pulling on pajama bottoms.

"You said something about food," he said with a grin.

"Actually, I said I was hungry," she laughed. "But I wouldn't mind some company." She giggled as he came to her and wrapped his arms around her, kissing the side of her neck.

"Mmmm..." he growled, nipping her earlobe lightly. "I'm hungry enough to eat you," he rumbled in her ear, his breath sending goosebumps across her skin.

"Food," she scolded him in a breathless voice as shivers ran riot up and down her spine, "Not sex." She pulled out of his embrace and turned on her heel, her stomach complaining more loudly. She glanced over her shoulder at him and her eyes widened as she read his expression. She gave a shriek as he lunged at her.

He chased her through the house, Angeline darting around furniture, laughter trilling through the rooms. He cornered her against the couch and made to grab her, his arms thrown wide. Angeline jumped onto the couch and ran across it to jump over the arm. She landed lightly and laughed as she saw his expression, both surprised and disgruntled all at once. She turned and flew into the kitchen, Devil hard on her heels. He caught her hand and pressed up against her until she was pinned against the counter. He lifted her up, seated her on the counter top, and kissed her silly, food temporarily forgotten as they indulged in an entrée of an entirely different sort. It was only when her stomach rumbled loudly that they turned their attention back to food.

She set Devil to chopping green peppers and onions while she grated cheddar cheese and chopped tomatoes. She rummaged in the 'fridge and found some mushrooms that she sliced thin. Devil whipped eggs into a frothy foam and added the onions and peppers. Ten minutes later, they were seated and happily eating omelets. They ate in compatible silence for several minutes until Devil cleared his throat. He looked her in the eye, his gaze steady and serious.

"I think you should move in."

Angeline dropped her fork in shocked surprise. She stared at him, her eyes wide, as the light over the table burned out with a pop. He chuckled at the surge of energy that flared around them as she gaped at him, letting the waves of surprise she felt wash over him; obviously, she hadn't regained much of her control.

"Move in?" She squeaked. Her forked trembled on the tabletop.

Devil reached over casually and stopped the utensil as it began to spin on its own. "Yes," he said slowly, with warmth in his tone. "You practically live here now, anyway. I'm sure that bob cat of yours would like to see you more."

Guilt pricked Angeline's conscience; she rarely spent the night at the hotel anymore, and only stopped in to change clothes and take care of Nicodemious. But to actually move in with Devil was something she hadn't considered. His next words made up her mind for her:

"It'll be harder for Jessop to harass you."

Angeline agreed and they finished their late night meal, neither of them realizing Chris Jessop was closer than they realized. Just twenty yards away, he stood within the shadowy tree line on the far edge of the back yard, his binoculars trained on Angeline as she laughed and played house with her dark haired protector. His teeth ground together until his jawed ached and his fingers itched to slip around her slender white throat, to feel her struggle against him as he punished her for this betrayal.

He watched her almost constantly now, the pressure to deal with Angeline and return to Portland increasing daily. His mother and boss were now calling several times a day and he was running out of excuses to prolong his absence. After witnessing the spectacular display of Angeline's abilities at the creek and the continued support of her new friends, Jessop realized his little notes had failed to do the job; although, truth be told, he was no longer certain what the final goal of the notes had been. He had been drinking the night he hatched that particular plan and had been forced to concede failure once he realized a few words on paper weren't going to dissuade the growing protectiveness Angeline's new friends felt towards her.

So now, he watched and waited, looking for the smallest opportunity for a snatch and grab. He'd been busy outfitting the basement of the old Larsen place for a private party between Angeline and himself. He had decided to give himself forty-eight hours to convince her to return home with him, using whatever means it took to do so. If, at the end of that time she still refused, he would kill her, telling himself the pleasure he would take in the act would help him move on. It had been so with the other girls with one exception: he really wanted Angeline to share his life. He hadn't loved the others.

He watched the lovers finish their meal and move from the kitchen; he crept through the yard and knelt in the shadows beneath the bedroom deck as the sliding glass door opened. Once sleep descended on the lovers he slipped away, slinking through the shadows, his mind replaying the sight of Angeline naked and writhing; his imagination placing himself in the picture.

~CHAPTER THIRTEEN~

"Tell me about Bounty Cove," Angeline said, later the next day. She and Devil lounged on a comfortable couch as they watched Nicodemious explore his new surroundings. "Why did Michael say no one would look twice at me?"

Devil tucked her securely against his side, the arm around her shoulders bent so he could run his fingers through her curls. "Are you letting it grow?" He asked as he enjoyed the silky texture.

Angeline shrugged. "I thought it might be a nice change," she trailed off. "And you're trying to change the subject; tell me about Bounty Cove," she said again, a little breathlessly as he leaned down to kiss her ear. She pulled away a little to lessen to impact of his lips on her skin. "Why did Michael say that?"

Devil sighed heavily. He had many things on his mind, and a lesson in local history wasn't one of them. "Because it's true," he told her. "Bounty Cove was settled by British and Colonial soldiers who were tired of fighting each other and everyone else. Others joined them and within a year, a town charter was written. In a nutshell it says anyone can find a home in Bounty Cove, no matter whom or what they are or where they come from." He sighed. "Then again, maybe it's because everyone you talk to around here either believes in UFO's, ghosts, or both." He grunted when her elbow dug into his ribs as she twisted around to gaze at him suspiciously.

"Don't tease," She said in a small voice. He returned her look with as much wide-eyed innocence as he could manage.

"I'm not," he assured her. "I'll take you to talk to Sue Beasley," he told her. "She's a widow who owns a bookstore in town and carries a wide selection of books on local history. She's also written a couple books herself, detailing the local legends." He chuckled as he thought of the plump little redhead that ran the bookstore; that was one woman he had always been afraid to get on the wrong side of. "Sue's a nice lady," he continued. "She can be a little overwhelming when you first meet her, but once you get to know her, you realize just what a warm, wonderful person she really is."

She stared at him, her eyes solemn and wide. She still felt a overwhelming sense of amazement and relief that Devil had been so accepting of her and her abilities. She expected to wake up and find that she'd been dreaming the last several months in Bounty Cove. She told him as much, keeping her eyes down, worried that her confession wouldn't set well with him. To her surprise, Devil's response to her confession was to pull her closer and kiss the nape of her neck.

"Did you know that Michael and I were in school together at the University of North Carolina?" He asked her in a mild, soothing voice. At her headshake, he continued. "Yeah. We were roommates, and I heard a lot about Bounty Cove in the four years we roomed together;

including the stories about some of the people who live here." He chuckled. "I didn't believe him at first," he admitted, ruefully. "So I came home with him for Christmas, and lo and behold, I met Sue Beesley. Within ten minutes of walking into her store, she'd told me a few things about myself that no one else knew. As I sat in her store, drinking coffee, she patiently explained to me that in this world, there were people, just like me, but with special talents, and Bounty Cove called to those people, brought them here. Sometimes they're people who have nowhere else to go, or people who need a place to hide away for a little while. Others are simply meant to be here," he added, gazing down into her upturned face. "Then a few years back, I decided to drop in on my old friend, and found him married to a little whirlwind of a woman and living in a haunted house." He paused, and then went on to tell Angeline Melissa and Michael's story. By the end of it, Angeline had silent tears on her cheeks; she had never realized the true depths of the Kemper's love for each other until Devil told her their story. She allowed him to turn her in his embrace and kiss the tears from her face. "I'm not going to run away screaming," he told her quietly. "Believe me when I say that there's nothing you could possibly do to top the things I've seen since I settled here." He held her silver gaze, willing her to believe him once and for all. The minutes stretched between them, unbroken and in silence. When she finally nodded and gave him a smile, he released the breath he hadn't realized he'd been holding; he wasn't sure he'd been able to find the right words to make her believe in him, in them. She turned in his arms, settled her back against his chest, and pulled a light blanket off the back of the couch to cover them.

He felt Angeline sigh and relax against his chest, her breathing deepening into slumber; he'd noticed she seemed to be feeling more tired than usual recently, but chalked it up to her recent loss of control and the resultant need to replenish her energy as well as their late night activities. He tucked the throw blanket around them more securely, and leaned his head back against the couch cushions. Nicodemious jumped up next to them with a little trill and settled down against his thigh, purring for all he was worth. Devil reached down and stroked the cat slowly, enjoying the feel of the warm fur beneath his fingertips. He closed his eyes, and let a soothing feeling of contentment ease across his heart and soul. As he joined Angeline in slumber, he decided there was something very nice about living a quiet, domestic life.

She was alone, walking along the shore, waves washing across her feet and erasing her footprints in the wet sand behind her, obliterating all trace of her passing. It was dusk, the moon rising like a pale face over the churning water. The sandy beach glowed darkly in the moonlight, the shadows seeming to reach out toward her, threatening to engulf her. She paused in her steps, and turned to peer across the sand; something was there, watching and waiting. "What do you want?" She called out to the shadows. "I'm not afraid." She felt, rather than saw, shadows shift, and felt something beckon to her. She stepped hesitantly away from the sea, knowing she should stay close to the water's edge to stay safe, but unable to deny the silent call. She walked several feet up the shore, and glanced back at the ocean, taking comfort in its constant presence. As she faced forward again, the shadows suddenly closed in around her, choking off the light, cutting off her escape route. She floundered through the dark, blind and disoriented. Something seethed toward her, stalking and slavering. She could feel its hot breath on her cheek, could smell its rancid breath. She cried out for help, but none came. She heard laughter all around her, taunting her, shattering her composure. She fell to her knees, her hands over her ears in a vain attempt to shut out the sound.

She knew she would die in this cold, dark place.

Her heart cried out against the unfairness of it; she still had so much to do, so many things to experience. In her mind's eye, she saw Devil's face, and the light of her love for him ignited in her chest, filling her with warmth and hope. She called out to him, her voice small in the darkness. She felt his touch and heard his voice; it dispelled the inky darkness around her. She blinked in the bright light, and returned to the water's edge...

Devil soothed her as she tossed and turned restlessly in the clutches of the dream, muttering and calling his name. He kissed her forehead, brushing the curls away from her face. She snuggled into his touch, and eventually calmed, a smile gracing her sleeping mouth. Devil tightened his hold around her small warm body and let sleep steal over him again.

Several days later, Angeline had the opportunity to meet Sue Beasley. She wandered into the other woman's bookstore, and within moments, realized she had found a new friend. Sue Beasley was perhaps five foot tall, plump, and red haired; Angeline felt positively tall standing next to her. Though Sue was tiny, she made up for it in attitude; she had a gregarious, outgoing personality and a sunny smile. She wore her auburn hair in a shoulder length style that accentuated high cheekbones and bright blue eyes. She had five children, four of them boys, and one daughter, and all of them much taller than she, though it was obvious she ruled the roost. Angeline walked into the small shop just in time to witness the small woman roundly taking down a tall thin young man; by his hair color, Angeline correctly assumed he was her son.

"If I had wanted the shelves rearranged, I would have done it myself!" She was telling the obviously chastised teenager. "Really, Anthony James, what were you thinking?" A small, plump hand bearing several rings gestured to the shop in general. The young man mumbled something under his breath, and Sue turned sharply to look at Angeline. "We'll finish this later," she told her son, "now please go and see about that new shipment for me." She dismissed her son and walked forward to greet Angeline with a smile.

"Welcome to Books of Bounty," she said in a friendly tone. "I'm Sue Beasley." She offered her hand.

Angeline shook the owner's hand and introduced herself.

"Of course I know who you are," Sue said warmly. "You can't live in Bounty Cove for long before everyone knows everything about you." She pulled a wry face. "Don't try keeping secrets; someone will find out."

Angeline felt herself grow a little pale. She swallowed hard. Seeing her visitor's pallor, Sue winked and patted the hand she still held in her own. "Don't worry, though," she said reassuringly, "No one will give a damn about any skeletons in your closet." She gave a little chuckle and motioned Angeline to follow her.

Angeline nodded wordlessly, wondering how the town's folk would react if they knew she could blow them up with a thought. She followed Sue down an aisle and watched as the woman began selecting books from various shelves around them. These she piled into Angeline's arms, a steady patter of conversation peppered with the occasional cry of delight coming from her mouth. She allowed the woman's energy to flow over her and felt the warm wash of her friendly nature and occasional starburst of absentminded preoccupation that emanated from her. Sue paused and stood, her eyes widening in surprise as Angeline continued to peer over the ever-growing stack of books.

"I'm sorry!" She exclaimed, taking half the pile into her own hands. "I get carried away when I'm excited." She motioned toward the back of the store with her bright head. "Let's bring these to the counter and we can have a cup of coffee." Moments later the two women set their burdens on the wooden counter and Angeline allowed herself to be led to a small café table that sat off to one side. As she settled into a little wrought iron chair, Angeline let her eyes wander around the store, and gave a start of surprise when something brushed across her ankle. Looking down, she found herself staring into the bright yellow eyes of a very large black cat. She smiled as the strange cat began to rub itself against her ankles persistently. She reached down and gently stroked the sleek cat from head to tail. A loud feline rumble filled the air and the golden eyes closed blissfully.

"Aren't you a handsome brute?" Angeline cooed to the black cat.

She started scratching behind its ears. The purring intensified and the cat leaned into the caresses until it was lying across the top of her feet, its eyes squinted in ecstasy. Angeline chuckled low in her throat over the feline antics. She continued to coo and babble at the cat, nonsense words flowing easily from her lips. She sat up with a smile as Sue returned with steaming cups of coffee on a silver tray.

She gave the cat a long-suffering look. "Just shoo Copernicus away if he becomes a bother," she instructed Angeline.

Angeline leaned down and regarded the bundle of fur stretched out across her feet. She gave him another scratch and said, "You're no bother are you? What a handsome thing you are," she continued. She glanced up and gave the other woman a smile. “I have one of my own,” she explained, “a Maine Coon named Nicodemious.” She straightened up and accepted a cup of coffee, laughing as Sue cast the cat on the floor an indulgent look and said, “Well, he isn’t pedigreed, but he’s certainly spoiled.”. After stirring cream and sugar into it, she took a sip, and widened her eyes in surprise; the coffee was hot and strong just as she liked it, but there was a hint of spice that she hadn’t expected but liked.

Sue watched the other woman’s expression closely. “It’s cinnamon and black pepper,” she said with a conspiratorial wink. “I like coffee with a kick.” She settled into the chair across from Angeline and regarded her for several long, silent minutes. Finally, as Angeline’s comfort grew less and less, Sue set her coffee mug down and took a deep breath.

“What can you do?”

Angeline gulped the hot brew quickly, scalding her throat. “I’m sorry,” she stammered. “I don’t understand what you mean.”

Sue took Angeline’s hand in her own, turning it palm up. She looked at Angeline’s hand for several minutes, saying slowly as she did, “I know these things.” Her sharp gaze captured Angeline’s frightened one. “You have a power that no one has seen in these parts in a very long time. What is it?” The long fingernail on her free index finger traced the lines of Angeline’s palm. When Angeline didn’t answer, Sue curled Angeline’s fingers into her palm, but didn’t release her.

“It’s all right, sweetie,” she said kindly. “While not everyone will ever know about it, you can’t hide it from me; I can feel the energy pulsing around you.” She paused, her eyes boring into Angeline’s for several, tense, silent minutes. “Something is coming,” she murmured, her grip on Angeline’s hand tightening, “Something frightening, something hungry. It's followed you, and it won't give up until it takes you or you stop it."

Angeline tried to pull her hand out of Sue's grasp; she felt suddenly claustrophobic, as if she couldn't take a deep enough breath. She felt herself beginning to tremble. The lights in the store flickered erratically and Copernicus raised to his feet the stare at her unblinkingly. Angeline shook her head and tried to control her emotions, but could feel herself slipping as her newly replenished control began to falter. With each breath, she lost a little more control until the bulbs in the light fixtures began to blow out one by one. She tried to stand, to get away, but Sue's grip tightened on her wrist.

"Relax," she said in a quiet, soothing voice. "There's no harm here, nothing to fear." Angeline felt her tense muscles responding to the calming energy that emanated from the other woman. She shook her head, clearing her mind, and took a deep, steadying breath. The few remaining lights steadied. She studied Sue in the dim light, trying to decide whether she could trust her. She swallowed hard, and gave a start when the black cat leaped lightly into her lap. She looked down at it, and felt something unwind as he continued to regard her placidly with his golden eyes.

Sue's grip on her wrist relaxed as Angeline sat back in her chair with a smothered sigh, and Sue shook her head and blinked as if waking from a nap. "Who are you?" Angeline asked when she finally found her voice. "What did you mean?"

"Just a woman," Sue said with a small shrug. "But like you I have abilities others don't." Her eyes sparkled behind her wire rim glasses. "I know when things great and small are about to happen, can affect my surroundings, and I have the ability to recognize others with similar talents. You," she continued quietly, "Are the start of something and you and your friends will have to stop it."

She patted Angeline's hand in a motherly fashion. "I'll help if I can. But until the time comes, just remember you're not alone." She took a deep breath and held it. She glanced down to the tabletop and Angeline followed her gaze, and felt her eyes widen in shock; the coffee in her cup was boiling as vigorously as if it were sitting on a hot stove, the dark brew slopping over the brim of the mug. Angeline drew in a loud gasp and felt her jaw drop. She lifted her eyes slowly back to Sue Beasley and felt a warming burst of trust well up in her chest. Her eyes prickled with tears and she struggled to find words. Sue patted her hand. "You are among friends," she told Angeline quietly. "No one will think you're a freak for what you can do."

Angeline opened up to Sue, telling her everything, and after several minutes, felt a knot she'd lived with all her life loosen and let go in her chest. She cried openly in relief to finally have found her place in the world and knew without a doubt she would never consider leaving Bounty Cove or Devil again.

~CHAPTER FOURTEEN~

She left an hour later, several books on Bounty Cove in a bag, including some that had been written by Sue herself. Angeline felt as if she was just waking up from a very long dream; somehow, spilling her heart out to Sue had lightened her soul, and now it felt as if she was seeing the world truly for the first time. She pulled out of the parking lot, cranked up the volume on her stereo, and sang every word of every song that played, a wide smile lighting her face. She puttered around Bounty Cove in her little car, stopping here and there to pick up this or that. By the time, she had finished with her errands and returned to Devil's house, the sun was starting to set in the western sky.

She glanced at her watch as she put groceries away in the kitchen and fed Nico; Devil had been called out on a carpentry job by Michael, and was due home later. She finished putting things away in the pantry, and skipped through the house to the master bathroom. In the middle of the room sat a sunken tub, big enough for two with water jets. She began running water and added a liberal amount of her favorite jasmine bath oil. Her hair had grown out to brush the tops of her shoulders in loose curls, and now she pulled it back into a stubby ponytail. She gathered a thick towel from a cupboard and hung her terry robe on the back of the door, and lit several candles about the room before turning off the overhead light. She closed the taps and sank into the hot perfumed water with a deep sigh of contentment. Nico padded in silently and hopped up onto the ledge of the tub to wonder yet again, why his human needed to immerse herself in water just to get clean. He proceeded to wash himself, just to show her, once again, how it was suppose to be done.

Angeline relaxed in the hot, perfumed water, the water jets caressing the muscles of her shoulders. She leaned her head back against the edge and closed her eyes, breathing deeply, and letting her mind wander. She still felt a shock of surprise every time she thought of her cup of coffee boiling merrily away on the table in front of her. Sue Beasley was the first person she had ever met in her life who had similar abilities to herself and she thanked the stars above she had met someone other than Devil and his friends who understood her. She floated lazily in the deep water, her body feeling as weightless as her heart.

She must have dozed off; she awoke with a start when she heard Devil calling her name just outside the bathroom door. She sat up quickly and called out to him, and smiled widely when he walked into the room. The water had only slightly cooled and she invited him to join her. She didn't have to ask twice; within minutes, he was sinking into the water with a groan. Angeline scooted until she was close enough to touch him and began lathering soap onto a washcloth. This she ran across his hairy chest and muscular arms. She took her time, soaping and washing his body, not saying a word, her eyes on his in a steady gaze. Devil watched as her eyes darken as she discarded the washcloth and continued to run her soapy hands over his body. He groaned as she flowed over him, straddling his hips, her fingers spearing through his hair as she leaned into him. He felt her soft breasts against his chest and raised his hands to cup them, his thumbs flicking across the rose-colored tips. Another groan was wrenched from his throat as she squirmed in his lap; he gritted his teeth and set his hands to her hips to hold her still. He could feel himself brush against her warm, soft flesh, and broke out into a sweat that had nothing to do with the hot water in which he was currently immersed.

Angeline's slight weight lay against him as she ran kisses up his throat and along his jaw. The touch of her wet tongue was pure heaven against his skin. His eyes closed as he allowed her free reign over his already hard and straining body, sucking in a hissing breath as her small warm hand caressed his body below the surface of the water. Her throaty chuckle sounded in his ear, and her hot breath across his cheek sent lightning bolts straight into his blood to pool there between his legs. When she finally brought her lips close enough to brush across his own teasingly, his control snapped. His arms clamped around her slippery body as he surged up and against her, sliding deep and smooth into her waiting body. She seemed to gasp and sigh, all at once, as she pressed against him, the tips of her breasts grazing the hair-roughened muscles of his chest.

It wasn't too long before they were both overcome, and gasping, fell into the burning embrace of rapture.

His heart thundered in his ears for several minutes as he lay back against the side of the tub and wrapped his arms around her. He realized with a start that no other woman had made him feel so much in such a short time; the women of his past had been mere conquests, playthings that he'd enjoyed as much as they'd enjoyed him. He'd never felt any keen sense of loss when the relationships had eventually cooled and ended. His fingers grazed down the length of her spine, and he grew cold as he imagined what his life would be like without Angeline in it. The thought that he needed to do something, to take some sort of step to keep her by his side raked across his mind, sinking hot talons into his heart; he knew there'd be a painful void left if he didn't do something soon and he lost her. He knew what he had to do, and thought ruefully he had never considered himself the marrying kind until Angeline had appeared in his life.

Angeline shifted until she was kneeling beside him, and leaned in to kiss him. "Finish up," she purred. "I'll cook dinner."

She rose, the water cascading down her lithe body, and gave a scream of surprise when he sat up and wrapped an arm around her waist and hauled her back down into the water.

"Not yet," he growled, capturing her mouth.

The water was considerably chilly by the time he let her go, and they ended up eating dinner much later than either of them had planned.

Over breakfast the next morning, Angeline mentioned meeting Sue Beasley the day before. "Did you know just how strong her gifts are?" She asked, giving him a pointed look.

Devil debated playing dumb, but in the end decided to tell her the truth. "Yes," he told her. "Most everyone around here knows; it was the only way I'd believe what she was telling me." He watched her, trying to figure out what was going through her mind. "I thought if you two met you would know you're safe here, that no one's going to think you're a freak of Nature."

Angeline took a bite of dry toast, and chewed slowly while she considered Devil's words; She had been feeling ill in thc mornings for the last several weeks and found only bland food first thing settled her stomach. She took a cautious sip of coffee and grimaced when it hit her stomach like a bomb; she clapped a hand over her mouth and bolted for the kitchen sink as a portion of her sketchy breakfast came back up violently.

The spasms passed several minutes later, and she leaned heavily against the counter, her hands curled over the lip of the sink, her head drooping. She panted lightly through her mouth until the queasiness passed, then, her hand shaking, filled a glass with water to rinse the bile from her mouth. She could feel Devil's eyes on her back as she made some mental calculations and came up with a number that scared the hell out of her. She turned to face him, wiping her mouth with the back of her hand, her body tense, and her gaze wary. She opened her mouth to say something, anything, but the still, blank look on Devil's face caused the words to die on her tongue.

Devil saw the truth in her silver eyes; his throat worked as he tried to say something. Unfortunately, his brain chose that moment to take a vacation, leaving his mouth gaping and his tongue glued to the roof of his mouth. Angeline broke the silence, her eyes fixed on her toes, her voice strained."I forgot to take a pill." A deep, dull red blush spread across her features, starting at her chest and rising to her hairline. She felt pressure building in her chest and she let out her breath in a rush. Energy flooded out of her in a small wave, causing her empty chair to move across the floor a few inches. Silence thundered loudly. It stretched unbearably between them and she swallowed hard, her throat dry. She turned away, her gaze fixed unseeing out the window into the backyard as Devil continued to stare at her silently with a blank expression on his face. She turned on the water, grabbed a sponge and cleaning powder, and began to scrub the basin clean, erasing the evidence of her recent vomiting.

The sound of Devil's chair scraping across the floor sounded like a shotgun blast in the quiet room and she jumped, her nerves stretched to the breaking point. She felt him move toward her, and knew when he stopped just inches from her back. His tension and some unknown emotion radiated off him, crashing against her back in waves; she shuddered at his voice when he finally spoke;

"When did you realize it?"

He sounds so distant, she thought bleakly, closing her eyes and willing herself to not feel.

She drew a shuddering breath and turned to face him. He stood mere inches from her, his hands hanging limp at his sides. Though he would appear relaxed to an outsider, Angeline knew him well enough to realize he was anything but at this moment; she could feel the tension rolling off him. Her lips parted, but no words came out as she suddenly realized she was afraid. Of him, of his reaction, of what this would mean for their future.

Devil, for his part, was trying to come to grips with the situation; the woman he loved was pregnant—*with his child.* So many emotions and thoughts were swirling through his brain he wasn't sure what was what anymore. He raised his hands to settle gently around her upper arms. He frowned when she flinched under his touch. "When?" He asked his voice low and hoarse, his gaze intense on her face. He hated the frightened look in her silver eyes, hated the way she trembled under his touch, and despised the emptiness that was growing as she quickly cut herself off from him. He leaned down and brushed her mouth with his lips, hoping to drag her out of the hole she was pulling herself into, and was swamped by the wave of uncertainty and fear that emanated from her.

Coldness flooded through him when he realized he was the reason she was feeling like she was; he hadn't exactly been acting like the ecstatic daddy-to-be in one of those pregnancy test commercials. He pulled her carefully into his embrace, his mouth nuzzling her ear. "It's all right, Angel," he told her quietly. He felt her fingers curl into his shirtfront, her nails digging into his chest as she clutched him and felt her body begin to quake with harsh sobs. He felt like an ass. Shame whipped him and he castigated himself for making her cry. He soothed her, whispering endearments in her ear, his hands rubbing the line of her back from hips to shoulders. "Ah, God, Angel," he murmured, "don't. I'm sorry; please don't cry." She pressed herself closer into his embrace, and his arms tightened, understanding she needed to be held more than anything at this moment.

He didn't know how long they stood there, him feeling like a world-class jerk with Angeline bawling into his shirt so hard that any words she spoke were incoherent, but it was quite some time before she cried until she made herself sick again, and he grimaced as more toast and coffee splashed across his work boots. He propelled her into her chair and then handed her a damp paper towel; while she dried her tears he cleaned up the mess on his boots and the floor. After handing her a glass of water, he pulled his chair close and laid a gentle hand on her thigh, his eyes on her face, silently compelling her to look at him. She took several shuddering breaths and glanced up quickly at him before succumbing to more tears. He sat and waited her out patiently, simply holding her hand silently until she was able to pull herself together again. When Angeline finally spoke, her voice was a whisper, and she couldn't look him in the eye as she pulled her hand free of his. "I realized just before you did," she told her hands as they lay in her lap. She drew a shuddering breath. "I didn't think you'd be so angry."

Devil's finger curled under her chin and he nudged it upward until he could look into her tear-streaked face. "I'm not angry, Angel," he told her, brushing the hair out of her face. "I'm a lot of things at this moment," *shocked, surprised, proud, possessive,* "but angry isn't one of them." He kissed the tears on her cheeks away before kissing her trembling mouth.

She leaned into him, seeking his strength, his warmth. "I'm afraid," she whispered.

Devil pulled her easily into his lap. "Of what?" He asked, settling her against his chest.

"That she'll be able to do what I can," Angeline wailed, sobs erupting again.

Devil let out a deep sigh and tightened his hold on her. "You silly little twit," he said, his tone turning it into an endearment, "haven't you learned anything? This is Bounty Cove; no one's going to care." He kissed the top of her golden hair. "He'll be treated like a normal kid here."

Angeline wanted to believe him, wanted to believe that no child of hers would ever have to face the loneliness and pain she'd had to growing up, but it was difficult. She kept her reservations to herself, however; she would deal with any situation that arose in the future, and worrying about it now would only serve to make her more miserable. Instead, she decided to worry about the moment at hand. "What are you thinking?" She asked, looking up into his face, searching for a clue to his emotions; hoping with everything in her that she hadn't just left herself open to unimaginable heartbreak.

Devil gave her a lopsided grin and she felt herself relax a little. "Now that I've gotten over the shock, I'm thrilled," he told her in her ear, his breath sending shivers through her body. "It makes it all the more important that I marry you."

Angeline wrenched herself out of his hold and leapt off his lap. "Marry?" She squeaked, shaking her head. "No," she said distractedly. "No, you don't have to..." She began to pace in agitation.

Devil grinned at her, feeling her confusion, her honest conviction that he didn't have to marry her; that she wasn't trying to trap him. "It's not a matter of what I *have* to do," he drawled, "it's a matter of what I *want* to do." He watched her, as she continued to pace and mutter to herself, expecting that at any moment she would realize it was the perfect solution. Whatever he had been expecting her to do when she finally stopped pacing and glanced at him, it wasn't what she did; she pivoted on her heel and ran from the room.

Devil jumped to his feet and tore after her. He caught her as she wrenched the front door open; he grabbed her wrist and swung her around to face him. His hand clamped down across her mouth as she opened it to say something, and he steered her until she was flat against the wall, his large body pinning her in place carefully, mindful of her suddenly more delicate condition. "You're not running out on me," he told her in a quiet voice, frowning at the frantic, almost hysterical look in her eyes. His hand caressed her soft belly. "You're not running out on *us;* that's my baby, too; I won't allow it to be born a bastard." He cupped her jaw, his thumb caressing her cheekbone. He gave a shocked shout when her head whipped to the side and her teeth sunk into the webbing of his thumb with a feral snarl. Devil jerked his hand away with a hissed curse as Angeline darted under his arm and ran out of the house. Moments later, she was in her car, driving away fast. Devil slumped against the wall, shaking, cradling his bleeding hand against his chest and watched her go, unsure what could be done when Angeline was so angry and afraid. A snarled curse split the silence as his fist knotted and slammed into the doorframe, angry that there was nothing he could do but wait until Angeline had worked through things on her own and hating the helpless feeling that swamped him and the sudden all encompassing, gut wrenching dread that he'd never see her again.

She pounded the palm of her hand against the steering wheel, the pain shooting up her arm and roosting in her shoulder. The physical pain blocked out her mental anguish and gave her a steadier control over herself, allowed her thoughts to clear so she could think. *I am pregnant,* she thought, and then said the words out loud. Doing so made it real, made it solid in her mind.

He wants to marry me.

She shook her head, the words stuck in her throat. She pounded the steering wheel again to stifle the swell of emotion that threatened to choke her. *Damn him!* She screamed her frustration. *How can he expect me to marry him? He didn't even really ask if I wanted to marry him; he just informed me that we're getting married!* Against her will, her body sent a thrill of excitement to her belly as she remembered being pressed against the wall by his strong, hard body. His words pierced her brain and her hands shook. A small voice told her to turn around, to go back, allow him to claim her completely, but she railed against it; she needed time alone to work things through, to untangle the knot of emotions that sat hard and hot in her gut.

She drove out to the cove, wanting the peace and solace the ocean would provide her.

When she arrived, there was a dusty, dark colored sedan sitting in the lot; she scanned the beach below, but found it empty. Hoping she would be left alone, she made her way down the steep trail to the beach below. She took off her shoes and jeans, leaving her thin t-shirt on. She quickly waded out until the waves lapped her hips, soaking the hem of her shirt. She took a deep breath and dove under the next wave that rose in front of her. She swam under the frothing waves until her breath ran out and she surfaced, sucking in a quick breath and ducking under another curling wave. She swam until exhaustion pulled at her muscles and her mind was fogged. She waded out of the water and collapsed, face down, on the sand. The last thing she remembered was seeing something coming toward her fast out of the corner of her eye. There was a flash of surprised pain, then nothing.

Chris Jessup stood over her unconscious body, breathing heavily. He had heard her car as he poked around in the ruins of the old Witcher house, and had followed her down to the beach. He had concealed himself from her behind the flat rock he had seen her sunbathe on all those weeks before, watching her. When she had fallen to the sand, he had acted, grabbing a small rock. He came upon her silently and brought the rock down across her temple just as she realized she wasn't alone. He leaned down, checked her pulse, finding it strong, and steady at her throat. Relief washed through him; all his plans would fall apart if he'd killed her. He stooped and picked her up, cradling her slight weight in his arms and began to long climb to his car. Once there, he stripped her of her remaining clothing and bound her ankles with her panties, her wrists with her bra. He tore her shirt into strips and used one to gag her and another to blindfold her. He threw a blanket over her still form and got into the driver's seat; her shoes and jeans he would leave on the beach; with any luck, they would be found and it would be assumed she had drowned.

He grinned to himself as he imagined the next forty-eight hours of enjoyment he had ahead of him.

~CHAPTER FIFTEEN~

The sun sank in the western sky, and Devil was frantic; Angeline hadn't returned home, and no one he had called had seen her all day. He had fully expected her to be home by now, ready to talk and, perhaps, ready to marry him. Although if he were honest with himself, he could have handled the proposal a lot better than he had; perhaps waited until he actually had a ring to offer her. Then he could have gotten down on one knee and done it properly, maybe gotten Melissa and Jessica to help by hosting a dinner party so he could ask her with their friends surrounding her. Something told him that Angeline would have been more receptive if he'd taken that route. But the love he felt for her had increased a thousand fold when he realized she was pregnant, and he'd acted impulsively. He sighed heavily as he paced the living room.

Face it, he sneered at himself, *you should have handled the whole thing a hell of a lot better.*

He shook his head ruefully, again feeling like an ass. He continued to pace through the house, alternately fervently hoping she would walk through the front door and tearing himself up that he hadn't handled this morning better than he had. Nervous, impatient, he tried to occupy himself as he waited, but the memory of the look on her face when she'd run from the house kept returning to haunt him, and he felt helpless to do anything to make it right again.

Unable to stand the thoughts chasing themselves around his mind any longer, and giving into the need he felt to be doing something, he called Michael and Melissa to let them know he was going out to look for Angeline. He dashed off a quick note to Angeline to stay home until he got back, and grabbed his keys and left the house. He drove slowly through town, looking for her little red car, but didn't see it. Then, his jaw set and his palms sweating, he drove out to the beach, determined to get on his knees and beg her to marry him, hell, to just come home, if he needed to. He didn't realize Michael and Melissa were in their own vehicle close behind, feeling Devil was going to need them.

When he saw her car, Devil felt a wave of relief that left him dizzy. He parked next to it and got out, his eyes quickly determining she wasn't asleep inside. With dread knotting his gut, he headed for the trailhead; almost running full tilt down it to reach the beach before the sun completely set and left the stretch of sand in darkness. He quickly found her shoes and socks, and moments later her jeans. He scanned the beach, but found no other sign of her. Panic washed over him as his gaze turned slowly toward the water, horror dawning across his features. The tide was coming in and he rushed into the water, screaming her name, searching the water in the falling darkness for any sign of her, the memory of watching her flirt with the rip current back in July haunting him. Desperate, terrified, he screamed her name.

He heard voices on the beach but ignored them, calling Angeline's name repeatedly, his voice becoming hoarser as fear clawed up his throat from his belly. Strong arms came around his chest and he fought against them, tearing himself out of the grip to plunge through the waves again. This time a hand grabbed the back of his coat and yanked him back and off his feet. Salt water mingled with tears as he struggled to his feet and fell into Michael's arms, his hands clawed and clutching at his friend for support.

"Ah, God, Mike," he cried, his eyes bright with desperation, "I can't find her! Help me find her!" He slowly sank to his knees, emotion bowing him and sapping his strength and will until he could no longer stand.

Michael held him up and helped him out of the water. Night had fallen and a stiff breeze had begun to blow off the water. Devil shivered violently from a mix of cold and shock. He turned bleak eyes up to Melissa as she stood in the light of a camping lantern; in her arms, she held Angeline's clothing. Her eyes were large and filled with sadness.

"She went into the water," he told her, shock numbing his words. "I drove her into the water. I don't think she came out. I killed her." He bowed his head, trying to come to terms with the enormity of his loss, truly believing Angeline was dead, unable to hear the small voice in his heart that told him otherwise.

Guilt raked savagely across his heart as he began to realize it was his fault she was gone; that it was his fault he'd never hold their child. He'd reacted badly to the realization that she was pregnant, had for all intents and purposes, demanded she marry him. He hadn't thought to ask her what she wanted, had assumed she wanted to marry him, that she loved him enough to want to spend the rest of her life with him. Raw, ugly sobs tore from his throat as he fell to his knees; cold, voracious sorrow bowing him forward until his face was in the sand. He wrapped his arms around the back of his head as he begged God to kill him.

His friends stayed by his side as he cried out his anguish and held him back when he tried to find solace in the ocean's cold embrace. Finally, numb and drained, Devil sat upon the sand, his arms around his knees and stared out at the water. They passed a cold night there on the sand, staying with their friend as he held his lonely vigil. When dawn broke, Devil walked the shoreline, his eyes scanning the water's edge for Angeline's body. Around midday, he allowed Michael to take him home; there didn't seem to be anything else he could do. He undressed mechanically and collapsed onto the bed, dragging the blankets over his shivering body. He reached out and pulled her pillow close and buried his face in it, sobs wracking his frame once again; it still smelled like her.

~CHAPTER SIXTEEN~

Angeline awoke to a pounding skull and shivers wracking her body. She tried to touch her head, but couldn't; for several disorienting moments, she tried to figure out why her arms wouldn't work. They were stretched over her head, and she twisted slowly until she could see the handcuffs that were wrapped around each wrist tightly; another set looped through the pair attached to her hands and clamped around the top rail of a metal bed frame. Another series of shivers coursed through her body, and that's when she realized she was naked. She moved her feet, heard the metallic clink of metal on metal, and felt the bite of leg irons around both ankles. Panic raced through her blood as she tried desperately to pull her hand through one of the cuffs encircling her wrists. She thrashed about on the bed, screaming her fear and rage, the sound travelling through the dark room, bouncing off the walls, and causing her head to pound. She fell back against the mattress, panting. A door opened somewhere in the dark, and she turned her head to the sound, her eyes straining to see through the inky blackness. A small light appeared, illuminating Chris Jessop's face, and Angeline lost herself to the fear all over again. She screamed in denial at the look in his eye, knowing she would never see Devil again. That realization crashed over her, and she fell silent as Jessop set the camping lamp on the floor next to her head and loomed over her.

Devil awoke with a start. The dream had been so real; Angeline had come home and gotten into bed with him. He could smell her shampoo mixed with salt water. He opened his eyes and looked around, expecting to find her sleeping softly beside him, but was faced with the grim realization that it had been a dream. He wiped an exhausted hand down his face and opened his eyes as Michael walked into the room.

"I filed the report for you," he said in a flat voice. "They're listing her as missing until they find her."

Devil nodded silently, the knot in his gut clenching tighter. He understood without his friend telling him that she would be considered missing until they found her body. He got off the bed and pulled his robe over his naked body as nausea kicked him hard in the gut at the thought of his angel's still and lifeless body. A wave of melancholy washed over him a moment later as he remembered Angeline wearing his robe that first morning they had awakened in bed together. He staggered as agony ripped through his soul and he clutched the dresser top to keep from falling to his knees. He breathed heavily, fighting down nausea as guilt began to chew on his innards again. He waved Michael off as his friend reached out to steady him.

Angeline gasped as pain ripped her away from Devil's side. She had seen his anguish and had tried to comfort him, but had been unable to reach out to him; she had been only able to stand by his side, her heart tearing to shreds as she watched him struggle through his pain. Now she was back in the dark, chained and naked, held in thrall to Jessop. She didn't open her eyes, but could feel him there, standing close, watching her. Slowly she opened her eyes and saw she'd been correct; Jessop stood close to her side, his blue eyes shining with a cold, manic light. When his eyes began to take in the sight of her naked body, she steeled herself to show no emotion, to not shrink away in a vain attempt to hide. "You should have been mine," he cooed, reaching out to run a finger along her cheek. Angeline flinched from his touch against her will.

"Go to hell," she spat. "You lost your claim on me the first time you hurt me." She watched Jessop's demeanor darken as fury hardened his features. Almost casually, he reached out and slapped her across the mouth. Undaunted, Angeline continued. "I'm not going back with you, Chris, no matter what you do to me. I mean come on! Do you really think this is the way to get a woman to marry you? I hate you, Chris, and I'll die before I let you touch me."

She saw the moment he lost his handle on his mad rage; she literally felt something snap in his mind and the waves of dull, unfocused madness suddenly sharpened into ice-cold spikes of hatred. She screamed as those spikes drove into her, tearing her apart from the inside out, doing more damage than his fists. Mercifully, darkness crashed through her and she sank into oblivion.

When she came to again Jessup was straddling a chair backwards at the foot of the bed, watching her closely. She unconsciously tried to cover her naked body with her arms and was surprised to find herself free. She sat up quickly and noticed her feet were unbound as well. She curled herself over her drawn up knees and watched him warily. Several minutes passed before he spoke to her, holding a thin white t-shirt out to her.

"There's food and water next to you."

Angeline instantly became suspicious.

"I realized that perhaps chaining you to the bed was not the right way to go about convincing you to come home with me."

Angeline wasn't paying attention; there was only one thing she wanted to hear from him. "How do you keep finding me?" She shivered as his face stretched into a gloating smirk.

He stood and she watched him with wary eyes as he turned away. When he turned back, Angeline saw that he held something white in his hand; in his other, he held something small and familiar looking—her cell phone, the one Chris had given her when they began dating. "GPS," he smirked, tossing the phone at her. It landed in her lap, and she flinched as if it was a poisonous snake, realizing that it was her fault he'd dogged her for so long; her cell phone was something she was accustomed to having with her at all times; it had been a part of her life for three years and it had never occurred to her to replace it when she went on the run. Silently, she cursed her own stupidity three ways to Sunday.

"You've been unconscious for hours," his suddenly flat tone yanked her attention back to the here and now and she looked up just as he lobbed the other object at her, "you must be at least thirsty by now." Angeline realized he'd tossed her a shirt, and clutched it to her as he came close again and leaned closer. His hand travelled across her shoulder and down her chest, pausing to caress her breast. She twisted away from him and pulled the shirt over her head as quickly as her sore and battered body would allow. "You shouldn't have made me hurt you like that Angeline," he said, an odd sorrow in his tone, "How can we play when you make me hurt you?"

"What do you want?" She asked, her voice gravelly. She didn't even glance at the food on the floor next to her low bed. She shrank away from him as his touched brushed across her cheek. Her breath hissed through her teeth as the side of her face gave a deep throb of pain under his touch. "To keep you, to control you, to make you mine and no one else's," Chris answered, his voice taking on an odd, lilting tone.

"Go to Hell," she spat viciously as she settled the shirt's hem about herself; the shirt was many sizes too big and sitting in a curled up position as she was, it covered her completely . Her spark of bravery died quickly as he slapped her.

Jessop sighed heavily. "How am I supposed to teach you manners when you refuse to learn?" He asked in a tone that one used on a stubborn child. "Give me a chance, Angeline; let me prove to you that I'm a wonderful lover, better than the one you're whoring for now. Come home with me, and let me take care of you." Without warning, he grabbed a handful of her hair and jerked her head back to ground his mouth against hers, his tongue invading her mouth, causing her to gag in revulsion. His free hand clamped over her breast, squeezing hard enough to leave more bruises. She whimpered in pain, and tried to use her fear to fight him off as she had the night he'd beaten her, but the pain he had inflicted and continued to inflict on her body and mind and her head injury distracted her, kept her from gathering her scattered thoughts. Emotionally, her energy was drained, leaving her numb and almost resigned to her fate and what little there was leaked away, feeble and unfocused. Unable to muster a defense, she turned off, going limp under his hand. He tore himself away. "You like it," he panted, his eyes bright with madness. “You like making me hurt you.”

Angeline shrank away from him, shaking her head furiously, his words snapping her out of her temporary stupor. “No,” she whispered, “Please don’t,” she begged, terror causing her voice to crack. Her eyes widened as he reached back into the shadows and brought forth a riding crop. She watched, frozen as he brought the tip closer, flicking it harshly across the tender skin of her flank. Pain raged through her body like an inferno, and she caught a sob in the back of her throat. She moaned as the crop fell across her belly and swayed back against the cinder block wall.

“It’s time to come home, Angeline,” he told her in that singsong voice of his madness. He applied the crop to her flank again, and she felt her skin erupt into an angry welt. The strike was followed closely by several more across her hips, her belly and her chest. “It’s time you started behaving like my wife instead of whoring for your dark haired lover.”

The thought of Devil put some steel into her spine; he would want her to fight, to do everything she could to make sure she and their child came home. She pushed away from the wall and scrambled around him clumsily as he raised his arm again, knocking the camp lantern over and shattering the bulb as she did so. She darted across the room in the dark toward where she remembered seeing the door open. She heard him behind her, and suddenly, she was transported back into her dream of running in the dark, something frightening pursuing her. She staggered as her feet tangled in unseen debris and she fell hard, knocking the wind out of her lungs. She struggled to her feet and lunged forward, coming up hard against the wall; her hands frantically searched the concrete wall on either side of her, her cold and clumsy fingers scrabbling desperately until she felt the wood of the door to her right. She found the knob and turned it, opening the door just as his hands came around her throat from behind, his body slamming into hers and pinning her face against the rough wood of the door, splinters gouging deep furrows across her cheek. She pried at his fingers as they dug into her throat, his grip burrowing into her windpipe, cutting off her air. Her lungs burned with the effort to draw breath and she saw bright explosions behind her eyes as pain bloomed through her skull. She felt his hot breath on her cheek, and felt the hard rise of his erection against her backside. Tears flowed down her cheeks as she realized she never see Devil again.

The last thing she heard was Jessop's voice telling her he was sorry it hadn't worked out.

The last thing she saw before Death claimed her was Devil's face.

Jessop stared down at Angeline's still body, shaking; he hadn't meant to do it this time, hadn't wanted his fingers to dig into her windpipe and slowly squeeze the life from her body, but once again, the compulsion had come upon him, and he'd been unable to stop it. Once again, a woman lay dead at his feet. Slowly, heedless of the tears that leaked from his eyes, he bent down and gently gathered Angeline into his arms. Straightening, he carried his small burden back to the iron frame bed and lowered it to the sweat stain mattress. He leaned over her, brushing wispy curls from her cheek; it was still damp from her tears of fear and pain. His fingers skimmed across the purple shadow that marred her cheekbone, his expression almost childlike in its sorrow. Kneeling beside her, he picked up a slender, finely boned hand, crooning at the sight of bloody, broken nails and swollen fingers; she'd tried to fight back, tried to defend herself, using her hands to shield herself as blows had rained down; blows caused by his hands. He blubbered as he gently straightened her too big shirt, pulling it down to cover the splotches of bruising that covered her thighs, anger beginning to replace the grief and sorrow that this beautiful angel was dead.

Why did she have to fight? Why didn't she just give in and marry him? He wouldn't have had to hurt her if she'd just stayed where she belonged and married him. If she'd just given him control...

Shaking his head, Jessop stood and gazed down at the broken angel as his common sense kicked back in. There were things to do; evidence to destroy, a body to wipe down and dispose of, a life to get on with. Sighing heavily, Jessop left the basement.

~CHAPTER SEVENTEEN~

Angeline had been gone for almost forty-eight hours. It felt like a lifetime to Devil. He vaguely remembered talking to the Sherriff, but other than that, he walked around in a fog. He ate only if someone told him to, but preferred to be left alone in his room. The sight of her belongings scattered about the room tormented him; everywhere he looked she was there—her toothbrush in the bathroom; her clothing in the dresser and closet; her nightgown draped over the chair; her perfume bottle and cosmetics on the dresser top. Every moment they'd spent together replayed in his mind, and he knew he hadn't appreciated that time nearly enough; that knowledge caused him to die a little more with each passing moment that she was gone. He was drinking constantly now, a bottle of scotch always within reach no matter where he went as he prowled the house. It took the edge off, but it didn't completely obliterate the pain.

When Michael came to tell him the news, he found Devil sprawled in an easy chair in the living room, Angeline's cat curled on his lap. Devil stared unblinking at the fireplace, not noticing the hearth was stone cold. Michael cleared his throat, and when Devil raised his eyes to look at him, Michael was shocked by the change the last forty eight hours had wrought in his friend; he was deathly pale, dark shadows marring eyes that were devoid of life. Grief had left deep lines in his lean cheeks.

Devil saw the grim look on his friend's face, and felt a shard of ice slip down his back. He sat up, tense, his hands clenching the arms of the chair.

"They found her."

It wasn't a question. Michael nodded.

"She was dumped on the side of the road near the cove; they've taken her to the hospital in Elizabeth City." Michael paused and swallowed hard, watching as Devil got to his feet and move to the bedroom. "She's badly hurt, Dev."

Devil was on autopilot, mechanically pulling jeans and a shirt, his only thought to see his Angel again, even if it was to say goodbye; it took several minutes for the meaning of Michael's words to penetrate the fog that shrouded Devil's mind. He had just tied his shoes when he stopped and actually thought about it. He roared Michael's name as he stalked back into the living room. He grabbed his friend by the shoulder and shook hard, his eyes dark and stormy as they searched his friend's face. Afraid to hope, but unable to stop himself, he licked his lips and asked in a ragged whisper, "She's alive?"

Michael grimaced as Devil's fingers bit into his shoulders, but answered him in a clear voice. "Barely; the Sherriff's posse found her naked and unconscious just before the turn off to the cove." He paused, his eyes skittering away from Devil's. "She's in bad shape, Dev. They don't think she's going to make it."

Devil pivoted suddenly and strode to the front door, grabbing his coat and keys as he went. "I need to get to her," he said over his shoulder. "Are you coming?" Without waiting for an answer, he walked out of the house and got into his truck. Elizabeth City was only a two-hour drive; he would make it before the sun went down. Somehow, it seemed like a deadline he had to meet. He started driving away even as Michael was closing the passenger side door. Devil sped away, kicking up gravel and dust, and hell bent for leather, his jaw clenched, and his hands in a white-knuckle grip on the steering wheel. He felt Michael reach across him, pull the seatbelt over his shoulder, and secure it before fastening his own.

Devil never quite remembered the details of the drive to Elizabeth City; he sped, doing eighty most of the way; why he wasn't pulled over, he would never know, but he arrived at the hospital in half the time. He paused at the reception desk long enough to learn which room Angeline was in and instead of waiting for the elevator, he sprinted up three flights of stairs. He crashed into the hospital corridor at a dead run, Michael close behind, and snagged a passing nurse.

"I'm looking for Angeline Carston, room three twelve," he barked tersely. The nurse pointed silently down the hall with her pen, her mouth open and her eyes wide. Devil heard Michael murmur to her, but didn't pay any attention; he was too intent on reaching Angeline. He jogged quickly down the hall, impatiently looking for the right room. It was the last room on his right, just past the nurse's station. The door was closed, and Devil realized his hands were shaking as he reached for the handle; he took a steadying breath and pushed the door open gently. Christian Witcher, Melissa, Jamie, and Jess all looked up at him, weary sadness and hesitant hope in all their eyes.

Devil staggered back half a step when he saw his beautiful angel lying so small and still upon the hospital bed; she was hooked up to a heart monitor and there seemed to be hundreds of intravenous lines snaking from both arms. Christian stood and came to him, putting a hand on his shoulder. Devil couldn't take his eyes off Angeline, and his voice cracked when he spoke.

"Is she..." He wanted to ask if she was going to be okay, but couldn't voice the words, afraid of the answer.

"She's alive," Christian said, understanding, "and they're doing everything to keep her that way."

Devil's eyes found Christian's. "What did he do to her?" Raw emotion made his voice shake.

Christian sighed, pinching the bridge of his nose. "Broken ribs, broken fingers, beaten, dehydrated, strangled..." He paused, not sure if he should continue; the look Devil gave him chilled his blood. "What else?" Devil said low, a muscle ticking in his jaw. When Christian paused, Devil's rage slipped. "Tell me!" He roared. "Did he, was she...?" Unable to voice the words, he stared at Christian, eyes blazing with grief and fury, willing him to answer.

"No," Christian said, sighing gustily, "Thankfully, given the rest of the things he did to her, she was at least spared being raped." He ducked quickly as Devil's fist collided with the wall beside his head; slowly, Devil's head fell forward to rest against his arm, sobbing with relief. Christian laid a gentle hand on Devil's arm. "There's evidence that she fought back," he said in a low voice. "They found skin under her fingernails, even though the bastard tried to clean up after himself. She went down fighting."

Devil felt a surge of pride in Angeline that was quickly buried under hot rage and crushing anguish. "She's pregnant," Devil said to no one in particular, straightening up and pushing away from the wall.

Christian nodded. “We know. They’ve drugged her so her body can heal, but, Devil,” his eyes were sad as they held Devil’s, “she may lose the baby.”

Devil shook his head, trying to deny the truth of Doc’s words. He moved to Angeline’s bedside, tears welling in his eyes, as he took the chair Christian had vacated. He picked up one small hand and ran gentle fingers over the dark bruises that marred her pale skin. He paid no attention to the others as they left quietly to give him some privacy. Devil watched the rise and fall of Angeline’s chest as she breathed; searching her face for any sign she was aware of his presence.

“Oh, God, Angel,” Devil whispered brokenly, “I’m so sorry I didn’t keep my promise to keep you safe.” He reached up to brush a curl from her forehead before leaning over to kiss her. “Please wake up; I love you so much.” He pressed his face against her hand, kissing the fingers gently as tears flowed. “Please forgive me.”

~CHAPTER EIGHTEEN~

She floated.

In a gray fog she floated, warm and serene.

Am I dead?

She reached out, touching a warm hand as a voice floated through the pale light that surrounded her; she strained to hear words, but all she could make out was the voice-

Devil!

She struggled to reach him, to soothe the pain she heard in his voice as he continually murmured to her, to finally, finally, hold him in her arms again but couldn't reach him. Something prevented her from breaking through the fog that surrounded her; she was aware of her body, but only distantly. She narrowed her concentration and felt the burning pain that wracked her body. Memories flooded back; dark, painful memories that frightened and angered her. She felt the rush of energy anger always gave her and she forced it out, causing the fog to thin a little. The effort exhausted her, and the fog regrouped, closing in tighter around her. She rested a few minutes, and then tried again, this time pushing the energy hard, forcing it out in a wall that broke through the grayness for a short moment. In that flash of clarity, she saw Devil sleeping, his head down, his face turned toward hers. Weariness had drawn fine lines upon the face she loved so much, had chiseled hollows under his eyes and created deep gouges across his cheeks.

Angeline's energy waned quickly and she panted against the waves of exhaustion that washed over her.

Devil, please, I am not dead!

She screamed the words into the grayness that surrounded her, begging for Devil to hear her, to awaken and pull her out of the fog, but they echoed back, ghostly and hollow. Exhaustion sank its teeth into her then, dragging her under, and she sank into dark oblivion as the words faded around her, seeking peace and comfort.

She just needed to rest;

Yes, rest; and soon she would be able to reach Devil and hold him again…

The weeks passed. Devil's time and energy was given wholly to Angeline as she continued to recover. He had given up trying to remember the faces in the parade of doctors that came to check on Angeline daily. No one questioned his right to be there, and no one challenged him when he slept in a chair beside her bed every night, his hand clasped over hers. As her injuries healed, they began to wean her off the drug that kept her asleep, and Devil began to see signs of her coming out of it; she muttered and talked in her sleep, her bandaged hands clenching in the blankets tightly, as if caught in a never-ending nightmare. He begged her non-stop to open her eyes, and sometimes shouted at her when his frustration grew too large to contain, angry that the whims of Fate had graced him with Angeline, only to now threaten to steal her away from him. Despite everyone's dire warnings, she hadn't miscarried their child, and as the weeks passed, her flat belly began to round. The first time Devil heard his child's heartbeat he cried.

Angeline was aware of her child growing in her belly, and surrendered as much energy as she could to keep the baby alive. She also knew the fog was shifting, lifting away from her, leaving her increasingly more aware of her surroundings, and every day she tested it, reached out beyond it to touch Devil. She became aware of more and more until, one day, she could hear Devil shouting at her to open her eyes, damn it, his voice ragged, pleading.

I am not deaf, she told him crossly.

Devil's voice stopped in mid rant. Light flooded around her, hurting her eyes, and she felt his warm hands grab her own.

"What did you say?" Devil breathed.

"I'm not deaf," she whispered through parched lips. Her eyelids opened until he could see slivers of silver.

His hands cradled her face. "Angel?" She felt his lips warm and firm on her own. "Can you hear me?"

"Stop shouting," she mumbled as her eyes opened further before shutting again quickly against the light in the room.

Devil jumped back, shouting for a nurse. Michael rushed in, and was amazed to see his friend dancing around excitedly. A nurse brushed past him and rushed to Angeline's side. She pushed a button and more nurses, Christian, and another doctor rushed in. Devil and Michael were firmly escorted from the room.

"What the hell's going on?" Michael demanded to know.

Devil kissed him loudly on the cheek. "She's awake!" He crowed. "She told me to stop shouting at her!" He danced around, laughing loudly. When a hatchet faced nurse bustled up and told him to quiet down, he laughed harder, grabbing the nurse and planting a loud kiss on her pursed lips. "She's awake!"He only sobered slightly, tense and hopeful, as Christian left Angeline's room, his bearing tired and worn; a smile played across his face however.

"She's awake," he confirmed to the small gathering of friends.

Cheers and shouts erupted in the hallway, and the charge nurse glared at them until they quieted their celebration. Devil waited impatiently for half an hour while Angeline was checked over, tested, retested, and finally bathed. When he was given permission to go to her, he found her sitting in the chair he had grown accustomed to sleeping in, pillows bunched and rolled into pads to help her sit up. Devil went to her, falling to his knees in front of her and buried his faced in her lap, his arms going around her body. He held her, silent and thankful, breathing in her scent and feeling her warmth flood through him. He kissed the mound of her belly, and chuckled when he felt the baby kick under his cheek. He closed his eyes as her fingers stroked through his hair, softly, gently. They didn't speak, no words needed between them, allowing the touches they shared to do their talking.

~CHAPTER NINETEEN~

Angeline's recovery quickened with each day; her bones knitted, the bruises faded completely, and the cuts healed. The pneumonia that she had developed while she'd been drugged stubbornly clung to life in her body, keeping her weak, but even that, too, eventually passed. Two and a half months after she was found left for dead beside the road, Angeline's doctors cleared her to go home; it was her thirty-second birthday, and though the land was held in the clutches of winter, Angeline felt as if it was the brightest, sunniest day of the year. After she had awakened, she was able to tell the police who had attacked her, and a warrant was issued for Chris Jessop's arrest, making sure they knew he'd used the GPS application on her phone to track her and stalk her; unfortunately, he had gone to ground, and no one knew where to find him.

The baby grew steadily in her womb, active, and according to the ultrasounds, healthy.

When they arrived home, Devil carried her through the front door, claiming he was practicing for their wedding day. Angeline laughed breathlessly, a blush coloring her still pale cheeks; they had discussed it, and though Devil had been ready to marry her immediately after she awoke, Angeline had steadfastly refused to be married from her hospital bed. She had placated Devil by promising to marry him once she was home and completely back on her feet. So, on the last day in January, Angeline stood with Devil in front of Reverend Thomas, her dress one of simple design, and vowed to love, honor, and cherish Devil as long as she lived. The baby kicked hard as they were pronounced husband and wife, and she made a sound that sounded like a laughing gasp. Devil bent over her, his mouth brushing her ear.

"The baby?" He asked, his hands gently curving around her belly. She nodded, and placed one of his hands over the spot in question. He felt the fluttering nudge beneath his palm, and grinned like a fool. "Take it easy, big fella," he chuckled before kissing Angeline.

Jessop stood in the shadows of the church, pale and shaky; he had never expected her to survive, had truly believed he had killed her. When she had gone limp under his hands, he had continued to squeeze until he was certain she was dead. No heartbeat had fluttered in her chest, no pulse had thrummed weakly in her throat; there had been no breath in her body, yet here she was, alive, pregnant and married! He'd read the announcement of the upcoming nuptials in the newspaper, and had risked being spotted to see for himself that she was alive, half expecting it to be a trick or a mistaken printing of an old announcement. Yet, there she stood, still frail but glowing with joy as she joined herself to her lover. Jealous rage seethed through his mind; how dare she marry someone else? *She was his, damn it!* He had offered her everything a woman could ask for, had held her life in his hands, yet she had thrown it away, had refused to see that she belonged to him. *How dare she?!* He ground his teeth together and slid further back into the shadows as the happy couple passed close by on their way out of the church.

Jessop waited until the church parking lot was deserted before venturing out; he knew about the warrant for his arrest, had seen the news report on the late news just before Christmas. Thankfully, he had bought the Larsen place over the phone, using a false identity, and wiring the money from one of his accounts to the realtor's bank, and signing all paperwork via fax; no one knew what he looked like save Angeline and her bastard husband. Even so, he bought new clothes, dyed his hair, ordered contacts, and shopped for necessities late at night in the neighboring town. He paid the utility and phone bills on-line. He spent several days cleaning up the basement, erasing all traces of Angeline's presence; unfortunately, the bitch had scratched him, leaving long parallel furrows across the back of his hand; and he had missed some skin under her nails when he'd cleaned her body. With a sigh, he shook his head. There wasn't anything for it but to kill Angeline and her husband and escape to Rio. Though truth be told, he did regret that he wouldn't be able to take Angeline with him. He checked to make sure no one was watching and departed, walking to his car quickly, his head down. He hoped Angeline enjoyed her marital bliss; he drove away, making plans to end it soon.

Michael and Melissa, in their large home, hosted the reception breakfast; Angeline noted with a grin that hundreds of fragrant beeswax candles provided all the lighting.

Melissa snagged Angeline's arm and leaned in close to whisper, "Like the candles?" At Angeline's nod, she continued. "I love you like a sister, but I thought we might spare the light bulbs today."

Angeline laughed, as her heart flipped over in appreciation of the understanding gesture.

Though the wedding had been a small affair, many of the local people were invited to the champagne brunch reception in order to wish the newlyweds luck and happiness; among the guests were Devil's older brother, Paul and his wife Lyn Dee, and his younger sister, Shannon and her husband, Jason, and Angeline's sister, Cassandra and her daughter, Maddie. Angeline's grandmother, Constance, surprised everyone when she arrived an hour into the party, her bright eyes seeking out and finding her granddaughters and Devil almost immediately. With the stately grace of a bygone era, Constance moved through the crowd, nodding her head in greeting to one and all as she passed. She came to a halt before Angeline and Devil, and rapped her fingers across Cassandra's hand. "Don't flirt with your sister's husband," she said in a stern tone. "It's not good manners."

Angeline was overwhelmed as her grandmother's words brought a scrap of memory back; she felt a spasm of pain across her heart, and she gasped. For a split second, Jessop's face floated before her eyes, chastising her for her lack of manners as she swore and cursed him to Hell, pushing him to anger so that he would eventually beat her unconscious again, understanding instinctually that he preferred to hurt her when she was awake. Nausea swamped her and she swallowed hard Shivering, she excused herself as bile worked up the back of her throat. Sue Beesley stopped her as she made her way to the powder room just off the living room, and pressed a small packet into her hand. "For the dreams," the red head whispered as she kissed her cheek. Angeline stood and watched the little woman disappear into the crowd. Moving slowly, steadily, she made her way to the powder room and breathed a sigh of relief when no one else stopped her. Angeline closed and locked the bathroom door behind her and leaned close to the mirror, setting Sue's gift on the counter. She dampened a washcloth in cool water to press over her eyes and practiced breathing slowly and deeply, trying to get herself under control to stop the waking nightmare in its tracks. Despite her efforts, however, as she closed her eyes tightly, she felt herself falling into darkness.

She fell into pain, violent eruptions detonating along her nerves as fear strangled her. Angeline opened her eyes, and found herself back in the dark, naked and chained to the bed, Jessop looming large as he brought the riding crop down across her chest yet again. She screamed, her body arching with the pain. Torn, broken sobs and whimpers burst from her split lips and she begged.

"Please. Oh God, please!" She screamed into the black void.

"Beg for it," Jessop whispered. "Beg for the pain." The crop came down again, lighting fire across her thighs. "Scream for it," he panted.

Angeline tried to stop the screams; she bit her lip until it was bloody, and for several seconds, she was successful. Then molten fire slammed through her belly and she screamed until her voice gave out. She was delirious and out of her mind with pain and fear as she screamed curses at him, damning him to hell, insulting him, questioning his manhood until Jessop fell upon her, fists flying and she lay beneath him, sobbing and crying out to God, to Devil. Crying, screaming for her father, her mother, anyone.

No one came as sweet oblivion pulled her down into darkness.

Angeline's eyes snapped open. She was in Melissa's powder room, far away from that place of torture and fear, the lights strobing frenetically. She looked down at her hands, the broken fingers healed and twisted around the damp washcloth and tried to stem to flood of power that was streaming from her. She closed her eyes, breathing slowly, evenly, counting each breath and heartbeat, forcing herself to calm, until the soft, Morse code *tinking* of the lightbulb filaments stopped. She licked her lips as she opened her eyes, and hissed in a soft breath of pain; she had bitten her lip sometime in the last several minutes, and blood oozed sluggishly from the cut. She dabbed her lip with the washcloth and tried her best to push the lingering memories away. She had been told to expect these flashbacks, to expect moments when it seemed as if she were right back in Jessop's dungeon; she never expected them to be this visceral, this real. She stared hard at her reflection, willing the memories into a locked corner of her brain. A soft knock on the door and a rattling of the knob brought her back to the here and now.

"Angeline?" Melissa called softly through the door. "Are you all right?"

"I'll be out in a minute," she called back, congratulating herself on how pleasant and steady her voice sounded. She cleaned the blood from her lip and applied a light coat of lip-gloss; the cut wasn't deep, but Devil would probably notice it, and she didn't want him to worry. She fluffed her long curls and gave herself a critical look; her eyes were still a little red, but other than that, no one would know she had had a waking nightmare. They would probably attribute her red eyes from tears of happiness. Satisfied she had her mask in place, Angeline unlocked the door and stepped out to give her friend a smile. At the last moment, she remembered Sue's gift and reached back to pluck it off the counter.

Melissa looked at the little package with curiosity. "What's that?" She asked, her face alight.

"Sue gave it to me," she replied as she opened it.

A few moments later, she sucked in a breath; sitting in the folds of tissue paper was a pendant of garnets and opals in a silver setting that had a thin ribbon of gold wrapped around it. Angeline picked it up by the long, thin silver chain it was looped on and held it up to the light, the opals flashing. Both woman oohed and aahed over the lovely necklace and Melissa immediately offered to help Angeline put it on. Angeline held her hair out of the way as Melissa worked the clasp behind her neck. It settled between her breasts, flashing and winking its fire.

Both women rushed backed into the bathroom to look at it in the mirror. Angeline touched the pendant reverently. "It's too much," she whispered. "I can't accept this."

"Of course you can," Sue told her calmly. She stood at the door, looking at Angeline in the mirror. "Silver the color of your eyes, white opals to light your way in the dark and blood red garnets for strength against all." She smiled as Angeline turned to face her. She tapped the pendant lightly. "Use it when you find yourself lost; use it to focus yourself when the darkness pulls you back."

Tears shimmered in Angeline's eyes as she clutched the pendant tightly. She was speechless and she threw her arms around Sue, hugging her tightly. "Thank you," she whispered, kissing Sue's cheek. "I'll never take it off."

A throat cleared suddenly, and all three women jumped. Angeline looked up to find Devil watching them. "Is this a hens-only party, or can roosters join?" He asked with a grin. His eyes fell to the necklace that glowed lightly against Angeline's chest. He lifted it gently, and studied it, then smiled at Sue. "Thank you," he told her. He, too, kissed Sue's cheek, causing the widow to blush like a schoolgirl.

She playfully slapped his arm. "You need peace; hopefully I can bring you a small bit, even if it is just to banish the nightmares."

The small group wandered back to the party. Devil held Angeline's hand, and kept her close, protecting her. Though these were their friends, he felt he needed to shield her from the questions that would inevitably come up. He knew she relived the horror of her captivity in her dreams each night and he worried she would be hurt accidently by a thoughtless word or question. Though the command was unspoken, everyone knew not to mention Jessop's name around Angeline, but people being people, someone might inadvertently slip and say more than he or she meant to. Therefore, he kept by her side, and steered the conversation as needed, protecting her the only way he could.

Angeline's strength waned as the morning passed into afternoon, and she gratefully accepted Melissa's offer to nap in the guest room for an hour or two. The party wound down quickly after her departure, and soon, only family and close friends remained. Maddie took the Kemper and Andrews children in hand and led them out to the backyard while the adults relaxed and kicked off their shoes. Cassandra all but devoured Devil with her gaze, and shot him looks full of sultry promise whenever she thought her grandmother wasn't looking; Devil, for his part, ignored her until she sidled up to him at the bar and pressed her full bosom against his arm, asking for a gin and tonic in a breathless little girl's voice. Devil mixed her drink and handed it to her, noting the sultry look she gave him. She took a sip and her eyes on his, ran her pink tongue over her bottom lip in a slow invitation. Devil's instinct was to run the other way, fast; he was use to women offering themselves to him, and until he'd met Angeline, he had always enjoyed the chase; but even if he hadn't just married Angeline, he didn't think he would have taken Cassandra up on her offer. It didn't take a genius to realize the woman was a barracuda. He felt certain she would chew him up and spit him out. Besides, he'd never been the kind of man to play sisters against each other; he'd never been that kind of crazy suicidal.

He stepped away as she ran a red painted nail down his chest, her fingertip slipping inside the buttons of his shirt to score his skin lightly. Her intended effect was to fire his blood; instead, it left him cold. He was in the process of disengaging himself from her when he saw a blur of motion out the corner of his eye. Cassandra drew back quickly with a piercing screech, her arms flailing wildly.

Angeline yanked her fistful of her sister's hair as hard as she could, pulling the heavier woman off Devil. As Cassandra whirled to meet her attacker, Angeline gave her no warning and slapped her as hard as she could across the face. While their grandmother kept the others from interfering, Angeline pushed her face into her sister's and whispered furiously, "Stay away from my husband."

Cassandra recovered herself enough to slap Angeline back, though her sister twisted, and she ended up hitting Angeline's shoulder instead of her cheek.

"Your husband, maybe, but you owe me," she spat back, "all those boys I made dance with you, go out with you, even though they didn't want to. The things I did to make sure you had a normal social life would straighten even your hair." She saw Angeline's eyes widen in understanding, but didn't anticipate the venom in her sister's next words.

"Don't act like it was a sacrifice to sleep with them, Cassie. You and I both know you enjoyed it."

"Of course I did!" Cassandra admitted, "But who would have looked at you twice? You were an ugly little freak; I figured if it was the only way to get someone to pay attention to you, then I might as well enjoy it." Her eyes narrowed to slits, a nasty smile lighting her face. "If it wasn't for me, you wouldn't have known how to attract your husband enough to get pregnant before the wedding. At least you got some experience between the sheets before you met him." Her grin grew more malicious. "Quite a bit, actually, the way I heard it."

Angeline's gasp was drowned out by Devil's roar. She had to step between her sister and her enraged husband to prevent Devil strangling Cassandra, knowing Devil would rather cut off his own arm than harm her. She faced Devil, placing a small hand in the middle of his chest to stop him.

"Let me deal with her," she said quietly.

Devil gave her a look of anger mixed with disbelief; he couldn't stand by and let his beautiful wife be insulted, not after he'd failed to protect her from Jessop, and his hands itched to throttle Cassandra where she stood. He didn't care that she was Angeline's sister, didn't care that to do so, no matter how much she deserved it would only serve to hurt Angeline worse. He stared down into Angeline's starlight eyes, words of protest dancing on his tongue, but as she continued to gaze at him steadily, those words died and he relaxed. Nodding and taking a step back, he gave in to her request. Angeline gave him an understanding smile and turned to her sister, her smile falling away to be replaced by a look of cold fury. Without a word, she grabbed Cassandra by the upper arm and propelled her into the library, kicking the door shut behind them, leaving a stunned and uncertain group of family and friends behind them.

Angeline leaned her back against the door, and studied her sister in silence as Cassandra seethed, her hands clenching and unclenching at her sides. "How dare you?" Cassandra spat, her cheeks coloring hectically. "How dare you embarrass me in front of all those people?" She demanded, flinging her arm out to indicate the assembly that was more than likely listening at the key hole.

Angeline straightened and took a moment to lock the door. She paced forward, the lines of her body tense, anger radiating off her in waves. The light bulb in the desk lamp blew out, sprinkling Cassandra with fine glass. Angeline was certain she heard Melissa groan on the other side of the door. "You must truly hate me," she said mournfully, almost to herself. She wasn't sure she'd spoken aloud until Cassandra replied.

"I don't hate you," Cassie hissed between her teeth. "I just wish you had never been born."

Her words stilled Angeline's heart for several long moments, stole her breath, and robbed her of her fury. For more seconds than she could count, Angeline was certain her heart was breaking. Childishly, she struck back.

"If you are embarrassed," Angeline said in a low voice, "you have no one to blame but yourself." She stopped in front of her sister, her arms folded across her chest. "I never asked you to sleep with those boys," she said, shaking her head and letting her hurt be heard, "I never asked for anything from you; anything you did was to make yourself look good." She adopted a stance of exaggerated simpering femininity. "Oh please," she gushed, batting her eyelashes at an imaginary boy, "won't you *please* dance with my sister? She is ever so lonely, and too shy to ask you herself. I'll be *ever* so grateful if you did." She took a suggestive step forward, allowing her hips to sway. "I'll do *whatever* you ask in return."

Angeline straightened and her face stilled. "It must have worked pretty well, considering all the dances and dates I got from the boys who hung out with you. Or were they the ones who approached you, tried to make themselves look good in your eyes?" Cassandra opened her mouth, but Angeline cut her off. "I don't care who made the deals. But just so there's no misunderstanding, let me be perfectly clear: *I owe you nothing.* You made the choices, not me. And if I catch you coming onto my husband again, *I will kill you.*"

This last statement was said in as deadly a voice as Cassandra had ever heard her little sister use, and felt the truth behind her words as Angeline let her sister feel the power of her convictions. Cassandra gulped and nodded, speechless. Tears welled in her eyes and spilled over as great gulping gasps poured out. "I'm sorry," she blubbered. "Ang, I'm so sorry. Please don't be angry with me!" She buried her face in her hands, sobbing hard. "Please don't hate me!"

Angeline let her anger evaporate, sparing the rest of the light bulbs in the library. She gathered her sister in her arms. "I don't want your apology," she said, firmly. "I want you to apologize to Devil for making him feel so uncomfortable."

Cassandra nodded, straightening up and wiping her tears stained cheeks. "I said something terrible," she said brokenly. "I might as well have called you a slut out there."

More tears spilled as Angeline chuckled. "You're lucky I didn't let Devil have you," she told her sister gravely. "Although he does know I was a virgin, he wouldn't have let the insult pass." She handed Cassandra a tissue from a box on the desk. "Stop crying Cassie. This is just sisters being sisters, not the end of the world." She turned and walked back to the door and unlocked it. As she pulled the door open, Cassandra's next words stopped her.

"Maddie can do it, too."

~CHAPTER TWENTY~

Angeline stopped in her tracks and slowly turned to face her sister. She closed the door again and walked slowly forward until she was standing in front of Cassandra.

"What?" She breathed faintly. She wasn't sure she had heard her sister correctly. "What did you say?"

Cassandra nodded slowly, her eyes large in her thin face. "Maddie can do it, too. She blows out light bulbs; she's fried three toasters, and made all the windows in her room shatter." She threw her hands up, frustration rife in her body language. "I wasn't going to saying anything until later, but what the hell? We're here now, and I might as well tell you."

"Does it happen when she's angry?" Angeline asked, her voice barely a whisper, deciding in a moment that whatever antagonism was between her sister and herself wasn't important enough to ignore the consequences of her niece being in possession of an out of control power.

Cassandra shook her head. "No, she does it all the time, Ang; it doesn't matter if she's happy or angry, or just yawning. I don't know what to do anymore, and Grandmother isn't as young as she was when she was helping you." She grasped Angeline's hands, her grip biting. "Please, Ang, I need your help."

Angeline pulled her hands free with some effort, and walked to the library windows, watching the kids as they played tag. Maddie, a tall, thin girl with dark hair, stood off to the side watching the younger children run and play, her eyes never leaving them. "She seems to be taking her role as babysitter very seriously," she commented as Cassandra joined her. "How old is she now?" She turned and looked at Cassandra. Her sister watched her daughter, a soft look of motherly love lighting her features.

"She's almost thirteen," Cassandra said with a misty smile. "She knows what she can do, knows that you can do it too, and it's made her a wreck." At Angeline's questioning look, Cassandra went on, "She's discovered boys, Ang."

Understanding dawned in Angeline's brain. No matter how pretty her niece was, she would be ostracized if any of her friends ever found out what she could do. And if her hormones became part of the equation before she was able to control her ability, the danger would be unimaginable; the first time a boy broke her heart could cause Maddie to accidently unleash a firebomb of power that could level a small city.

Cassandra nodded, reading her sister's thoughts as she paraded across her face. "I want to ask you if Maddie can come live with you for a little while; it wouldn't be forever, just until she's more comfortable and can control it." Angeline watched as Maddie comforted one of the girls who had fallen and skinned her knee. Though her expression was friendly, she obviously wasn't as carefree as a girl her age should have been. Angeline turned and walked to the library door and opened it. Sticking her head out, she called to Devil to join them. When he arrived, she outlined Cassandra's request, careful to keep her own thoughts and feelings shielded so he would be able to make his decision without any outside influence. Devil watched the girl outside the window with her mother and aunt, and saw Angeline's gentle nature in her actions and movement.

Angeline said nothing as she watched Devil thinking it over; she knew she and Cassie were asking a lot of him on his wedding day, and hoped he wouldn't feel pressured. Her heart skipped a beat as he turned to her and smiled widely.

"I just realized this is my niece we're talking about, too. She's part of my family now, and we Damiens take care of family." He turned his gaze upon Cassandra, and nodded at her. "When you get back to Portland, send whatever she needs." He rubbed his hands together briskly. "Don't you think we should break the news to her?"

Cassandra gave Devil a small hug, her sister's words still ringing in her ears; after casting Angeline a sheepish look, she left to go fetch her daughter, leaving Angeline and Devil alone. Angeline walked to Devil and slid her hands up his chest to wrap around the back of his neck. "Thank you," she said simply before kissing him. Devil's arms came around her and he returned the kiss delicately; he gave a start of surprise when she pulled him closer and deepened the kiss, clinging to him almost desperately.

They had spoken of her experience and though Angeline had fragmented memories of her captivity. "All I truly remember is the pain, when I do actually remember," she had told Devil. "Most of the time I was somewhere else, somewhere away from my body; I can't explain it any better than that," she said, frustration lining her brow. The doctors had all agreed she may never recover the memories, and that was probably the best thing for her. Unfortunately, when she dreamed, she lived through the experience all over again; the pain, the humiliation, the hopelessness. Angeline was determined not to let what Jessop did to her ruin her life, and put her energy into living her life with Devil, especially after she was so certain she would die at Jessop's hands. She was determined to put it behind her, and begin making new memories with Devil.

She felt Devil pull away, and felt a brief flash of senseless rejection, though all he did was shift until he could lean a hip against the desk. When he recaptured her lips under his own, all other emotions were buried beneath a rising tide of want and need. Though her logical mind told her this wasn't the time or place for a afternoon quickie, she plastered herself against his hard frame, seeking and taking whatever she could while she could. She could feel Devil holding back, and though all she wanted at the moment was a complete surrender to the pounding in her blood, she also realized he was probably the only one in their right mind at that very moment. She allowed him to break of the kiss reluctantly, and snuggled against his chest with a sigh, closing her eyes and allowing the warmth of his embrace cradle her. They stood like that for several minutes, simply holding each other, Devil's hands kneading the muscles on either side of her spine at the small of her back. She leaned into his touch with a little groan, arching her back like a cat and sighing with bliss. Neither of them spoke, they just held onto each other tightly, neither in any hurry to let go.

Cassandra returned with Maddie a short time later, and Angeline asked to speak to her niece alone. Devil led Cassandra out of the room, offering to get her another drink. When the door shut behind them, Angeline sat down on a divan next to her niece, and gave her a long look, which the girl returned. Maddie was dark haired and green eyed like her mother, though she seemed to have inhcritcd her father's bone structure.

"You mom tells me you've been blowing up toasters," Angeline finally said, a smile letting the girl know there would be no teasing, no recriminations. When Maddie nodded silently, her eyes on her hands, Angeline leaned in and whispered in her ear, "ever had to try and explain how you blew up the television?" At the girl's startled look, Angeline laughed and put her arm around her shoulders. "You and I can do some pretty wicked and wonderful things, can't we?"

The girl shuddered in her aunt's embrace and leaned into Angeline's shoulder. "How do I make it go away?" She asked in a frightened whisper.

"You don't," Angeline told her truthfully. "You figure out what makes it go haywire, and you control it. Now," she said, sitting Maddie up and taking her hands. "Your mom wants you to live with me and your Uncle Devil for a little while; she thinks I might be able to help you so you stop blowing things up and scaring the neighbor's small dogs. Would you like that?" She watched as the girl nodded silently, her eyes once again lowered.

Maddie looked up suddenly, a worried expression on her face. "But all my things are in Oregon," she said in a worried tone, "My pillow, my clothes." She chewed her bottom lip.

Angeline patted her hand. "It's okay, sweetie," she reassured the girl. "Your mom will send anything you want out; you just make her a list, and she'll make sure you get what you want or need." *Or she'll have me to deal with,* Angeline added grimly to herself.

A smile broke out across Maddie's face as she tried to stop the tears that had gathered in her eyes from falling.

Angeline reached over, snagged the box of tissues off the desk, and gave it to Maddie.

"Dry your eyes and we'll go let everyone know okay?" At Maddie's nod, Angeline stood, and doubled over as the baby kicked particularly hard. She gasped then chuckled, and waved Maddie away as the girl made to offer assistance. "It's okay," she said a little breathlessly, "your cousin is feeling a little rambunctious is all."

Maddie coming to live with her aunt and uncle was greeted with enthusiastically; and Cassandra was made to understand that the list of items she was to send Maddie was, indeed, very important to her daughter's happiness. Maddie was initially aghast that her Auntie told everyone about what she could do, but relaxed when she realized no one thought she was some kind of freak. Her self esteem had been raised several notches by the time she, Devil, and Angeline left the party, and by the next morning, she was chatting away like a magpie, already becoming comfortable with her new surroundings.

When Maddie started school in Bounty Cove a week later, Angeline found herself as nervous as her niece; though she knew most of the kids Maddie would meet wouldn't think twice about Maddie's ability, she still worried about rotten apples spoiling things for Maddie. Therefore, when she saw Sue Beasley's daughter loop her arm through Maddie's and lead her into the school laughing, Angeline felt the need to stop by the bookstore and invite Sue to breakfast.

Since the store wasn't scheduled to open for another hour, Sue gladly accepted Angeline's invitation. They seated themselves across the table from each other in Auntie June's diner, and after a minute of perusing the menu, each decided on bacon and eggs with toast, coffee for Sue and orange juice for Angeline. When the waitress had left to put in the order, Angeline leaned forward and took one of Sue's hands. "I wanted to say thank you for being such a good friend to me; I never imagined I would ever find somewhere where I could truly feel at home, and I have. It's so good to know I'm not alone, and now it looks like Maddie won't be, either." She explained seeing Sue's daughter, Courtney welcoming Maddie to school.

Sue waved Angeline off with a ringed hand. "Honey, there's nothing for you to thank me for; Courtney and Maddie are very much alike in more ways than most people know. If you didn't notice, those two girls are so similar in appearance they could be mistaken for the same person." Sue's eyes softened a little. "She takes after her father." Her gaze took on a misty, faraway look for several long seconds before she shook herself and leaned closer, her voice dropping. "Courtney can sense others like herself, the same way I can; she knows from painful experience what it's like to be considered 'weird' by the other kids. She'll make sure Maddie is taken care of, no matter what." She leaned back as their breakfast arrived.

The two women ate in compatible silence for several minutes. "Have you lived here all your life?" Angeline finally asked. Sue dabbed her mouth with her napkin, the rings on her fingers catching the light and throwing off rainbows. "No," she said after a moment, "like you I found Bounty Cove by accident." She shrugged lightly. "It's not a really dramatic story; my friends and I were driving up the coast from Georgia, and we stopped to get some sleep. We were fresh out of high school," she said, remembering. "My girlfriends and I wanted to see a little more of the world than the little patch of dust we'd grown up in. We arrived the day before the Fourth of July, and decided to stick around for the fireworks the next night." She sighed wistfully. "I met my husband, Richard, under the rocket's red glare." She laughed, years falling away from her face as she did. "He kissed me that night, and although I knew I shouldn't let him, I did. After all, I figured I would be leaving soon, and I had this crazy idea of leaving broken hearts wherever I went that summer. The next day, my girlfriends continued their road trip, and I stayed behind." She took several bites of her breakfast. "It took me a little while to trust anyone enough to let them know what I could do, but when I told Richard, he just smiled this funny little smile and told me the same thing I told you when we met: this is Bounty Cove, and everyone is welcomed, no matter what."

Angeline sat back, enjoying Sue's story. "Richard and I had four boys, one after the other, and then, we were surprised by Courtney. Thank God she got to have her daddy for a few years."

Angeline's throat clogged with unshed tears over the sadness she felt radiating from her friend. "What happened?" She asked in a gentle whisper. Sue brushed impatient hands across her cheeks. "He suffered an aneurism," she answered flatly. "Richard had always had trouble with his blood pressure, and one day, it caught up with him."

"I'm so sorry," Angeline said in a stricken voice. "I didn't mean to pry." Sue smiled brightly. "Of course you didn't," she said, reassuring Angeline. She pushed her plate away, and glanced at her watch. "I'm due at the store in ten minutes," she said. "Want to come along?" At Angeline's nod, Sue dug money out of her purse and tossed it on the table. When Angeline protested Sue picking up the tab, the other woman brushed her off. "You can pick up next week's breakfast," she told Angeline.

Angeline agreed reluctantly and followed Sue to Harbor Books, and watched as Sue went about opening the store. She met Sue's oldest son, A.J., and listened with half an ear as mother and son went over an order that had been delivered just prior to opening. She wandered among the shelves, perusing titles and pulling out ones that interested her. She heard the bell over the door ring several times as customers from town came in to make purchases or to shoot the breeze. Angeline learned more in a few minutes' time than in the almost year she'd lived in Bounty Cove; it seemed Sue dealt in not just books on Bounty Cove, but news of its residents, as well. For instance, she had learned Katie Bishop, eldest daughter of the mayor, had decided to elope with the Travers boy over the weekend, and that Mrs. Bishop had gone to bed with a headache, and hadn't stepped foot in public since. Angeline was starting to get a good idea of how everyone seemed to know who she was shortly after arriving; no one was exempt from the grapevine newscast—young, old, rich, poor, stranger, or native. All were included and discussed at length. Angeline vaguely wondered what had been said about herself in the weeks following her arrival.

The bell over the door chimed again, though Angeline ignored it. She found herself seated at the same table she had shared with Sue on the morning they had met, engrossed in a historical romance that featured dashing heroes, creepy villains, swooning heroines, and several ripped bodices. As she read, she became aware of a prickling that spread between her shoulder blades. Glancing up, she noticed Sue looking over at her, and she smiled, and then returned to the story. The insistent feeling that she was being watched increased, and began to make her uncomfortable. She raised her eyes and glanced around the store surreptitiously. No one seemed to be paying any attention to her, but the feeling lingered, bringing with it chills that raced along her spine and set goose bumps along her arms. Deciding she was simply tired, Angeline closed the book and paid for it, and said goodbye to Sue and A.J. She gave the store cat a pat on the head and left, never noticing the man who watched her from the shadows.

~CHAPTER TWENTY-ONE~

When Devil came home around lunchtime, he found Angeline fast asleep in their bed. After kissing her brow, he pulled the quilt higher over her shoulder and left the room quietly. He wandered around the house, noting the small changes she had wrought in just a few weeks; flower arrangements adorned side tables and the fireplace mantle, throw pillows in bright colors and a variety of textures graced both couches and their bed. Though the additions were few, they made his former bachelor house into a home. He paused at the door of the newly christened nursery, and spent several moments picturing her in the padded rocking chair or standing at the changing table. He moved to the crib and looked down into it, trying to picture their baby sleeping peacefully among Pooh and friends; though they would soon be a family of three, he still found himself shaking his head in wonder. Less than a year ago, he had been a bachelor between short-term relationships. Now he was married with a baby on the way; it still boggled his mind at odd moments.

Devil left the baby's room and walked into the kitchen, his step light. After rummaging through the 'fridge, he threw together a sandwich that he ate while standing at the sink, washing it down with a glass of milk. His gaze wandered out the window into the backyard, his eyes focusing on a movement just inside the tree line that separated the yard from the creek; a vague shadow shifted then stilled. He stood, his gaze fixed on the spot, his body tense. Jessop was still at large, and though it would be suicidal to remain in the area, Devil was certain Jessop would try to finish what he had started if given the chance. The shadows remained still and undisturbed and Devil relaxed, shaking his head as he looked away. He missed the flash of movement as Jessop drifted deeper into the dim light under the trees. After checking on his sleeping, pregnant wife one more time, Devil locked the front door and returned to work.

Unshed tears sparkled in her eyes as Maddie shook with the effort not to cry; if her first morning in the new school had been an unqualified success, the afternoon had proven to be just as disastrous. It had started at lunch when she and Courtney sat down to eat. Courtney had been an unparalleled guide, showing Maddie around and pointing out important landmarks such as the front office, the library, and the girls' room, as well as pointing out who to turn to for friendship and who to avoid. Overall, Maddie had been greeted well; unfortunately, she accidently stepped on a few toes when she turned down an invitation to have lunch with Sissy Adams, Prima Donna of the eighth grade, in order to eat with Courtney.

Since then, Maddie had found herself seated next to Sissy in every class, enduring the mean and catty remarks the girl hissed at her whenever the teacher's back was turned. Most of it Maddie could ignore; she knew her fashion sense was just as good, if not better, than Sissy's and knew her family was probably wealthier than Sissy's, so the juvenile insults pretty much slid off her back, unnoticed. And, being the new kid, Maddie hadn't expected to make friends with everyone she met, but when Sissy's words turned more personal, Maddie felt the cut.

"I heard your mother didn't want you anymore," Sissy said in a loud voice right before gym class.

She faced Maddie, her expression haughty. Maddie glanced around and saw every eye on them. Sissy stood, facing her from the opposite end of the locker room like a gunfighter calling her out. "That's what everyone's saying, you know," Sissy continued meanly. "They're saying your mother didn't want you so she dumped you on your poor auntie, and really, she doesn't want you, either. Is it true your mother slept with so many men that she doesn't know who your father is?"

Maddie winced inwardly at the sting of the cutting remarks. While they were not true—her father had passed away suddenly in a car accident just two years ago—Maddie was certain by the end of the day, the lies would be held as gospel. The whispers had already begun among the girls surrounding them, drifting up and over them like a restless breeze. Maddie stood, outwardly calm and relaxed while inside she could feel a churning, hot maelstrom seething in her gut. She clenched her fists at her side, willing herself to remain calm and unruffled, striving to maintain control. She began to sweat as the air around her began to crackle with static electricity and the temperature rose.

The gym teacher arrived at that moment just as a stray breeze teased the curls that clung to Maddie's sweaty cheek, dispelling the tension and shooing the girls out into the gymnasium. The girls filed past her, their heads close together as they whispered.

"It must be true," Sissy was heard to say. "She didn't even try to argue."

The class passed with miserable slowness for Maddie as she ran her laps, warmed up, and was picked last for dodge ball teams. Though normally graceful and athletic, Maddie found herself distracted into clumsiness. Her classmates' laughter and taunting grew in volume and intensity until she could take no more and she turned on her heel and marched out of the gym, ignoring the teacher's order to come back immediately. She moved quickly and silently about the locker room, and with quick, efficient motions showered and dressed. She was sitting in a far corner of the cavernous room by the time the class returned.

"Oh, who cares where she is?" Sissy's voice demanded, echoing gratingly off the metal lockers and tile walls. "I hope she ran all the way back to Oregon," Sissy continued. "Who needs white trash like that here?"

Maddie heard a garbled question and Sissy's derisive answer. "I heard her mother's such a whore that she planned to teach her the family business."

She laughed nastily as someone gasped and cried, "That not true!", and Maddie recognized Courtney's voice.

"By the time I'm done, no one will know the difference."

Maddie had jumped to her feet by now and she saw Sissy disappear into the showers, towels wrapped around her head and body. She stalked forward as the rest of the girls fell back, and waited until Sissy had turned to say something else. She watched as Sissy's eyes widened in surprise and her face grew a little pale.

"Take it back," Maddie demanded in a low, shaky voice, "take back what you said about my mother." Her hands clenched at her sides.

Sissy smirked. "Why should I?" Her voice was saccharine sweet, and her eyes were wide with feigned innocence.

Maddie took a step forward. "Because," she said slowly, as if to someone of limited intelligence, "if you don't, I'm going to make you very sorry." She reached up and wiped the sweat from her eyes. She was shaking uncontrollably now, and she felt her grip on her temper slipping dangerously. She could feel her anger roaring inside her, demanding to be allowed free rein to devour and destroy. The fluorescent lights flickered fitfully overhead.

Sissy laughed and sauntered forward. "Are you going to tell on me?"

She pouted prettily and she tossed her hair, laughing in Maddie's face. Before anyone knew what was happening, Maddie's fist clenched tight, and she pulled it back. She punched Sissy in her laughing face and knocked her to the floor. Sissy sat on her bottom on the wet shower floor, her legs splayed comically in front of her, her hands clutching her face. She began to shriek like a banshee.

Maddie stood back as Sissy's friends rushed to help her, feeling her fist slowly unclench. Though the whirlwind still raged in her gut, the anger quieted a little, and her control strengthened as she felt a grim satisfaction in seeing Sissy knocked on her butt. Her feeling of contentment vanished the moment she saw the look on the gym teacher's face, and Maddie didn't bother to protest her side of the story when the teacher ordered her to the principal's office.

~CHAPTER TWENTY-TWO~

The shrill ringing of the phone on Devil's nightstand awakened Angeline. Groggily she answered it, and came awake in an instant when she heard Maddie's tear filled voice on the line. She was dressed and calling Devil to meet her at the school in three minutes, and pulling into the parking lot in another ten. She rushed into the front office, and was directed to the nurse's office where she found Maddie slumped in a plastic chair, her knees drawn up to her chin. Her dark hair swung forward to hide her face. Angeline took a step forward just as Devil crashed into the room. At the sound of his arrival, Maddie's head snapped up, and her pale, defiant expression caught Angeline's heart; she felt a clenching in her chest at the haunted look that Maddie couldn't quite keep from her expressive eyes. She rushed to Maddie and fell to a knee beside the girl's chair. She reached up and brushed Maddie's hair out of her face, and in a soft voice asked, "What happened, Sweetie?"

Maddie's face crumpled and the tears she had been fighting back broke free, coursing down her cheeks as ugly sobs tore through her slender body. She threw her arms around her aunt's neck and clutched her tightly, her face buried in the side of Angeline's neck.

"I'm sorry!" She sobbed. "I tried really hard, I really did! Please don't make me leave!"

Angeline cast a bewildered look over her shoulder at Devil and comforted her niece. Out of the corner of her eye, she saw the school's principal, Mr. Sweeny, and Devil leave the room. She untangled herself from the death grip Maddie had on her neck and pulled another chair close. She sat down, and holding Maddie's hands in her own, waited the storm out. There was only one thing she needed to know, and as soon as Maddie's sobs had quieted, she asked the question;

"Did you lose control?" At Maddie's headshake, Angeline let out a loud breath. "Tell me what happened."

Haltingly, the story came out. Though not as bad as she had anticipated, Angeline was still worried.

"You channeled your anger and hit her?" She asked, more than a little shocked.

"Not *all* of it," Maddie said defensively, "I didn't want to *hurt* her; I just wanted to make her shut up."

"Still," Angeline said slowly. "Fighting isn't the answer, as I'm sure you've heard a thousand times before." She shook Maddie a little bit. "No matter how cruel and nasty Sissy Adams was, once you hit her, she became your victim; people are going to naturally take her side now." Angeline watched as miserable understanding cascaded across Maddie's features; it was like watching a devastating avalanche as it obliterates the landscape.

"So now I'm the unwanted daughter of a slut *and* a bully," Maddie said bitterly, her face hardening. She gasped loudly as Angeline's hand connected with her cheek, slapping her forcefully.

"Don't you *ever* speak like that about your mother!"

Devil and Mr. Sweeny chose that moment to walk into the room.

Angeline closed her eyes with groan as Maddie sank her face against her chest, sobs shaking them both. Angeline stood up and managed to transfer Maddie from her embrace into Devil's.

"Just let her cry," she whispered as she slipped out the door to follow the principal.

She followed the older man to his office and slid gratefully into a padded chair, her knees shaking and her back aching. With a sigh, she raised her eyes to the man, noting the thinning hair and dark brown eyes that twinkled behind wire rimmed glasses. He offered her a small, genuine smile and sighed in commiseration.

"I've talked to all the girls in class who saw what happened," he began. "And though all Sissy did was call Maddie and her mother names, from the sound out it, the black eye Sissy now has was dearly deserved." He held up a tired hand, forestalling anything Angeline might have said. "I'm not condoning what Maddie did, and she will be punished, but so will Miss Adams; I've already spoken to Sissy's parents, and they are shocked and embarrassed that their daughter would be so cruel, especially to a new student. They fully support any punishment I see fit for her behavior at school, and have assured me that she will be punished at home, as well."

Angeline nodded, and then paused, wondering how much she should tell him about her niece. Finally, deciding the whole truth would be the best course, Angeline took a deep breath and said, "There's something you should know about Maddie."

Mr. Sweeny waved her into silence. "Miss Franklin has already given me a demonstration of what she can do. Quite impressive, I must say." He chuckled, holding up a twisted fountain pen for Angeline to see. "I'm starting to think I should just change my name to Dr. Xavier, to save time." At Angeline's questioning look, the principal smiled. "Dr. Charles Xavier? X-Men comics? No?' He sighed, perhaps a little sadly. "Look, Mrs. Younger, there are more kids with extra-special abilities in this school than even you can imagine; I don't know if their families are somehow called here or if it's something in the water that produces some many kids with special gifts. All I know is I've been doing this job here in Bounty Cove for thirty years, and in that time I've learned how to cope with the occasional outburst of temper fueled gift."

Angeline stared at the man in front her, her mouth gaping open and speechless. He sat placidly, his hands folded on the desk blotter, a benign smile on his face and watched as she slowly pulled herself together. "Where were you when I was a kid?" She finally asked with a shaky laugh. She took a deep breath to force down the sudden bubble of hysterical laughter that was threatening to burst forth; it was a wasted effort. The giggles rose until they threatened to choke her, and she pressed her hands to her mouth in a vain attempt to control them; they spilled forth regardless, and Angeline found herself laughing. Laughing until her sides ached and tears ran down her cheeks. Like a catharsis, the laughter released the knot of tension that had settled in her belly the moment she'd received Maddie's call; Mr. Sweeney sat silently, and allowed her to laugh until she could stifle the worst of her outburst.

"I'm sorry," she gasped, wiping tears from her cheeks. "You must really think I'm completely off my rocker." She paused and took a deep breath, calming herself more. "It's such a relief to know we don't have to hide anything from you," she explained. "Or worry about making excuses for things that Maddie simply can't control right now."

Sweeney waved her explanations off. "No need to explain, Mrs. Damien," he countered, "I'm just glad we can work together to make sure things like this don't happen anymore." He leaned forward, and gave Angeline a small smile. "I'll be keeping Maddie after school for an hour each day for two weeks; Miss Adams will be joining her here in the office. I think a couple weeks of having to work together without the distraction of their peers will give the girls a better understanding of each other."

Angeline released a breath and nodded. "I agree," she said whole-heartedly. "While I don't expect they'll become best friends, I'm sure it'll at least give them some respect for each other."

"Exactly," Mr. Sweeney said, standing up. He walked around the side of the desk and helped Angeline to her feet. "I'll expect Maddie to report to the office right after final bell on Monday." Angeline nodded and allowed him to escort her to the door. She shook his hand.

"Thank you," she said quietly. She gave him a smile and left, leaving the older gentleman shaking his head at the rush of sincere appreciation he'd felt in her words; it left him feeling truly heroic.

"She cried herself out," he said quietly, slowly getting to his feet. He hitched Maddie higher against his shoulder. "She may be tall for her age, but she doesn't weigh all that much," he commented as he moved toward Angeline.

Angeline reached up and brushed Maddie's hair out of her sleeping face. Her niece hiccoughed in her sleep, sobs still causing her breath to hitch every now and then. "Let's go home," she murmured to Devil. "I'll tell you about Maddie's punishment when we get her settled."

Devil nodded and Angeline led the way to her car, opening the passenger door so Devil could settle Maddie in the seat. He carefully secured the seatbelt around her and rolled up his jacket to cushion her head against the headrest. He walked around the hood of the car and leaned down to kiss Angeline.

"I'll see you at home," he said, closing the door gently.

Once Maddie was settled in her room, still sleeping, Angeline and Devil met up again in the kitchen and sat down at the table. Angeline told Devil about her meeting with Mr. Sweeney, and Devil agreed with the punishment Maddie would serve with Sissy.

They sat quietly, each in their own thoughts until Angeline asked in a quiet voice, "Devil, what are 'X-Men'?"

Devil roared with laughter, and spent an hour explaining Wolverine, Storm, and Magneto to Angeline. Maddie walked in during his explanation, and seeing her aunt's look of confusion, told Devil to rent the movies next time he was in town.

~CHAPTER TWENTY-THREE~

Maddie reported to Mr. Sweeney's office right after last period the following Monday. She caught Sissy alone for a moment and apologized for giving her a black eye. Sissy, still sullen, and now a little frightened of Maddie, mumbled her acceptance, and breathed a sigh of relief when Mr. Sweeney arrived to give them their assignment; he expected them to work together to clean all the chalkboards throughout the school. The two girls worked together in strained silence for an hour until Mr. Sweeney found them and allowed them to go home. They walked out of the school together.

Maddie saw Sissy wave at her father who was waiting for her in the parking lot. She put her hand on Sissy's arm and stopped the other girl as she began to walk away.

"I really am sorry," she told Sissy sincerely. "I didn't mean to hurt you."

Sissy glanced down at Maddie's hand then looked up at the taller girl. Her right eye was thickly covered in makeup, but it didn't completely hide the bruising. She raised her fingers to her eye, and then shrugged. "I had it coming," she said quietly. "Why didn't you sit with me at lunch?" The words burst forth, hurt lacing her tone. Tears glimmered in her bright blue eyes. "I just thought we could be friends," she whispered, looking down at the ground.

"I promised Courtney," Maddie told Sissy. "I didn't want to break my promise." She nudged Sissy a little, making her look up. "We can still be friends, if you want," she said slowly.

A smile broke across Sissy's face. "I'd like that," she answered. "I think it would better than always fighting with you." She laughed a little. "I don't think there's enough make up in the world to cover up all the bruises you'd give me."

Maddie laughed and skipped down the steps beside Sissy, feeling a weight had been lifted from her shoulders. She stopped Sissy again and fumbled in her backpack for a scrap of paper and a pencil. After jotting down a phone number, she handed the paper to Sissy.

"Call me later," she said. "Maybe we can figure out how to wash the blackboards faster."

She giggled as Sissy rolled her eyes. Saying goodbye, the two girls parted, not yet best friends, but well on their way to being such.

Sissy did call that night, and every night after that. Devil was heard to complain that he didn't understand what the two girls had to say to each other after spending hours together at school. Angeline listened to Maddie giggle and caught the look of exasperation her niece gave him.

"Uncle Devil," Maddie said in a tone that said he'd never understand, "this is *girl stuff.*"

Angeline had chuckled and kissed him, giggling to herself at his grumpy expression.

Weeks passed, and soon, spring arrived, bringing with it warm breezes and sunny days. Angeline grew round as the baby she carried thrived; she was due to deliver at the beginning of June. She grew more and more restless as April waned into May, and more often than not, found herself cleaning the house and organizing the nursery. At night, she lay in the circle of Devil's embrace, wondering aloud whether she would ever see her feet again, or whether their baby would look like Devil or herself. Unspoken was her worry that the baby would in some way being impaired due to Angeline's ordeal and the medications she'd been given during her recovery. More and more she found it harder to sleep at night as these thoughts ran around and around in her mind, like rats chasing their tails and her shape and size made it difficult to get comfortable. Unable to sleep, Angeline took to walking along the creek, letting the sounds of the night and the water soothe her troubled mind.

It was a night like several others. Angeline couldn't sleep, and had risen from Devil's side to walk the creek side trail to the Kissing Temple. She sat on the stone bench and leaned her head against a fluted pillar, gazing out at the gurgling stream. The sound of the water soothed her frayed and anxious thoughts and she let her mind drift like a leaf on the water.

The hand came from behind and clamped over her mouth, cutting off any sound she would have made. Angeline held herself still, terror rippling through her system. The sound of Jessop's voice in her ear turned her blood to ice.

"You're mine," he panted.

His free hand wandered down the front of her shoulder to fondle her full breasts. She struggled against him, screaming against his hand as he laughed rudely. His hand continued down her body, stilling when it encountered her round belly.

"You whore," he said, almost tenderly.

His hand fell away from her belly, and she felt him fumble with something behind her back. She heard the soft hiss of metal, and her eyes widened as he brought the hunting knife in front of her eyes. He placed the tip at the corner of her eye and let it travel down her cheek, pausing to nick her jaw before travelling down her chest to her belly.

"You whore," he repeated softly in her ear. "I'll make you pay."

He moved his head to her other side, and she felt his hot, wet tongue lick the line of blood that trickled from the cut on her jaw. She breathed shallowly, fighting the panic down as she blocked out the feel of his tongue against her skin. His fingers dug into her cheek as he continued to torment her with the tip of the knife, almost caressing her with it. Memories flooded through her brain, and she remembered everything; her mind's eye showing her the cruel things he had already done to her; she saw herself begging him to stop, saw herself pretending to cooperate just to end the pain and humiliation. She saw his gloating face as she promised to do anything he asked if he would just stop.

Fury—hot, wild, and unfettered—raged.

She felt it build in her belly, rise through her chest, and fill her soul with a dull, red flame that licked greedily and hungrily. Perspiration poured from her and she shook with the effort to contain the rage that flooded her senses. Static built around them, the air crackling with energy as she took a deep breath and held it. Rage burned hot, fast, and clean, but she didn't want that. She wanted Jessop to finally understand the true meaning of the words pain and fear.

For once, she wanted him to truly be afraid.

Of her.

A girl's voice floated through the still night, calling Angeline's name, distracting her and causing the rage slip a little and Angeline smiled grimly to herself; Maddie was going to see the truly destructive side of her ability up close and personal. She saw the girl's trim outline just a hundred years away on the other side of the creek, a flashlight beam bobbing in the dark. Angeline called to her, a quiet whisper that sounded like a shout in the stillness. It floated over the burbling creek, and for a moment Angeline was afraid it had missed her niece, but then the light played across the creek to the temple, and shone in Angeline's face. She heard Maddie squeak shrilly. Angeline felt the knife tip slip against her chest, and felt the sting as a trickle of blood flowed.

"Tell her to stay back," he grunted in her ear. "Do you want your little niece to watch as I kill you? On second thought," he continued, his tone taking on a leer, "Go ahead and invite her over; when I'm done with you, I can play with her."

Angeline tensed as her eyes closed. "No," she whispered, going limp as Maddie's form retreated to the house without Angeline telling her to. Relief flooded through her; Maddie would awaken Devil and help would come. She thought of Jessop's threat against Maddie and allowed the fury to build; she'd die and take him with her before he laid a finger on her niece. The rage still seethed in her, but it wasn't enough; she needed to feed it, to turn it into more than it was, make him understand that he would never torment her again. She closed her eyes and let the memories flood through, waiting for the pain and fear and humiliation to feed her anger; but surprisingly, they didn't come. In a split second of clarity, she understood: she wanted vengeance; she wanted Jessop to burn in Hell for what he had done to her and Devil, but she wasn't afraid of him, nor did she feel any shame over the things he had done to her. After all, it was only her body he'd almost broken, not her spirit; he had never actually touched her soul, and she'd never given him the satisfaction of staying conscious long enough for him to violate her. Then the truth hit her.

"You never wanted me," she gasped, struggling against him, "It was my virginity you wanted. Once I told you I was a virgin, you changed, became more possessive," she continued, understanding, "That's why you beat me after the dinner party. You were pissed because you thought I was trying to give away what belonged to you." The rage twisted, changing. "I thought I was being clever, making you so mad that you'd hit me until you knocked me out, but you weren't interested in my body anymore, were you? The minute I gave my virginity to Devil, you decided to kill me; if you couldn't have me, then no one could, right?"

Jessop grunted in her ear. "Figured it out, did you?" He snarled, yanking her back against his body like a shield, "Unfortunately, you didn't have the good grace to die the first time I tried to kill you." He nuzzled her ear, the knife nicking her again. "You should have died, Angeline." He shook his head, "So many needless deaths to see to after yours." He didn't sound regretful at all; instead, he sounded almost impatient to get on with the bloodletting.

Angeline gasped. "No," she moaned, thinking of Sissy and Courtney, spending the night with Maddie, and imagining the horror that awaited them if she didn't stop Jessop. Like fire-strengthened steel, Angeline felt the moment her anger coalesced and hardened as fear finally flooded through her. She knew as the energies gathered around her that she would probably destroy herself along with Jessop and felt a flood of regret that Devil would never know his daughter, and that small ocean of remorse fed the gathering strength in and around her. She closed her eyes and pictured the energies twisting around them; saw the blue flash of lightening as it sparked around them through her eyelids. She turned in his grasp, looked up at him as her arms came around him. She stood on her toes, her face tilted to his.

Devil broke through the tree line and shined his light toward the temple just as Angeline kissed Jessop. He skidded to a halt in stunned disbelief, almost falling head first into the creek. Maddie and her two friends, Courtney and Sissy, plowed into his back and he stumbled forward, his bare feet squelching as mud squished between his toes. Fury built as he watched Angeline press her body tight to Jessop's as she kissed him with what appeared to be passionate enthusiasm. A low growl began in his throat, and without a thought, he waded across the creek, the cold water numbing his feet in moments. He stalked up the opposite bank and roared his wife's name.

Angeline jumped and turned in Jessop's embrace to face Devil as he stood below the temple rail, his feet braced wide apart, his shoulders stiff and squared, his posture radiating aggression. She had expected this; had expected to see the fury, the pain, the disbelief, but it still hurt. It still cut deeply to think he didn't believe in her. Her heart quailed in her chest, threatening to stutter to a standstill as the torment crashed through him and he whispered her name brokenly, reaching out a hand to coax her back to his side. Tears flooded her vision as she drew on the raw emotion emanating from the man she'd soon die loving.

"I'm sorry."

Her words were a mere whisper of breath, but they held the full weight of her love for him. They rang in his ears and a cold realization dawned as he watched her return to Jessop's embrace. The bastard flashed Devil a look of triumph before he lowered his head to kiss Angeline deeply. He saw the light begin to grow around them, and it took several seconds to realize it wasn't the color of gold, the color of Angeline's passion; it was silvery white, the color of white-hot heat. It swirled around them, the energy's sound growing into a deep, dull roar. Devil staggered back several feet as the heat within the temple rose and spilled beyond the structure's railings. He heard a small sound behind him, and turned in time to catch Maddie as she ran past him. She screamed for her aunt as she struggled in his grasp, tears coursing down her cheeks and the white light pulsing from the temple glowed in her green eyes, turning them almost colorless. Devil held her tight as she fought to break his grasp, and he could feel her fear and anguish rising off her in waves, pulsating in rhythm to her wildly beating heart. He clenched his jaw as biting cold enveloped them. He shivered violently as the cold pierce his bones until he felt brittle and worried that one wrong move would cause his entire being to shatter. The cold was so horrible it caused him to moan in pain as he felt the last of his body heat slip away. He ducked his head to peer at Maddie, to protect her any way he could. Expecting to see fear and anguish in her face, he was shocked to find that her lovely little face had become a blank mask of utter concentration. In a flash of understanding, he realized that it was Maddie who was producing the bone-chilling freeze, that it was she that had sucked the warmth from his blood and bones; somehow she'd siphoned the heat from her surroundings and converted it to bone chilling, all encompassing cold; it emanated from her, it turned the air around them so cold their breath puffed from between their lips in a heavy mist and the ground beneath their feet erupted with a bloom of ice crystals.

Angeline had heard Maddie's screams but from a distance; she instead concentrated on pulling any and all energy from all around her, willed herself to tap into the girl's almost endless supply of power, gathered her frantic fear slowly, startled by the icy coldness of the power that streamed heartbeat by erratic heartbeat into her. She gathered it into a loose knot, layered in her own fury and the revulsion kissing Jessop ignited in her soul, tied it together with Devil's pain and anguish, and added the agony of never seeing Devil or Maddie or any of her friends again; she knew when she finally unleashed everything within her grasp she'd incinerate herself as well as Jessop.

She slowly raised her hands to Jessop's face, cradling it as a lover would, and broke the kiss. She opened her eyes to Jessop's smug and satisfied look, and felt a wave of nausea as she spoke words she never thought she would ever speak:

"Take me with you."

The knife clattered to the worn stone floor at their feet and Jessop gloated. "Beg me," he commanded her. "Beg me and try to convince me." His hands slid up her arms and tenderly came around her throat, squeezing ever so gently, the pressure increasing by small measure as the seconds slowly ticked past. "Convince me that I could ever want you again."

Angeline's eyes fluttered closed, and one word slipped from between her pale and trembling lips; "Please. I was wrong; I should never have left."

Jessop's laugh was low and ugly. The pressure of his hands suddenly grew painful and she struggled to gasp for breath as her eyes opened wide. Her hands clamped down on Jessop's wrists, her nails digging deep furrows into the skin and muscle. The power thrumming through her blood lent her inhuman strength, and she used it now to bend him to her will. Blue flame burned deep in her eyes as Jessop tried to get away from the demon who now forced her mouth over his, kissing, licking, sucking the life from him. Pain and pleasure raced through his nerves and he moaned deep in his throat. He tasted blood on his tongue and it caused his body to grow instantly hard. His blood began to boil in his veins as the heat between them rose to a fevered pitch; his arousal became painful and he ground his hips against hers in a desperate attempt to relieve the ache.

Angeline waited until his hold on her throat loosened before stepping back and breaking the kiss with a wrenching motion. She allowed the sickened energy of his twisted lust to fill her, feed her. Her silver eyes narrowed as Jessop looked at her in confusion a split second before rage contorted his features. As he reached for her, she stopped him, placing her hand over his heart, her touch enough to hold him in place. She held her breath and opened herself to the wave of energy that had built up around them, became a conduit between Jessop and the maelstrom that seethed around them. Jessop's eyes widened as she touched him, and at first he didn't notice the trickle of pain that lanced through his body; it was too well hidden among the passion she had awakened in him by her kiss. He reached for her, and tried to pull her close, but she stayed just out of his grasp. "What are you doing?" He asked. "Don't tease, Angie."

"I'm not teasing, Chris," came her voice, strangely detached sounding. "I'm killing you."

She opened herself wide to the power then and let it pour into her body and through her hand into Jessop. She flinched slightly as his hands scrabbled at her, a finger catching on and snapping the thin silver chain around her neck. She caught the broken necklace as it fell from her neck, absently looping the chain around her fist as she did, not noticing the way the pendant burned the tender skin of her inner wrist.

Jessop's screams were drown out by Maddie and Devil's as they watched the fire roar to life inside the small confines of the stone temple. Shock settled quickly over Devil and his hands fell to his sides as he realized what Angeline had done. He didn't notice Maddie rush up the bank to the side of the temple.

Maddie had felt the pull of her energy toward the temple, had known on some primitive level what her aunt had been doing, and in a rush of desperate instinct, had added a small thread of protective energy to the strand of cold that connected her to her aunt, and now she followed it. It wasn't much and wouldn't last long, but it was better than nothing. She dashed into the temple, and holding her shirt over her mouth and nose, searched frantically for Angeline. A burned hand reached up through the thick smoke and clutched at her, and Maddie screamed in fright before kicking it away. Another step brought her to a small cleared area in the smoke; Angeline huddled on the floor as if in a bubble. Her hair and clothing were singed, but otherwise she seemed unharmed. Maddie bent low and helped Angeline to her feet, slipping an arm around her waist. They stumbled to the door of the temple, skirting around the edge of the room. The smoke was heavy but the fire seemed to be confined to a darkened mass in the center. In the distance, Maddie could hear sirens blaring as volunteers were called from their beds to answer a cry for help.

Maddie and her aunt burst out of the temple and into the fresh night air just as Devil arrived, panting. Maddie listened to her uncle rant his fear and relief to find her safe as she carefully supported her aunt's weight. "If anything had happened to you," Devil continued as he took Angeline in his arms, scooping her up and carrying her away from the temple. He glanced back over his shoulder to make sure Maddie was following close behind. They reached the water's edge and he gently laid Angeline on the creek bank to gently splashed cool water on her face, uncovering the small cut Jessop had made on her jaw, still chastising Maddie for her recklessness. The chilly water brought Angeline around and she stirred weakly in his arms. Her silver eyes opened and took in the dark brown eyes she loved so much.

"I'm not dead?"

Her voice croaked from her throat but Devil understood her just fine, and the moment he heard her voice, he forgave Maddie for scaring him so badly. He hugged Angeline to him tightly, relief causing tears to spring into his eyes. He kissed her face repeatedly, murmuring his love to her in broken and disjointed phrases. Angeline was stunned and briefly wondered how it was that she was alive, and was marshalling herself to ask, but her thoughts were cut short by a clenching pain that ripped across her abdomen.

The pain passed within a minute or two, leaving Angeline breathless and anxious all at once. She struggled to sit up, and pulled on Devil's arm to give her the leverage her awkward shape needed. She pulled herself to her knees, panting and a little dizzy as a second pain thundered through her muscles. She gasped loudly and her vision swam. Devil's face came into view and she grabbed at his hand, clutching tightly until the pain passed.

"The baby," she gasped through pale lips.

Devil's expression went from concerned to downright panicked in the space of a heartbeat. He gathered her into his arms and surged to his feet, stumbling slightly and almost pitching them both into the creek. He regained his balance, splashed through the shallow water to the opposite bank, and stumbled up the embankment into the back yard. He barely paid any attention to the girls as they led firefighters in the opposite direction to put out the remaining fire in the temple. Within minutes, he had gained the living room, and gently placed Angeline on the couch while he phoned Christian at home. Angeline struggled to her feet, moved slowly into their room, gathering her pillow and her overnight bag, and was waiting patiently for Devil at the front door when he rushed past. She waited with a small, tired smile on her face until he realized where she was. Though she felt drained, she found a small amount of reserve energy from somewhere deep inside her and tapped it; she managed to stay on her feet and not sway drunkenly as she waited for Devil. He finally found her and helped her out to the car, fastening the seatbelt around her bulky midriff tightly. As he stepped on the gas, Angeline grabbed his arm.

"Wait!" She cried sharply. Devil slammed on the brakes.

"What?" He said loudly. "What's wrong?"

"The girls," Angeline panted as another pain wracked her frame. "Call someone; we can't just leave them here. Call Sue to come get them."

Knowing she was right, Devil pulled out a cell phone and called Sue. He explained what was going on, and asked her to please come get the girls. A few minutes later, he had snapped the phone shut and put the car in gear. As he backed out of the drive and pointed the nose of the car toward town, Angeline's hand clamped down on his thigh as another contraction gripped her. By the time this one had passed, he was halfway to Christian's clinic. Angeline slumped in the seat, relaxing and resting, gathering any reserves she could. A sudden wash of warm, wet fluid flowed over her and she cried out in surprise just as Devil pulled into a parking spot.

Devil came around the car as Christian and his partner rushed up with a wheel chair.

"Oh, for goodness sake!" She grumbled as the three men fussed over her. She hobbled to the chair and sat gratefully; cocking an eye to Christian, she said quietly, "My water just broke." She saw Christian nod as Devil came along side and took her hand. She looked up and caught the blazing look of love her gave her; she felt strength flow through their clasped hands from him into her. She took a deep breath and held it, allowing herself to calm and accept his energy; she knew she was going to need it later.

In a few minutes Angeline was changed and in a bed. Christian spent several minutes examining her for any injuries she might had gotten during her encounter with Jessop, and found a splatter of melted silver metal on the inside of her wrist. He carefully peeled the metal away, and dressed the burn; then with a nod and a grin, he left Angeline and Devil alone for a few minutes.

Devil kissed her on the forehead and tensed as she gasped and clutched his hand tightly. She held her breath against the pain, struggling not to become overwhelmed by it. He talked to her in a low, steady voice, willing her to relax, to breathe. Angeline reacted to the sound of his voice, and she began to unclench her fingers from around Devil's hand. As the contraction passed, she relaxed against the pillows and gave Devil a small smile.

"Piece of cake," she whispered.

Twelve hours later, Devil was out of his mind with worry. The contractions were growing harder and faster, ripping through Angeline's small body mercilessly; she grew so weak she could no longer cry out, could no longer keep her head up or her eyes open. She lay against the white pillow, her complexion gray, barely breathing. She mewed pitifully as the pain gripped her again and again. Devil touch his forehead to hers, his eyes closed, as he murmured to her, coaxing her to breathe, to fight. He felt her shallow breath against his chest and heard her whisper.

"I love you." Her lips touched his cheek as her blood pressure suddenly bottomed out and alarms went off in the room.

~CHAPTER TWENTY-FOUR~

Angeline opened her eyes. She found herself in a place of warm, white light; she was alone and silence rang through the place. She gave a start and looked down at her side as a small hand slid into her own and her gaze came to rest upon the visage of a little girl with dark curls and silver eyes. The little girl's bottom lip trembled and tears filled the bright eyes.

"Where am I?" She asked. "Where's my mama?"

Angeline knelt on the floor next to the little girl and hugged her tightly, tears flowing freely.

"I'm right here, baby," she sobbed. The little girl pulled back and studied Angeline's face gravely.

"What's my name?" She asked in a small voice.

Angeline reached up and brushed away dark curls that clung to her daughter's tear streaked face. She smiled sweetly, love for her daughter welling up inside her chest.

"You name is Caytie, baby, and I've waited for you a very long time."

The little girl smiled. "The lady told me to wait right here," she said earnestly, her eyes big. "She said if I waited patiently my mommy would come and get me."

There was a sense of movement from behind them and Angeline looked up to see a woman walking toward them. She was short and sported an abundance of red hair.

"Sue?"

The woman smiled. "Of course," she said impatiently. "Who else was going to make sure you didn't leave your daughter all alone?"

The burn on the inside of Angeline's wrist gave a small throb and she rubbed it absently.

"How?" She stammered.

She noticed a wink Sue gave Caytie, and looked back at her daughter who had covered her mouth with her hands, muffling noises that sounded suspiciously like giggles. Angeline picked Caytie up and stood, and felt a rush of emotion as the little girl's head rested against her shoulder. "What's going on, Sue?" She asked tersely. "Are we dead?" A chill ran through her at the thought.

Sue shook her head. "No, not dead," she said calmly. "Think of it more as a waiting room."

"So what are we waiting for?" Angeline asked, impatience coloring her words.

Sue waved her tone away, and settled her hands on her hips. "You're waiting for you to make up your mind," she said bossily. "Are you going to stay here with your daughter, or are you going to go back to Devil?"

A chill washed through Angeline and her arms tightened around Caytie. "What kind of choice is that?" She asked, trembling. "I want to take Caytie back with me. And how is it you're here anyway?" She asked suspiciously.

Sue laughed. "Sweetie," she said, shaking her head, "remember that pendant I gave you?" At Angeline's nod,

Sue pressed on. "When I made it, I was able to infuse it with a piece of myself—a piece of my spirit, if you will. When you wear the pendant, that part of me is always with you; that's how you were able to sleep without dreams. I kept them away."

Angeline's hand went to her throat, and then dropped.

"The pendant's gone," she said sadly. "It melted in the fire."

Sue reached out and took Angeline's hand, pulling the bandage from her wrist. Underneath was a shiny, red burn in the vague shape of a heart; the edges glowed silvery in the pearlescent light. "That's where some of the silver melted on to me," Angeline explained needlessly.

Sue nodded. "That's why I'm here," she said. "When the pendant melted and touched your skin, it transferred its powers into your body."

Understanding was slow to dawn; Angeline walked around the empty space cuddling Caytie to her. The little girl murmured sleepily in her ear and she smiled. "That's why I couldn't feed on the memories," she finally said. "You took the pain and fear away."

She saw Sue shrug. "In a roundabout way," Sue said lightly. "I helped you heal in your dreams, tried to siphon the hurt away until all you would ever feel if you ever remembered everything was rage."

"You should have left a little of the pain," Angeline said lightly. "If you had, I wouldn't be standing here; I wouldn't have used up so much of myself—I could have incinerated Jessop without getting Maddie involved." Her eyes widened. "Maddie!" She suddenly barked. "Where is she? I need to tell her what I did."

Sue laid a gentle hand on her arm. "Don't worry," she said soothingly, "Maddie knows what you did; she was able to put a little something extra into the energy you pulled from her and was able to shield you from the worst of the storm."

Angeline nodded, the explanation making sense. "So," she began slowly, "you became my anti-boogey man, I get that. But how is it that Jessop didn't kill me the first time? We hadn't had time to really get to know each other before that happened."

Sue shrugged. "From what I've been able to figure out, it was your friends who protected you; since coming to Bounty Cove you've made a handful of friends that have become willing to lay down their lives for you, whether they realize it or not. That type of love and loyalty shield you, makes it harder for those who intend you harm to do so."

She stood back and looked beadily at Angeline. "Now," she said briskly. "Have you made up your mind?"

Angeline's head bowed as she held her daughter tightly. She didn't want to leave her little girl, but could feel her heart pulling her inexorably back to Devil. She closed her eyes against the tears that threatened, but they fell anyway.

She kissed Caytie's forehead and whispered, "I love you, baby."

The white warm light flickered and began to fade to black.

She closed her eyes and buried her face in Caytie's dark curls, memorizing Caytie's smell, the feel of Caytie's arms around her neck, the warm, solid feel of Caytie in her arms...

~CHAPTER TWENTY-FIVE~

She opened her eyes to Devil's smiling face. An overwhelming sadness enveloped her heart as she turned her face away from his, burying it in the pillow; she didn't want to hear to news she somehow already knew: Caytie hadn't returned with her. She felt Devil's hand push back the hair from her forehead and a moment later, his warm lips kissed her. His tenderness compounded her grief until it grew into a living creature, writhing and twisting inside her, taking over, filling her with coldness as it ate away at her heart and soul, leaving her feeling empty. She wondered if she would ever feel warm or happy again.

Devil frowned, puzzled. He eased himself down onto the side of the bed and gently pulled her unresistingly into his arms. "I love you," he told her quietly. To his shock, Angeline began to quietly cry, garbled words tumbling from her lips as she shook with the force of the tears.

"I could have stayed," she bawled. "I held her in my arms; I told her what her name is."

Devil's confusion grew. "Who?" He murmured in her ear. "Who did you hold?"

Angeline sat up and pulled away, her tear filled eyes barely meeting his. "Caytie," she said miserably. "Our daughter." Brokenly, she told Devil of her journey, of meeting Caytie. "She was so beautiful," she whimpered. "I knew the moment I saw her she was our daughter."

"Oh, Angel," Devil whispered, brushing tears from her cheek. "It was a dream, that's all. They had to knock you out when they did the c-section."

Angeline didn't understand his words, and tried to make him understand. "I *died*, and Caytie met me," she told him insistently. "Sue was there; I think she's some kind of guardian angel or something. She told me I could stay there with Caytie, or come back to you." She looked away. "I left her alone," she whispered, ashamed. Devil's finger tucked under her chin and drew her gaze back to his.

"You didn't die," he insisted. "They made you go to sleep so they could get the baby out, that's all. The drugs made you have a very real, very strange dream, that's all." He kissed her and laid her back against the pillows. "Rest, Angel," he told her quietly. "Go back to sleep. Everything's fine."

Angeline couldn't understand why Devil insisted on acting as if everything was okay, but found she didn't have the energy or the will to fight with him, to make him understand. Memories flooded into her drowsy mind; memories of how it felt to hold Caytie close, and tears leaked out from beneath her closed lids.

"I'm sorry, baby," she whispered sadly, as sleep claimed her.

Devil sat and watched as she drifted into sleep, his brow furled into a frown of concern. He worried she had done herself damage during her struggle with Jessop, either mentally or emotionally. He watched as tears continued to leak from beneath her lids as she cried in her sleep. He gently caressed her drawn and pale cheek, and leaned down to kiss the frown from between her eyes. A sound brought him up and he turned to see James standing in the doorway. The older man looked tired and worn out.

"How is she?" He asked as he came to her bedside. Devil stood and moved out of the way, as Christian checked her incision and the burn on her wrist. Devil sighed heavily, pushing his fingers through his hair.

"She woke up for a minute," he said, his voice low. "She was really upset about something; she thinks she died and met our daughter." His eyes skittered up to Christian's. "She seems to think she left the baby somewhere."

Christian nodded. "Don't worry," he said, laying a hand on Devil's arm. "It's the drug we use; it causes some women to have very vivid, disturbing dreams. Once it's burned out of her system, she'll be fine." He stood and clapped a hand on Devil's shoulder. "Go home," he instructed. "Get some sleep; I don't think she's going to wake up until tomorrow." He wasn't surprised when Devil shook his head.

"No," Devil said roughly. "I don't want her waking up alone."

Christian sighed, and gave Devil a commiserating look. "I'll have my nurse bring you a pillow and blanket," he said quietly. Devil nodded, not really paying attention, and sat down in a padded chair near Angeline's head as Christian left the room.

Angeline awoke in the white light again. "Caytie?" She called, her eyes searching everywhere for her daughter. The light pulsed and shifted, and Angeline could make out a figure moving toward her and hope flared in her chest, only to die a moment later as the figure resolved itself into that of Sue Beasley.

Angeline tried to hide her disappointment with a smile, but Sue saw right through it.

"Caytie's not here," she said quietly. As Angeline began to protest, Sue held up a hand and stopped her. "She's fine," she said, reassuring the young mother. "She's just fine, surrounded by people who love her." She wagged a finger at Angeline. "You shouldn't be here," she scolded mildly. "You made a choice; you need to stick to it."

Angeline grabbed Sue's hand and held it tightly. "I made a mistake," she said desperately. "I changed my mind. I can't leave Caytie here all alone; I should have stayed and let her go instead."

Sue's brow wrinkled in confusion, then cleared as understanding dawned. She laughed and pulled Angeline into a tight hug. "Oh you poor thing," she crooned, "Caytie isn't here anymore because she went back with you. Look!" She turned Angeline as the white light parted, and Angeline gasped loudly, her hand covering her mouth as tears poured from her eyes.

There was Devil, holding his daughter in the crook of his strong arm, his other hand holding her own as it lay on the blanket that covered her. Behind him, she could see Michael and Melissa, Jamie and Jess, and there was Maddie, standing on her toes to peer over her uncle's shoulder at her baby cousin. The baby yawned and everyone laughed, though Angeline couldn't hear the sound. She turned to Sue, mystification shining in her eyes.

"I don't understand," she said haltingly. "You said I had to choose between here and there; between Caytie and Devil."

Sue shook her head gently, a small smile on her lips. "I never asked you to choose between your daughter and husband." She held up her hand and she pointed silently to a new scene as it faded in over the family scene. There she was, holding Caytie tightly, the little girl's arms wound around her neck, and there was Sue. Angeline listened as Sue gave her the choice again:

"Are you going to stay here with you daughter, or are you going to go back to Devil?"

The scene froze.

Angeline turned to Sue again. "You told me to decide between them!" She cried insistently.

Sue shrugged lightly, a smile twitching her lips. "That's one way to interpret my words," she said, her voice shaking with laughter. "Or you could have heard what I truly meant: take your daughter and choose between life and death."

Angeline shook her head, still confused. "I chose to go back," she said, trying to understand. "I left Caytie here, with you; how could I have left her here, but she's there?" She sank to her knees, unable to stand any longer. Her head hurt, and it throbbed sickeningly. Sue knelt beside her, brushing her fingers through Angeline's hair.

"Caytie was never in any danger; *you were."* As Angeline tried to make sense of her words, Sue pulled her into a tight hug. "Caytie was here because she's part of your soul, bound to you by blood. But she's also bound to Devil, her father; had you stayed, she would have returned to her father, leaving that piece of her soul attached to you behind. Instead, you returned together." She kissed Angeline's forehead. "Go home," she said gently. "You don't need to be here any longer; your husband and daughter need you."

They stood together, questions whirling in Angeline's brain like a swarm of bees. "I don't understand," she stammered. She looked up to find herself alone. "Go home," she heard Sue's voice say as it faded from her hearing.

Angeline turned and looked at the scene of Devil holding her daughter, and felt a rush of emotion swamp her. *Why didn't he tell me?* The scene shiftcd until she saw herself awakening, for the most part raving and unwilling to listen to Devil's words and actually hear them. *He tried,* she answered herself. *I wouldn't listen.* She felt a momentary flush of embarrassment; if she hadn't so busy feeling sorry for herself for all the wrong reasons, she would have spared herself a second trip into—well, wherever this was. She shook herself and took a deep breath as the scene faded and her eyes closed.

~CHAPTER TWENTY-SIX~

Several days later Angeline walked slowly up the front walk of her home, Devil behind her, cradling the small form of their daughter, Caytie Michelle. She pushed open the door and staggered back as a loud cheer rose from the interior to wash over her and Devil. She smiled in puzzlement as Devil caught her eye and before either of them could speak, people were rushing out of the house to surround them, their faces alight with happiness, their voices a cheerful babble.

Angeline stood in stunned amazement as she accepted hugs and kisses of congratulations that were restrained in deference to her recent surgery. Angeline had been appalled at the sight of the incision that transversed her abdomen; it had been swollen and tender to the touch, and when the surgical staples had been removed she had had to clutch Devil's hand in order to subdue the waves of nausea that washed over her. The worst had been the first time she had sneezed; the force of the spasm had made her think she would split in half at the abdominal pain she had experienced. After that, she had made sure a small pillow was nearby so she could hold it tightly against her belly whenever she coughed, laughed, or sneezed. Even now, almost a week after the surgery she found it difficult to stand straight, though Christian had assured her in a couple more weeks she would feel good as new.

The small party spilled into the house, Melissa pulling Angeline ahead of the group in order to show her the decorations that had been put up in her and Caytie's honor. The living room was a riot of color; flowers of every kind and color from the flower shop in town filled the room with their perfume while streamers and balloons hung from every imaginable surface. In the center of the room stood a large pile of brightly wrapped gifts. Angeline laughed; it was the only way she could deal with the surge of emotion she felt. She turned to Melissa.

"Did you do this?" She asked, her eyes shining.

At Melissa's nod, Angeline threw her arms around her friend and hugged her tightly. "Thank you," she whispered, kissing her friend's cheek.

They drew apart as the revelers piled in behind them, and before Angeline knew what was happening, Caytie was taken out of her carrier and passed to her great-grandmother, Constance. Angeline blinked hard, looking around. She saw Maddie and Cassandra laughing together near the punch bowl as they watched Nicodemious chase after a stray curl of ribbon, her grandmother cooing over Caytie and Devil sharing a laugh with his brother, Paul. She stared hard at Devil, willing him to turn and look at her. When he did, she gestured around the room with a wide smile, but Devil saw the shadows that still lurked behind her eyes. He spoke a quiet word to Paul, who looked over Devil's shoulder at her as he nodded in response. Devil paused beside Constance and claimed Caytie with a quiet word that caused the older woman to blush, and then sauntered over to

Angeline, murmuring words into the baby's ear as he did. Angeline looked up at him expectantly as she took Caytie, her face tilted invitingly up to his. Without hesitation, Devil took the invitation and placed a lingering kiss on her lips, his fingers curled under her jaw.

Angeline felt her breath leave her lungs and a small groan crawled up her throat. All of a sudden, the party around them disappeared and all that mattered was her daughter in her arms and Devil's lips on hers. Colors swirled behind her eyes as her blood heated, and warmth flushed her skin quickly, the yearning for his touch taking her by surprise. Devil stepped out of the kiss suddenly, leaving her feeling mildly bereft and intensely annoyed. A feral growl of longing rumbled through her chest causing Devil to give a bark of laughter. He leaned down and his lips caressed her ear.

"We have company," his voice said silkily.

Angeline turned her mouth to his with a small pout and just before she kissed him again, she whispered, "Tell them to go away."

Devil stepped away before she could sink herself into the kiss and pull him after her with a laugh. "Behave," he said, laughter flavoring his tone. The pout she gave him was singular in its unspoken promises and intensity. He looked up as Michael walked over.

"Hey you two," he said jokingly, "get a room."

As Devil laughed, Angeline felt a surge of hot prickling irritation; though she loved her friends and family for the surprise party, at the moment, all she wanted was to get Devil alone and all to herself. Devil leaned in close and kissed her quickly.

"Later," he said huskily, setting her body temperature soaring.

Michael had seen the heated kisses between them, and had decided to distract them before one of the guests was burned in the incipient inferno that was threatening to erupt between them. He snagged Devil's arm and pulled him away from his wife before she absconded with him in the middle of her own party. Melissa steered Angeline to her favorite chair and within moments, had her settled comfortably, her feet resting on a small footstool, and Caytie sleeping peacefully in a bassinet close by.

"Now," Melissa said briskly. "Stay here, and let us wait on you." Angeline sank back into the chair's cushions with a sigh of encroaching tiredness. She perked right back up as Sue Beesley came forward, a wide smile wreathing her face. Angeline started to rise, but Sue just waved her back into her seat. Sue pulled a chair close and took Angeline's bandaged hand as she sat down. She slowly peeled back the gauze and silently looked at the heart shaped burn that was traced in silver. Her finger lightly traced it. After a moment, she gave Angeline her eyes and smiled. The two women sat like that for several minutes in silent communion; no words were necessary between them as each one spoke silently from her heart.

They finally broke the eye contact as Caytie awoke and began to squall lustily. Devil appeared suddenly as Angeline slowly stood. She took her daughter and with Devil's hand at the small of her back, she left the room for the privacy of the nursery in order to feed Caytie. She handed their daughter over to Devil, sat down in a rocking chair, and adjusted the front of her blouse. Within another minute Caytie was nuzzled against her mother's chest, noisily eating.

Devil stood in the doorway, his shoulder leaned against the frame, his dark eyes soft, and watched his wife and daughter. His previous imaginings had never quite conveyed the sense of contentment he felt in reality, and he felt a lump form in his throat when he realized how close he came to losing them both. A shiver worked its way through his body and he quelled it with a shake of his head. He wouldn't dwell on the past; his daughter and wife were here, alive and well. He straightened and stepped into the room as Angeline stood slowly uncounted minutes later. He took Caytie, already asleep, from her mother's arms and laid her gently in the crib, pulling the small blanket over her tiny body. His touch gently caressed her smooth cheek and he smiled as she sighed deeply. He turned as Angeline buttoned her blouse and stopped her hands in order to finish the task himself.

Angeline stood still, barely able to breathe as Devil slowly rebuttoned her blouse, his fingers warm against her skin. She felt the desire pooling hot, heavy in her belly, and swayed against him, seeking his touch, his warmth.

Devil watched her face and saw her bright eyes darken as she moistened her lips with the tip of her tongue. His body throbbed hot and tight as his head dipped to taste her breath. He stiffened and let out a quiet groan as a throat cleared itself behind them. Devil turned slowly.

"This had better be good," he growled.

Jamie stood in the doorway, looking uncertain and embarrassed. "Uh, yeah," he stammered, his face bright red. He cleared his throat again and pressed on, gesturing to the party behind them. "There's someone at the door, saying he's your cousin and needs to talk to you." He turned abruptly and scurried away; mortified he had interrupted a private moment.

Devil gave Angeline a pained look and sighed ruefully then he rested his forehead against hers. "We can't seem to catch a break today, can we?"

Angeline's expression was just as disgruntled. "Go see what's going on," she told him with a gentle nudge; the sooner he did, the sooner they could be alone again.

Reluctantly Devil left her with the baby and prowled through the house, his movements impatient; it had been close to six months since he had been able to touch Angeline in the way he craved. Frustration gnawed on his innards, causing him to be short tempered and impatient with the world. The people crowded around the front door parted as he arrived and Devil was able to see the back of the uninvited guest's head. Recognition prickled in his brain then roared to full blown life as he caught sight of the man's profile.

"Chance!" He roared happily, as he grabbed the man in a bear hug. "What the hell are you doing here?" He heard a groan and turned his cousin around. Dark, raw bruises covered the side of his face. "What the hell?"

Chance moved stiffly out of Devil's reach, his right arm held tight against his side. "My bike," he panted. "Laid it down about a quarter mile from here. Idiot cut me off."

Devil hollered for Christian, and when he had arrived, the two men each put an arm around the injured man and helped him into the house. The three men staggered past Angeline on their way to the kitchen. Angeline's eyes were wide as she took in the tall, sandy haired man that stumbled between Devil and James, noting the scrapes and bruises on his face. Devil looked back over his shoulder at her. "Go get Paul," he ordered her in a loud voice. He barely saw Angeline nod as she scurried off in search of his older brother.

Angeline found Paul standing in a knot of people, holding court as only he could. She could hear his low rumbling voice as he regaled his listeners with some story about him and Devil as boys. Laughter rang out as she reached the small knot of people. She gave Paul an anxious look.

"Devil needs you in the kitchen," she said quietly. "Someone's been hurt."

Paul set aside his drink and excused himself before following Angeline out of the room. Out of deference to her, he kept his pace slower to match hers. "Who is it?" He asked quietly as they negotiated to crowd of people.

Angeline shook her head. "I don't know," she responded. "But he could barely stand on his own."

They reached the kitchen and Angeline hung back as Paul surged forward with a loud shout. He recognized the new arrival instantly. "Chance!" He called as he reached the group. He helped get his cousin into a chair, noting the whiteness around his mouth, and the painful stiffness that he held himself. "What the hell happened?"

Chance sucked his breath in through his teeth as Christian began to remove his leather jacket. It hurt to move his arm, and breathing made his ribs burn painfully. Afraid he would scream if he tried to talk, Chance clenched his jaw tight and remained mute. He closed his eyes against the nausea the pain kicked up in his belly, and listened to the annoying buzzing in his ears. Behind his eyelids, he felt the world tilt crazily on its axis. Without warning, he threw up. As the spasm passed he cracked his eyes open long enough to look at his cousin Devil and his wife. "Heard you got hitched; thought I pop in and see if it was true," he mumbled almost drunkenly just before he passed out.

Paul caught his cousin as he slid from his chair and with minimal effort righted him in his chair and held him steady while Christian finished his cursory exam.

"Broken collar bone for sure," the doctor said, straightening up. "Probably a couple ribs, too. We should take him to the clinic so I can get him patched up."

Paul nodded and between himself and Devil, managed to get Chance into Doc's car without waking him up. Devil straightened up after making sure the seatbelt was tight around his cousin and faced Angeline. Indecision lit his brown eyes as he regarded her.

Angeline stood on her toes and kissed him with a smile. “Go on,” she told him softly. “I'll be alright.” She gestured to the people behind her. “I don't think Melissa's going to let me do more than sit and look pretty anyway.”

Devil leaned down and kissed her. “I'll be back as soon as I can,” he promised. He climbed into his truck and drove away, following Christian's car closely.

Angeline raised a hand, waved goodbye, and watched them until she couldn't see the vehicles anymore. She dropped her hand with a sigh and turned to her friends and family. The corner of her mouth quirked up into a bit of a smile.

“Where were we?” She finally asked. She found herself swallowed up by the crowd and let it propel her back to her comfortable chair by the fire. She sat for an hour, opening gifts for the baby, watching the clock and glancing out the window anxiously, awaiting Devil's return.

~CHAPTER TWENTY-SEVEN~

By the time the last guest had departed, Angeline was feeling very tired. Despite her protests Sue, Melissa, and Jess sent their children home with their husbands and stayed behind and helped her clean up the mess. Angeline finally sent them on their way once the dishwasher was running and the garbage had been taken out. She took a long hot bath, and fed Caytie, and soon, she was laying in bed, trying to read, her ears pricked for the sound of Devil's truck.

It was close to midnight when Devil returned. He found Angeline curled under the blankets, a paperback novel lying in her limp fingers. He settled her under the covers and laid the book aside before checking on Caytie. Finding his tiny daughter and wife sleeping, Devil decided he should do the same; he felt more tired than he could describe, exhaustion burning a deep ache in his muscles. He dragged his clothes from his body as he made his way to the bathroom. Once naked, he took a hot shower, allowing the hot water to wash away the worry and stress he had carried for so long. Jessop was dead, Angeline and

Caytie were alive, and Maddie was adjusting well to her new life in Bounty Cove, making friends, and tying up the phone line for hours every night. The drama of the past almost year seemed far away and inconsequential now. He tilted his face into the spray and let the tears of relief fall.

He showered until the hot water ran cold, and his body began to shake with shivers as the needles of icy water peppered his skin and awakened his brain. Cleared minded and suddenly awake, he stepped out of the shower and toweled off, wrapping the fabric around his hips. He heard a noise as he left the bathroom, and following it, found himself once again standing in the door of Caytie's nursery. A small tabletop lap cast a small pool of muted golden light, highlighting the curls of Angeline's burnished hair, and giving her pale skin a warm glow. She sat, slowly rocking and humming to their daughter as she finished her midnight snack.

Angeline glanced up to see Devil in the doorway, naked, but for the towel around his waist, and damp. She smiled softly at him as her body reached for his, as her soul called softly to him. When Caytie had her fill and had given her mother a cursory burp, Angeline put her back to bed, and after kissing her daughter on the top of her soft head, she went to Devil. She took his hand and led him silently to the bedroom, pausing long enough to make sure the baby monitor was turned on. She slipped her robe from her shoulders at the side of the bed, let it fall in a silky rush of fabric to her feet, and held her hand out to him.

Devil took her hand and pulled her close, wrapping his arms around her small body. At the touch of her lips to his all thoughts and worries fled, and he lost himself in the kiss. Conscious of her healing body, Devil touched her gently, carefully, even as her fingers sought to touch him with fierce and consuming need. They fell to the bed, taking comfort and seeking reassurance in the feel of each other's touch.

Angeline awoke early the next morning, a feeling of contentment and well-being pervading every fiber of her being. She lay on her side, her head pillowed by Devil's arm, her back pressed tight against his chest as his free arm curled around her waist and held her securely to him. She sighed sleepily as he nuzzled her neck and giggled softly when his whiskers tickled her jaw. She turned her head enough to reach his mouth, and kissed him slowly. Caytie began to fuss from her room and with a whispered good morning, Angeline rose slowly from bed and went to her daughter.

Devil lay back against the pillows, his hands behind his head, and listened to Angeline's voice as she talked to Caytie, her voice sweet and melodic. He heard Maddie's voice, low and indistinct, and decided it was time he, too, got up. Yawning, he padded on bare feet down the short hall that separated the nursery from the master bedroom and peeked in to find Angeline changing Caytie's diaper, Maddie hovering close and talking baby gibberish to her cousin. As he took in the scene, it hit him suddenly that Maddie had shot up another inch or two; her pajama bottoms seemed pretty short. With a smile, he entered the room, saying good morning as he did, and gave each of his girls a kiss. As Angeline settled into the rocking chair to feed Caytie, he and Maddie left to make breakfast.

Angeline joined her husband and niece half an hour later, cradling a full and drowsy Caytie in her arms. She gently place her little girl in her swing and turned it on to its lowest settling, and sat down at the table with a jaw cracking yawn. She watched Maddie and Devil work as a team to make waffles, and laughed as Maddie swatted Devil's arm when he reached out behind her back to tug on the end of her ponytail. Her stomach growled a loud grumble when a plate overflowing with a large waffle was placed in front of her.

As Maddie and Devil joined her at the table, Angeline was surprised by Devil's words.

"We need to take Maddie shopping."

Angeline traded a look with Maddie, whose mouth was hanging open, a sparkle of excitement lighting her eyes. "Okay," Angeline answered slowly, confused by how out of the blue his announcement had come.

"Yeah," Devil continued, more gruffly, "I noticed her pajamas are a little short." He ducked his head as a flush rose in his face.

"Um, Uncle Devil?" Maddie began in a choking voice as she tried not to giggle, "They're Capri style bottoms." At his uncomprehending look, Maddie sighed and shook her head sadly. "They're supposed to be a little short."

A look of pained consternation crossed Devil's face and he muttered, "Oh." Then, straightening and giving them a defensive look, he went on, "I'm sure you both could use a new outfit or two, anyway." He watched Angeline and Maddie exchanged an unreadable look and was taken by surprise as they both stood and moved to each sit on one of his knees and wrap their arms around him. They both kissed his cheeks, and hugged him tightly.

"Poor, uneducated man," Angeline sighed in a mournful tone, "He has no clue what he just got himself into, does he?"

Maddie's response was a girlish giggle.

"All right, all right," he grumbled half heartedly, "Give the man a break," though his arms came around them to hold them tightly. He suddenly couldn't imagine his life without these two females or his daughter. Emotion clogged his throat for a moment, before he cleared it gruffly. "The next kid better be a boy," he murmured in his wife's ear. "Maybe then the playing field will be more level." He felt her laughter all the way to his toes.

The lighthearted atmosphere was temporarily dissipated by the arrival of Matt Dixon, Bounty Cove's sheriff. There were several follow up questions he needed to ask Angeline before he could close the file on Chris Jessop's death. Once he was satisfied that Angeline had acted in self-defense, Sheriff Dixon assured her that her part was finished, and left the little family alone to enjoy the beautiful spring day.

~CHAPTER TWENTY-EIGHT~

They made the trip to Raleigh a week later, after Maddie's last day of school. She had convinced her aunt and uncle to let her invite Courtney and Sissy along, citing that they, too were growing girls, and probably would like to get an outfit or two, as well. And so, on the last day of school Courtney and Sissy rode the bus with Maddie home, each girl carrying a backpack stuffed with all things vital for a weekend long sleep over.

Angeline greeted the girls cheerily and didn't miss how all three seemed to watch her closely. She gave them each a bright smile as she continued to pat Caytie's back to coax a burp from her daughter, and told them there were fresh cookies in the kitchen. Maddie was the last to leave the room, her step slow as she watched her aunt closely. Since the night of the attack, Maddie had been reluctant to let Angeline out of her sight, and it was only Devil putting his foot down and insisting that Maddie finish out the two weeks of school that she even left the house.

"Maddie?"

Angeline set Caytie in her bassinet and went to her niece. Taking her hand, Angeline frowned, realizing Maddie's fingers were ice cold. She reached up and brushed a lock of hair from her face. "Sweetie, are you all right?" She grew more alarmed when she noticed the pale shimmer in Maddie's green eyes. Suddenly, Maddie was gasping for air, her cold fingers beginning to heat at an alarming rate, and her body trembling violently. Her green eyes flashed from green to silver repeatedly, as Maddie struggled to control herself.

Angeline froze as she realized Maddie was trapped in a cycle of powerful emotion so erratic that it was turning Maddie's emotions inside out and producing so much energy that if it weren't bled off soon, it would rip its way out. Angeline wasn't worried about the electrical appliances so much as she was worried about Maddie. Thinking quickly, she slapped Maddie across the cheek, hoping the shock would end the vicious emotional circle Maddie was just starting to ride. It worked.

With a gasp, Maddie's fingers rose to touch her cheek gingerly. Tears sprang to her eyes, extinguishing the silver light that had blazed in them. She blinked, and shook her head, normal anger and hurt in her voice as she asked, "Why did you do that?" Her lower lip trembled and Angeline was quick to wrap her arms around her niece to comfort her.

"I'm sorry, sweetie," she whispered, rocking her niece gently, "It was the only way." At Maddie's look of confusion, Angeline sighed and led her to the couch. "Don't you know what just happened?" She felt the resentment flare in Maddie and squeezed her hand tightly. "Maddie," she said, her voice low and calm, "You almost lost control; don't you remember?"

Maddie's anger evaporated in a flash as horror masked her expression. "No," she whispered, shaking her head.

She frowned as she struggled to think back over the last couple minutes. "One minute you were telling us about the cookies, and the next, you were slapping me." She threw a sullen look at her aunt.

Angeline felt chills race along her spine. When she was younger, she'd had an episode that to this day she couldn't remember; a boy had been hurt, badly burned by the fire that had resulted from short circuiting boom box. She shivered as the chills crawled over her body. Slowly, gently, she touched Maddie's cheek; it was still a little warm. "Honey," she said calmly, swallowing her fear, "What's wrong?"

Maddie's face crumpled and for a moment she appeared to be several years younger, then her face smoothed out, and a cool light replaced the look of fear in her eyes. "Nothing," she muttered with a shake of her head, "That I can't handle."Then before Angeline could press her for more information, she jumped to her feet and left the room. A moment later, Angeline could hear Maddie's laughter as she joined her friends in the kitchen; the sound was brittle and forced. Before she could pursue any line of thinking however, Caytie began to fuss, spooked by the strange tension she sensed around her. With a sigh, Angeline went to comfort her daughter.

Later that night, though Angeline watched her niece closely, she couldn't find any hint of the rage she'd sensed earlier in the girl; it was almost as if the episode had never occurred, and Angeline wondered if she'd exaggerated the danger she'd felt when she witnessed Maddie's eyes flashing green to silver and back rapidly. What she couldn't know was that Maddie was as disturbed by the incident as her aunt, and she struggled mightily to push it away, determined not to let anything ruin her friends' fun.

Devil was aware of the tension between aunt and niece the moment he walked in the door that evening, and when he tried to talk to both on separate occasions to find out what had happened, he'd been gently but firmly rebuffed. He watched his wife and niece in studied silence, allowing the chatter of Maddie and her friends flow around him. He noticed the frequent looks Angeline sent Maddie's way; looks rife with concern and a tinge of fear. He also took note of the way Maddie steadfastly ignored her aunt with a single-minded determination. It was late before the three teenagers settled down for the night, and he waited quietly in bed for Angeline to join him.

"What happened today?" He asked quietly as he held her and kissed her shoulder. He felt the sigh she heaved throughout his body, and his arms tightened around her in response. Then, without another word from him, Angeline was telling him what had happened.

"I'm not worried by how hard she struggled to keep control," Angeline finished, her fingers picking at the comforter, "because that means she's really trying hard. It's the fact that she doesn't seem to remember any of it until I slapped her." She sighed again. "If she were any other teenage girl, I wouldn't be so worried about it, but this is Maddie, not some over-hormonal drama queen; it's not like her to be so sullen and angry."

Devil wasn't sure what, if anything, he could say to alleviate her worry, so he simply held her until they both slept.

~CHAPTER TWENTY-NINE~

Maddie awoke in the small hours of the morning, hot and cold waves breaking over her in turn, her stomach knotted in nauseated twists. Moonlight filtered through her sheer lace curtains and she was able to see her friends sleeping peacefully in their sleeping bags on the carpeted floor. So she hadn't cried out this time; no one knew she'd had another nightmare. She reached over to snap on the bedside lamp, and wasn't surprised when it didn't light. Nor did the flashlight she pulled from under her pillow. Her stomach was starting to settle, but she was fairly certain she wouldn't sleep again before the sun came up. She shivered under her heavy blanket as another wave of cold washed over her. With a heavy sigh of frustration, Maddie got out of bed and fumbled in the dark until she was able to find her robe and shove her feet into her slippers. Then silently, she tiptoed around her friends and out of the room. Silently, ghostlike, she stole through the house to the kitchen, intent on a glass of chocolate milk and a cookie. She reached around the doorframe of the kitchen door and flipped on the light as she entered the room, and came up short with a sound of surprise.

Devil heard the startled squeak of surprise and turned to find Maddie standing in the kitchen door, her dark hair in wild disarray around her pale face. Dark shadows marred the smooth skin beneath her green eyes, and the skin over her face was drawn. She seemed to hesitate there in the doorway, as if she were afraid to come into the room. He spoke her name quietly, making his voice as soothing as possible. She visibly relaxed, though her steps were still slow and hesitant as she made her way to the kitchen table. He frowned when she fell into a chair and, elbow propped on the tabletop, covered her eyes.

"Could you please turn off the light?" She asked in a shaky voice, "The light hurts my eyes."

Instead of pointing out to her that she'd been the one to turn on the light in the first place, Devil flipped the overhead light off and sat down across from his niece. After a moment or two of silence, he cleared his throat. Maddie jumped. He frowned.

"What's wrong?"

Why she felt she couldn't tell her aunt about what she was feeling, Maddie didn't know, but Uncle Devil was someone she felt comfortable confiding in, and to her shock, she began to cry, loud, shuddering sobs shaking her violently. When Devil came to her side and knelt, she turned until her face was buried against the side of his neck, her arms clutching him tightly.

"I'm having nightmares," she sobbed. That confession opened the floodgates, and Devil was stunned to hear how shaky Maddie's emotional state had been since the night Jessop attacked Angeline at the creek.

Since the night Angeline had killed Jessop, using energy drawn from Maddie.

In a flash of insight, Devil was certain that the energy Angeline and Maddie had shared that night was responsible for the turmoil Maddie was now experiencing. He patted her back, making soothing noises in an effort to calm the sobbing girl and simply waited for the worst of the storm to pass. Finally, Maddie seemed to gain a little control over herself and sat back, wiping her eyes with the backs of her hands and sniffling. Devil stood and handed her a paper napkin to blow her nose.

"I have a suggestion," he told her once she'd dried her eyes, "And I'm pretty sure you've thought of it yourself, though you seem reluctant to take your own advice." He waited until Maddie looked up at him, her eyes wary. "You need to talk to your aunt," Devil told her carefully. "She's the one who knows what's going on with you, and she'd be the one to best know how to help you." He gave her a crooked grin and shrugged. "All I've got is a shoulder to cry on."

Maddie nodded, her eyes on her lap. "I know," she whispered so quietly, Devil had to strain to hear her voice, "But every time I try, all that happens is I get mad, and then everything goes blank."

A slight noise reached Devil's ears, and he looked up to find Angeline standing in the kitchen door, her hand on the frame, her body statue still. Her face was as pale as Maddie's and her eyes were wide with confusion and uncertainty.

Devil cleared his throat and gestured for Angeline to join them. "Maybe now's a good time for the two of you to work this out," he suggested, moving across the room to make coffee.

Maddie looked up and watched as her aunt slid slowly into the chair across from her. Though she couldn't see her aunt's hand because they were hidden in her lap, Maddie was fairly certain they were clenched tightly together; her aunt's shoulders were tense, her face drawn. Maddie swallowed hard and said into the tense silence, "I'm scared." Then, before she could lose her courage, she rushed on. "Ever since that night, I get scared that something bad is going to happen; and every time I try to talk to you about it, I get mad."

Angeline felt herself grow colder; until that night, she'd never imagined there was any way to actually share energy. Until then, she'd been able to siphon needed energy from those around her, but had never considered the possibility of sending energy back the other way; she wondered if, in the chaos and confusion of that night, she'd inadvertently pushed some of her rage back to Maddie, had accidently infected her niece with the gruesome memories. She took a shuddering breath.

"I heard you say you've been having nightmares," she began, hoping whatever she heard wouldn't be as bad as she feared. She watched Maddie nod slowly, her eyes downcast.

"How did you live through that?" She asked, her voice a bare whisper. "In my dreams, it's happening to me, even though I know it's not real. And it makes me angry that I can't do anything to make it stop," she finished through clenched teeth. The table between them rattled loudly before Maddie managed to clamp down on her emotions.

Angeline felt sick. How had it happened? How had she passed her memories to Maddie that night? How had Maddie not lost her mind in the weeks since the attack? She was a child, unable to effectively deal with memories so real, so alien, that she may as well have had it happen to herself. Pity and sorrow rose in her heart as she stared across the table at her niece. She searched her mind; desperate to find something she could give Maddie to help the girl rid herself of memories that weren't hers.

"What do you do when you get mad?' She finally asked, her voice trembling.

Maddie shrugged. "I push it down. I imagine a giant hole and push everything down into it." She glanced up at Angeline, her eyes haunted. "It worked, at first, but it's getting harder to do. Now, it just jumps out at me, all the time."

Angeline nodded. This was something she knew how to handle; Maddie had lost her ability to keep herself centered, and as a result, her emotions and nightmares were spinning out of control. She glanced up at the clock that ticked softly on the wall; it was five a.m. Courtney and Sissy wouldn't be awake for a couple more hours. Making her decision, she stood, saying as she did, "Get dressed, Maddie." She winced at how stern and sharp her voice sounded in the early morning quiet. She willed herself to soften her words. "Be sure to wear your swimsuit." She waited until Maddie left the room and turned to Devil. "She's off kilter, right now. I think if I can help her get her balance back, this will go away. Can you handle things here for a couple hours?"

Devil nodded wordlessly before kissing her forehead. "Be careful," he said softly.

Angeline gave him a weary smile. "I will," she promised, before turning and leaving the kitchen to get dressed. Devil watched her go, worry taking root in his chest. He stayed, held in place, his breath held until he heard Maddie and his wife leave the house, closing the door quietly behind them. Only then did he move to the living room to watch as they got into Angeline's little car and drove away into the foggy early morning light.

~CHAPTER THIRTY~

Dawn was creeping silently over the horizon as Angeline wordlessly navigated the car out of town. Beside her, Maddie was tense, and in an effort to help her niece relax, Angeline reached over and patted Maddie's leg. She didn't like the way Maddie flinched. "You need to learn how to relax," she said quietly. "For me, going to the beach always help. It may not be exactly what you need, but it couldn't hurt until you find a way of dealing with the excess for yourself."

From the corner of her eye, she saw Maddie nod silently, her brow wrinkled in confusion. Finally, Maddie spoke."Is that what's wrong with me?" She asked, the barest glimmer of hope in her voice, "I just have too much building up inside me?"

Angeline sighed with relief; it seemed as if Maddie was already starting to understand. This time when she patted Maddie's leg, the girl didn't flinch. "I never considered that I could feed energy to someone else," she said in an apologetic voice, "I knew I could affect how someone was feeling, but I didn't know I could infect someone with my memories. Until you came along, there was no one else who could do what we can." She sighed heavily. "I suppose, if I'd taken a moment to think about it, I would have realized it could happen." She glanced over at Maddie, a sad smile twisting her mouth. "I'm sorry, baby."

Maddie's eyes filled with tears; it seemed as if she was crying a lot lately, and it made her impatient with herself. Until a few weeks ago, she'd never cried much. "It's not your fault," she managed to say through the tears that clogged her throat; "I didn't know it, either."

They passed the rest of the trip in silence. Angeline was aware of Maddie's sudden interest as they pulled into the makeshift parking lot above the trail to the beach below. She turned to see her niece surveying their surroundings keenly.

"Isn't this where Mr. Kemper almost died?" She asked in that morbid curiosity that most teenagers had.

"Yes," Angeline sighed heavily. "That's what the story says." Before Maddie could ask anything else, she got out of the car, and waited for Maddie to do the same. She half expected a return of the sullen teenager, but was pleasantly surprised; it seemed the moment the fresh ocean breeze touched Maddie's face, she relaxed. Turning, she gave her aunt a grin.

"I feel better already," she sighed, coming around the nose of the car. She grabbed Angeline's hand and swung her arm lightheartedly. "Lead on," she quipped, reaching up and brushing wind teased hair out of her face.

Hand in hand, they walked down the dirt trail to the beach below. Reaching the water's edge, Angeline breathed deeply, enjoying the taste and smell of the salty water. The sun was just above the horizon now, and seagulls cried and wheeled in the sky above their heads. Squinting slightly, she was able to pick out the sleek grey silhouettes of a small pod of dolphins out beyond the breakers. Turning to her niece, Angeline was surprised to find Maddie with her eyes closed, her face serene. Her breathing was slow and even, and Angeline knew in that moment that her instincts had been correct.

"It's important for us to stay balanced," she murmured, leading Maddie away from the water. "Think of it like a cup of water, half full. The empty half is all the room you've got for the extra energy you produce or take from others around you. When you add too much, it over flows and makes a mess." She sat down on a rock and took off her shoes. Maddie did the same, and seemed to take immense pleasure in the feel of the warming sand between her toes. Angeline went on, her voice light and low. "I feel better in the water," she said, pulling her shirt over her head, "It always makes me feel as if everything just washes away." She stood and pulled off her sweats. "It might be different for you."

Maddie nodded as she too stripped to her bathing suit. Then, without a word, she took off down the sand. Angeline watched as Maddie ran into the water and moments later, dove into a wave. She laughed as her niece resurfaced almost immediately, gasping. Even from the distance, she could tell the girl was beginning to shiver. She shook her head and went to join Maddie in the waves.

"What do you do in the winter?" Maddie managed to gasp between shivers.

Angeline laughed. "I suck it up if it's bad enough," she said, touching her temple. She took a deep breath and dove in, forcing her body to accept the cold shock of the water against her warm skin. She stayed submerged until her body had adjusted to the temperature of the water. When she resurfaced, Maddie was watching her, awe in her expression. "Come on," Angeline invited, beckoning to her, "Just let yourself go. Forget everything but the feel of the water against your skin, the sound of the waves and the seagulls. Forget everything except what your body feels."

Maddie gave her aunt a doubtful look; how in the world was she supposed to relax and let herself go when her body was threatening to slide into hypothermia? But her aunt seemed so carefree, so certain this would work for her, and she was so desperate to end the nightmares, that she forced herself to dive back in. Before too long, she began to realize that her Aunt Angeline was right; as long as she concentrated on what her body was feeling, she was able to forget everything else. By the time she left the water to flop, exhausted onto the sand beside her aunt, Maddie was feeling a thousand times better. They lay in silence, allowing the warming sun to dry their skin. Finally, Angeline turned and propped herself up on an arm.

"The first thing to do," she began, "Is get your body relaxed; when your body is tense, it's harder to focus on getting your energy and emotions unknotted. The more tense you are physically, the closer you are to breaking, emotionally, and that's when accidents happen." She sat up as her niece did. "I'll show you how to bleed the excess of the quick and dirty way another time, because it should only be done in an emergency; for now I want you to learn how to do it safely."

Maddie listened, intent and eager as her aunt taught her how to center herself.

"Close your eyes," Angeline instructed, "and simply breathe, deep and slow. Concentrate on the sound of your breath, your heart, let it relax your mind and calm you."

Maddie did as she was instructed, initially finding it difficult to block out the sound of the waves washing up the sand. Eventually, though, she was able to blend the sound with that of her breathing, and felt herself reach a new level of relaxation. As she did so, she became aware of a hard, sullen knot in her gut. Curious, she reached out and touched the pulsing, sickly tangle, and her eyes snapped open and she gasped in pain. She found Angeline watching her closely.

"It hurts, I know," she murmured sadly, "But you have to face it and not be afraid of the pain." She felt her heart twist with the knowledge that she wouldn't be able to do this for her niece, that Maddie had to face the hurt, pain, and anger on her own, and learn to rid herself of it. "Don't rush it," she instructed as Maddie closed her eyes again, "It's like when you have a bruise and you poke it every now and then to see if it still hurts as badly as it once did."

Maddie nodded and steeled herself against the pain she would feel, and felt the moment her shoulders stiffened. She blew out her breath and heard the slight sounds of Angeline getting to her feet. "I'll be close," was all she said as she walked up the beach.

So, Maddie began again, breathing deep and slow, allowing the sound to calm her until she once again saw the poisonous knot of anger, then, nervously, she touched it, surprised to find that it didn't hurt as badly this time. Confidence growing, Maddie set to work, unraveling the tangled skein, patiently working knots loose until the entire thing fell apart and dissolved. When that happened, she felt as if an invisible weight lifted off her, leaving her feeling as if she could almost float. She opened her eyes and looked for Angeline, finding her sitting up the beach on a flat rock. She scrambled to her feet and jogged to her side. With a heartfelt sigh, she took a seat beside her aunt and gave her a nose-wrinkling grin.

"Better?" Angeline asked, her own lips twitching. At Maddie's nod, Angeline raised her arms above her head and stretched. "Good. Now remember this from now on. The next time you start feeling it building up, take care of it immediately." She watched Maddie nod soberly before allowing the grin she felt make its appearance. "Now, how about that shopping trip?" She asked.

Maddie's eyes sparkled and her laugh was light and merry; much more in keeping with the girl Angeline knew. She felt the last little bit of doubt and tension bleed away as Maddie grabbed her hand and practically dragged her up the path to the car.

~CHAPTER THIRTY-ONE~

Devil noticed the difference the moment his wife and niece walked through the front door; the two of them were laughing, their arms wrapped around each other's waists as they tried to keep each other from falling over. Caytie was fed, burped, bathed, changed, and dressed, and Maddie's two friends were both in the kitchen, happily chowing down on waffles and scrambled eggs. To his surprise, Maddie was completely honest with her friends when they wanted to know where she'd been. When he gave Angeline a surprised look, she'd simply winked and gave him a sunny smile that warmed him to his toes. When she left the room to go and shower, he followed, a piece of paper tucked into his back pocket.

He caught up with his wife as she moved around their room, picking out clothing for the day. Coming up behind her, he wrapped his arms around her waist and dropped a kiss onto her shoulder. "Happy Anniversary," he murmured in her ear.

Angeline turned in his loose embrace, puzzlement written across her face. "Anniversary?" She asked in bewilderment. She watched as Devil dropped his arms and turned away, pulling something from his hip pocket.

"Don't tell me you forgot," he said in mock hurt as he turned and handed her a folded piece of paper.

Angeline took the paper, a frown marring her features and slowly unfolded it.

"We met one year ago today," Devil told her, watching her face as she read the contents of his gift.

Angeline had stopped listening. It took several attempts at reading the words before their meaning sunk in and she understood.

"Partnership?' She asked, weakly, her eyes rising to his.

Devil grinned then. "Joe Carter is willing to offer you a partnership. He'll take care of the large animals, and you'll treat the house pets; you get an office and he's offering a decent yearly salary." He made a face. "You'll have to do your own filing and such unless you want to hire someone yourself."

Angeline's brain began working again. Michael Carter had a veterinary clinic just outside of town. His animal hospital and offices were large, clean, and well kept; Angeline had met him within the first month of her arrival, and had been impressed by how well his patients had been cared for.

"Joe's wanted to expand and treat smaller animals, but he hasn't had the time or the opportunity to do so," Devil was telling her. He tapped the paper that she still held in a loose grip. "This is his offer to you; you can accept it or not. It's entirely up to you."

"Has it really been a year?" Angeline asked in a whisper, still staring at the paper in her hands. She didn't really expect him to answer; it was simply the first coherent thing her brain had come up thought.

Devil began to feel a little worried; she didn't seem to be enjoying his surprise. "I know you wanted a clinic of your own," he said quietly, reaching for the paper, "You don't have to accept the partnership if you don't want it." He tugged on the paper and frowned when she didn't let go.

"How did this happen?" Angeline asked, shaking herself and pulling the paper out of his reach.

Devil gave her a cocky grin. "Didn't I mention the job I've been working on for the last couple months was out at Joe's place?" Angeline shook her head. "No? Yeah," he continued, pulling her close, "he had an addition added on to the hospital and had his basement sealed; I've been overseeing the construction. We got to talking a few weeks back, and I mentioned you specialized in small animals, and was hoping to set up practice in the near future. Joe's the one who came to me this week and made you this offer." He stopped and watched Angeline's face closely. "So, what do you think?" He asked slowly.

Angeline frowned a little, and she made a funny gesture of a cross between a shrug and a head nod. "I think," she began slowly, as if choosing her words with care, "That I should probably go out to Joe's on Monday and discuss terms with him." She laughed suddenly and threw her arms around Devil's neck, pulling him down to kiss him.

The trip to Raleigh passed in giggling good cheer; Devil spent most of the day wearing a mock martyred expression as he waited outside dressing rooms and gave his opinion of too many outfits to count. By lunchtime, his stomach was complaining, and he wondered if teenage girls drew strength and sustenance from half off sales and name brands. When they finally sat down at a table in the food court, Devil could see that Angeline's energy was beginning to wane, and she was growing edgy; Melissa had offered to babysit Caytie for the day, and it seemed that his wife was starting to feel their daughter's absence keenly.

Maddie and her friends had just agreed among themselves that they'd had enough shopping for one day; there was a dance at the school that night-the first in a series of summer dances to be held at the school—that they all wanted to attend, and they wanted to get home with plenty of time to spare.

So, after lunch, Devil helped load bags and boxes into the car and watched as the girls climbed into the back seat. Angeline stood by her door, waiting until Maddie was completely inside before closing the door, and then slid into her own seat, pulling the passenger door closed. As she pulled the seatbelt across her lap, she felt Maddie's fingers touch her shoulder. Angeline turned her head and gave her niece a smile as she covered Maddie's had with her own.

"Thanks, Aunt Angeline," Maddie said quietly, leaning close to kiss Angeline's cheek, "For everything."

Angeline squeezed Maddie's hand before releasing it. "Anytime, Sweetie," she replied as Devil slid behind the wheel.

They were soon out of Raleigh and on the highway. From the silence in the back seat, Devil guessed all three girls were napping. He glanced sideways at Angeline, and found she had leaned her head back and closed her eyes. He reached over and gave her leg a squeeze, causing her to open her silver eyes and smile at him. "Tired?" He asked softly, letting concern flavor the words.

Angeline nodded and smothered a yawn behind her hand. "A little," she confessed, laying her hand on top of his. "Sometimes it feels like all I do is sleep anymore." Her complaint was said lightly, though Devil heard the seriousness that lay underneath.

"Doc said it was to be expected," he reminded her. "It takes time for your body to bounce back from everything you've gone through." He deliberately didn't recount everything she'd been through, not wanting to awaken any painful memories.

Angeline realized this and appreciated his attempt, and didn't allow the dark memories show themselves. "I know," she replied quietly. Then she sighed, closing her eyes again. "I'm simply use to being on the go," she murmured over another yawn. It didn't help that the June day was sunny, bathing her in warmth; she always got sleepy when she was warm. "How am I supposed to go back into practice if I'm taking catnaps all the time?" The last was muttered as sleep overcame her.

Devil chuckled to himself and continued to hold her hand as the ribbon of the highway unwound in front of him.

~CHAPTER THIRTY-TWO~

Maddie awoke just as he turned onto their street. She frowned as she spied the strange car parked in the driveway. “Who’s that?” She asked, her voice a little rough from sleep. She stretched as much as she could without hitting Courtney in the head, and Devil heard her jaw crack as she yawned widely.

He shook his head, a frown between his eyes. “I don’t know,” he admitted slowly, turning into the drive. As he put the car in park, he noticed the man in the gray suit standing on the porch. It appeared he’d just knocked on the door when he noticed their arrival; his hand was still raised.

Devil awakened Angeline gently. “I want you and the girls to stay here until I find out who this is,” he told her, not taking his eyes off the stranger. Sissy and Courtney stirred behind him. He heard one of them stage whisper to Maddie, “What’s going on?” He heard the slight sound of Maddie’s voice as she replied, though he couldn’t hear the actual words. Giving Angeline a cautious look, Devil opened the door and got out.

The stranger smiled brightly and met Devil on the front walk, his hand held out. Devil shook his hand. "Colin Brubaker," the stranger introduced himself. "Chris Jessop's attorney."

Devil didn't reply; how the hell had Jessop managed to invade their lives once again, even after he was dead?"

"What can we do for you, Colin?"

Angeline's voice was calm and low behind Devil. He turned and scowled at her, but she brushed past without looking at him, keeping her eyes carefully from his; in a flash, he realized he was blocking him out, keeping him from feeling her emotions. But he knew she was wary, even frightened by this man's arrival; despite her brave front, he saw the way her fingers trembled as she shook hands with the man, and noticed the smile she offered wasn't as bright and open as it could have been. He moved in behind her, silently offering protection and support.

Colin Brubaker smiled in reply and opened the attaché case he held at his side, seemingly oblivious to the undercurrents swirling around him. "If we could sit down for a few minutes," he said, rifling through papers, "I'll explain everything."

Angeline nodded briskly, and turned to face Devil. "Why don't you help the girls bring everything in while I talk to Mr. Brubaker," she suggested, giving him a smile and reaching out to brush at the frown on his face with her thumb; he had to marvel at the way she continued to try and comfort him, when she was the one in need. She leaned closer. "I've known Colin for a couple years, and he's harmless. But if it makes you feel better, I'll scream my head off if there's a problem," she promised in his ear as she kissed his cheek. Devil didn't like it, didn't like the brittle way she seemed to be holding herself, but wasn't really sure what he could do or say to stop her. He harrumphed and nodded. She gave him another smile and turned to their visitor to escort him inside.

By the time he'd helped the girls carry their shopping up to Maddie's room, Angeline and Colin Brubaker were seated at the kitchen table, their heads close together as they read a piece of paper together. He cleared his throat as he entered, and was surprised by the stricken look of shock on Angeline's face when she looked up at him. "Is it all right to tell my husband?" She asked, her voice a little shaky. Devil didn't like how pale she was, and went to stand beside her immediately. He gave Brubaker a hard look.

"Tell me what?" He asked in a gruff voice, not at all appreciative that this man had upset his wife.

The attorney cleared his throat, clearly unnerved by the threat Angeline's husband presented. "No reason not to," he said hastily, handing the paper to Devil. "My client named your wife, Angeline, in his will."

Devil read the document in silence for several minutes. Finally, he cleared his throat. "This names Angeline Elizabeth Carston Jessop as the sole beneficiary of his worldly goods," Devil said slowly, frowning. "He even names her as his wife." He waved the paper angrily. "She never married him."

Brubaker wiped his brow nervously, Devil's growing anger causing him to sweat. "That's why I'm here," he began, taking the will back, and trying to placate the glowering man, "Because Angeline married you and not Mr. Jessop, and he didn't rewrite the will before his death, there's a problem." He took a deep breath and pulled another paper out. "As per his standing will, in the event that Angeline dies, or they have not yet married at the time of his death, then everything goes to his mother, Marianne Jessop, and Angeline is perfectly fine with that. However," he continued, giving Angeline a commiserating look, sorry that he had to dredge up unwanted memories, "Mrs. Jessop believes that Angeline has earned some kind of compensation for," he glanced at the new paper, and read, "Pain and suffering received at the hands of Christopher Jessop."

Devil glanced down at Angeline at the small gasp she made. Her eyes were wide, and her hands gripped the table edge tightly until her knuckles shone white. Mr. Brubaker went on smoothly. "I have been given permission to write you a check in the amount of five hundred thousand dollars, to be used as you see fit."

Angeline bolted to her feet, knocking her chair over. "But that's everything!" She protested, aghast. She turned an accusing look on Colin. "Just a minute ago, you were telling me that you were simply here to let me know I'd been named in the will, but it was going to his mother! You said nothing about this!" The attorney's calm expression did nothing to soothe her. "I don't want anything for him!" She stormed, her eyes brimming with tears. "He hurt me, he stalked me, and he held me prisoner and tried to kill me and my baby! I don't want anything from him or to do with him!" Only Devil noticed the way the light over the stovetop flared and began to flicker erratically and felt the distinct chill in the air. Moving swiftly, he reached out for Angeline and pulled her close, cradling her head in his large hand, pressing her face against his chest. He murmured soothing sounds in her ears, cautioning her, calming her, yet even as he watched, ice crystals began to form on the glasses of lemonade Angeline had served for herself and Colin. He caught Brubaker's eye, and realized with a start that the man knew what was happening.

The attorney nodded solemnly in answer to Devil's silent question. He absolutely knew about Angeline's unique gift; he'd seen it firsthand one morning when he'd arrived at her clinic and accidently startled her. The florescent lighting fixture above his head had made a loud crackling noise, popped, and went dark. By that time, he'd been witness to too many other occasions of electrical malfunction when Angeline was near to be coincidence; when he pressed for an explanation, she had told him after swearing him to secrecy, and even then, he had never been sure she'd told him everything. Now, he stood slowly and went to Angeline and her husband, reaching out to gently touch her shoulder, ignoring the low growl of warning that rumbled from Devil's chest. "Ang, Chris was my client, but I hope I can say that you are my friend. Marianne knows what happened to you, thanks to all of the media coverage, and wants to do something for you. She wants to make it up to you in the only way she knows how." He paused, giving Angeline's shoulder a pat. "She hopes you'll use the money to do the things that make you truly happy."

Angeline moved out of Devil's embrace and paced the floor, biting her thumbnail in concentration. Chris' mother had always been a sweet and gentle woman with hidden iron will that she wielded with extreme efficiency when needed; there was simply no way she would have stood aside and allowed her son to continue harassing Angeline if she'd known what was happening. This offer was Marianne Jessop's way of apologizing for not recognizing the situation and stopping it. She struggled to calm herself in order to think clearly; it was difficult to do because of the hellish memories that kept intruding and muddying her thoughts and emotions. Once again, the lights started flickering and plates rattled inside the cupboard. She took a deep breath and tried to distance herself from the turmoil of emotions churning through her. "So it's her way of compensating me for my pain and suffering?" She managed to ask, her voice as tight as the fists at her side.

Brubaker nodded, beginning to relax a little as she seemed to understand. “That’s it in a nutshell,” he told her, taking on the formal role of attorney again, “Mrs. Jessop asked me to give you this letter and asked that I leave her phone number in case you wished to speak to her.”

“Will you be in Bounty Covc long, Colin? I think it would be a good idea to speak to Marianne before I make a final decision.” She gave him a smile that wasn’t as tight as it could have been. Devil let a sigh of relief slip out as the lights steadied and the constant hum of the dinnerware rattling disappeared.

Brubaker began gathering up his papers and putting them neatly into his briefcase, nodding as he did. “I’ve been instructed to stay as long as it takes,” he said, his voice and expression more relaxed and cheerful. He paused and gave Angeline a gentle look. “She really wants to do this,” he told her quietly, “Ever since she found out what he did to you, she’s been very determined to do something to make your life better from now on.”

Angeline looked at her husband, love shining in her starlight eyes. “It already is,” she answered softly as the attorney stood and let Devil escort him back to his car. She stood in front of the kitchen sink, her eyes staring unseeing out the window. She jumped when Devil spoke her name.

“Are you all right?” He asked from the kitchen door.

Angeline sighed and hugged her arms to her belly. “It was just a surprise,” she replied, her voice calm and steady, “It was like getting slapped in the face to hear his name again.” She shivered and rubbed her arms as she glanced at Devil. “Is it cold in here?” She asked, moving to the coat closet to retrieve a sweater.

Devil chuckled as he helped her slide the sweater over her arms. “Just you,” he replied, kissing the nape of her neck. With a sigh, Angeline went to the kitchen table and picked up the piece of paper Colin had left behind. She studied the elegant hand of Marianne Jessop and felt a pang of regret that such a lovely woman could have had such a monster for a son. Without turning, she spoke to Devil, keeping her back to him as she did.

"I need to be alone for a little while," she told him in a steady, quiet voice. "I won't be gone long." She turned to see Devil's reaction. Her husband nodded, his expression understanding. "Will you be at the cove?" He asked, moving closer to reach out and touch her cheek. Angeline nuzzled her face against his hand, her eyes closing. "No," she replied, opening her eyes again. "I'm just going to take a walk; this isn't something that's about to explode inside me, just something I need to think about. I'll stay in the area, I promise," she added moving closer to stand within the circle of his arms. She placed her hands on his shoulders and stood on her toes to kiss him. Then, before Devil had the chance to deepen the kiss or distract her in anyway, she slipped out of his arms and was simply gone.

Shaking his head, Devil went in search of Maddie and her friends. It was coming up on dinnertime, and he wanted everything ready by the time Angeline got home; she was sure to be very hungry by the time she'd finished her walk.

~CHAPTER THIRTY-THREE~

Angeline stayed true to her word. She simply took a walk along the creek. Since the night Jessop died, she hadn't been back to the Kissing Temple, having subconsciously avoided the marble gazebo anytime she'd been out on a walk. Now however, she forced her feet along the path and up the stone steps. The fire that had consumed Jessop had left barely a trace of itself on the polished surfaces of the interior, and it took several minutes of searching on her hands and knees to even find the minute shimmer of opal and garnet that had fallen into a small fissure in the floor where she'd stood. With a small sigh, Angeline got to her feet and moved over to one of the stone benches and sat, wondering if she would ever be able to remember happier times here without the taint of Jessop's death at her hands. She sighed heavily and wiped a tear from her cheek. Thinking too hard about things and feeling sorry for herself would only make her crazy and make things worse in the long run. So, she closed her eyes, steadied her breathing, and let calm steal over her.

While Angeline allowed her mind to simply drift along the paths it would, Devil supervised the girls in setting the table and preparing a salad. Once he was certain things were under control, and while the grill heated, he went into the living room to call Christian Witcher to check on his cousin, Chance. Though he and Chance kept in contact, and had been close while growing up, his cousin's dramatic arrival a week ago had been nothing short of surprising; Chance usually let him know if he was dropping in to visit. Devil wondered what had prompted the visit. Not that he wasn't always glad to see Chance, but for him to just arrive out of the blue was out of character for him.

Doc answered the phone on the third ring, and after trading pleasantries, was able to tell Devil that Chance would make a full recovery in a few weeks. His collarbone and wrist were broken, and he'd sustained a nasty case of road rash, but otherwise, he was healthy and doing fine.

"Matter of fact," Doc said with a chuckle, "I'm not sure it would be good to keep him here much longer; he's already got Mrs. Nesbitt in a huff, and I fear she may poison his food tray in the near future."

Devil laughed, remembering how impatient Chance had been, even as a kid; Chance hated being sick or injured, and was usually a cross and grumpy patient. Devil vividly recalled having the chicken pox and being confined with his cousin for the duration of the illness. While Devil had been content to lie in bed and read, Chance had been impatient and eager to do something. It was only when Devil's mother threatened to tie Chance to the bed that he settled down, though he continued to whine and pout.

"Let him know I'll come and get him once you release him," Devil told Doc, "He can stay at my place until he's good to go."

"I'm sure he'll be happy to hear that," Doc replied dryly. "Shall I send a set of restraints with him?"

"I'll think about it," Devil laughed and said goodbye. As he hung up the phone, he heard the girls giggling in the kitchen. With a glance out the window at the slowly falling dusk, Devil made his way back to the kitchen and began grilling steaks for dinner.

When Angeline returned an hour later, dinner was just being served. She took a deep breath, the smell of steaks and baked potatoes making her mouth water and her stomach growl loudly. She hung her sweater in the closet next to the kitchen door, having finally grown warm enough to not need it anymore, and sat across the table from Devil with a grateful smile.

Devil studied his wife's face closely, noting the way her eyes seemed a little swollen, and her nose and cheeks pinker than normal. But other than that, there was no tense set to her shoulders, no stiff mask of anger, nothing that led him to believe she was feeling anything than content and happy to be right where she was. He watched her eyes close in blissful enjoyment as she took a bite of steak, and had to chuckle when she sighed, her entire body seeming to melt a little as she slowly chewed the bite. When her silver eyes opened and she caught Devil watching her, she grinned sheepishly.

When dinner was finished, the dishes were washed, and Caytie was fed, bathed and put to bed, Maddie and her friends retreated to her room to dress for the dance being held at the school. While Devil waited to drive the girls to the gymnasium, he and Angeline settled together on the couch in the living room to watch a movie. Wrapping his arms around her, Devil pulled Angeline as tightly to his chest as he could manage without hurting her. To his surprise, she snuggled even closer until it seemed as if she were trying to fuse their bodies together.

He recognized the signs of a very uncertain woman, and when she pulled his arms tighter around her body, he allowed it, knowing she was seeking reassurance. He waited her out in silence, allowing her time to marshal her thoughts. When she finally did speak, her voice was low.

"What would you do?"

Devil sighed. "Honestly?" He asked, as he stilled her hands' restless fidgeting as she worried the hem of her blouse, "I don't know." Several moments of silence passed as he wondered what was going through her mind. "I'm not the one who suffered so much," he finally continued. "I can't begin to imagine what you went through; it's easy to know what he did to you physically, but emotionally, mentally?" He shook his head. "How do you quantify something like that? How can anyone put a price tag on that?"

Angeline was silent as she listened to his low deep voice rumble in his chest under her ear. "Part of me wants to accept her offer," she finally admitted with guilt in her voice, "It would certainly help pay for college and we wouldn't have to worry about finances for a long time, but," she continued, her voice heating up with anger, "The other part of me wants nothing to do with him or his family ever again."

Devil kissed the top of her golden head. "Why don't you talk with Marianne first, and make a final decision afterwards?" He suggested, his lips wandering over her ear to her jaw. Angeline tilted her head a little to allow him freer access.

"Mmm," she breathed, considering his words, "I had already planned to talk to her," she admitted with a sigh, "But I'm not sure what to say to the offer. On one hand, I don't want the money, but on the other, I don't want to hurt her feelings."

This was one of the things Devil loved most about Angeline. No matter what it might cost herself, she was always concerned about those around her. He kissed her slowly as she turned slightly in his embrace, but before things could get more interesting, the three girls bounced into the room, giggling. With a sigh and a whispered promise, Devil hauled himself to his feet and trailed Maddie and her friends out the door.

Angeline awoke late the next morning, her body feeling relaxed, but her mind still a knotted tangle. After a cup of coffee and a light breakfast, she got dressed and took Courtney and Sissy home before stopping off at the bed and breakfast on Main Street.

She found Colin Brubaker sitting in the dining room, a newspaper in one hand, a cup of coffee in the other. As she drew closer, Angeline noticed the page he was reading contained the Sunday comics; whatever he'd found humorous left him smiling and chuckling to himself. She spoke his name quietly, trying not to startle him.

Hearing his name, Colin looked up. Seeing Angeline, he smiled widely and set aside his paper. He invited Angeline to join him. As she sat, she asked the waitress for a cup of coffee, and took her time stirring in creamer and sweetener. Colin watched and waited in silence, sensing her reluctance to bring up the topic. Eventually, she set her spoon aside and pinned him with a straightforward look.

"I will be calling Marianne this afternoon," she told him, her voice steady and betraying no emotion. "I still don't know if I can accept her offer, but I'm willing to talk to her at least."

Colin took a sip of coffee, nodding as he did so. "That's all she wants, really," he told her. "The money is just her way of trying to make things right again." He watched as a look of anguished uncertainty flickered across her features, and hastened to reassure her. "No one will think any less of you if you take the money," he told her, reaching out to place his hand over hers and give it a squeeze, "If that's what you're worried about."

Angeline sat back, subtly pulling her hand out from under his. "I'm not taking the money," she said, making up her mind in that moment. "I want you to set something up that can have the funds transferred to a trust account. I want the money to be donated to charities that help women get out of abusive relationships." She paused, taking a deep breath and steadying her shaking fingers. "I got out, and he still tracked me down," she finally continued, "And I almost didn't survive. I don't want that to happen to anyone else."

She sat back, suddenly aware that she'd been leaning over the table. Brubaker pretended not to notice and rubbed his jaw with one hand, covering the smile he felt beginning to stretch his face; that she was completely sincere was obvious, and he didn't want to give the impression that he wasn't taking her seriously. He hadn't had much opportunity to get to know Angeline while she was engaged to Jessop, but what he'd heard about her and learned for himself had made it easy to predict what she would end up doing with the money. Realizing she was watching him expectantly, Colin cleared his throat and nodded.

"If that's the direction you want to go, then that's what will happen," he told her, noting her sigh of relief that encompassed her entire being, "I'll get the paperwork drafted up and have my firm fax me copies. I'll have the papers ready for you to sign by tomorrow afternoon," he promised, taking another sip of coffee.

Angeline exhaled loudly; she suddenly felt as if a weight had been lifted from her shoulders, and she relaxed enough to smile at the attorney. "You think I'm being foolish, don't you?" She asked.

Brubaker shook his head. "No." He told her with finality, "I expected this to happen; I knew Chris since we were in school together; he always had to have things his way and did whatever it took to get what he wanted, even if it meant hurting others." He reached out and took her hand, this time not letting go when she tried to pull away. "I wish I could've warned you," he told her quietly, giving her a sad smile, "But I really thought he'd changed when he met you." Colin shook his head.

Angeline finally pulled her hand from his and gave him a brittle smile. "It's not your fault;" she told him slowly, "Chris fooled a lot of people, including me." Then, without waiting for his reply, she stood, holding out her hand to shake his. "Thank you for doing this, Colin. I'll see you when you have the papers for me to sign." Then, without another word or backwards glance, she left, her back straight, her head high. Colin felt a pang of sadness that he hadn't met her before Chris.

~CHAPTER THIRTY-FOUR~

The next day, Devil drove to the clinic to pick up his cousin Chance. He stifled a grin at his cousin's disgruntled expression, and just laughed at Chance's growled greeting.

"Took you long enough."

Devil shook his head and chucked Chance on his uninjured shoulder with his fist. "Don't worry, cuz," he said, tossing Chance's saddlebag in the backseat, "you're sprung, and there's a hot meal waiting for you at the house."

Chance leaned his head against the headrest and tried to shift his arm into a comfortable position. This however, was a lost cause; his collarbone was broken and his right arm was immobilized in a sling, and the shoulder strap of the seatbelt rubbed against his sore shoulder. It was no wonder his mood was surly and aggravated. He gritted his teeth until his jaw ached to keep from swearing a blue streak when Devil drove over each of the five new speed bumps that had been put in along Main Street to slow down traffic. Despite his best efforts, a groan slipped out from between his clenched teeth, and he gave his cousin a look, daring him to say anything. Devil simply rolled his eyes and kept his mouth shut, for which Chance was grateful.

Devil breathed a sigh of relief when he pulled into the driveway. It was plain to him that Chance was in pain, but Chance being the way he was, Devil knew better than to offer any kind of sympathy. So, he carried his cousin's saddlebags into the house, and didn't offer any other assistance. *One of these days*, Devil thought, watching his cousin get awkwardly from the car, *that damnable pride of his is going to get him in trouble.* Then, as he stood aside watching Chance, Devil saw something that made his jaw drop; Angeline came out of the house, moving with light steps to Chance's side. There was a moment of murmured conversation between his wife and cousin, then, without another growl or grimace, Chance allowed Angeline to help him the rest of the way out of the car.

Chance was shown to his room a short time later, and accepted a dose of aspirin without complaint when Angeline offered it to him. Devil stood, leaning a shoulder against the doorframe as Angeline went for the pills and gave his cousin an assessing look. What he saw was a man in more pain than he would admit and Devil shook his head.

"You might as well drop the tough guy act," he advised Chance quietly, "Angeline can see right through it; she'll know what's really going on whether you want her to or not, so don't even try and hide the pain from her."

At Chance's questioning look, Devil straightened and moved out of his wife's way as she returned to the room. "I was just telling Chance that pretending it doesn't hurt isn't going to work around you," he told her as she handed Chance the aspirin and a glass of water.

Angeline gave Chance a smile and said brightly, "I would have to say on a scale of one to ten, right now you're feeling about a seven in pain," she gave him a steady look, "Aren't you?" Her smile melted away and her expression grew serious.

Chance swallowed the pills with a gulp of water and almost choked. He wiped his mouth with the back of his hand, and gave Angeline a narrowed look and slowly nodded. "Yeah," he managed to say, his voice rough, "Should I even bother to ask how you know that?"

Angeline laughed as she felt Chance's surprise and skepticism. She patted his hand and sat down on the edge of the bed with him. "It's a little trick I have," she explained, making light of her abilities, "It helps me quite a bit when I meet someone as stubborn as you are." She laughed lightly at Chance's disgruntled expression and got to her feet. "I know Doc wants you to take it easy, but you don't have to do it lying on your back or even in this room. Whenever you want to join us, feel free to do so." She moved across the room to Devil's side, and said over her shoulder as she left, "Otherwise, we'll see you at dinnertime."

When Chance awkwardly rushed out of his room a few moments later, it was to find both Devil and Angeline waiting for him at the end of the hall, wide grins on their faces.

The weeks passed quickly, and soon, Chance was able to go without the sling that immobilized his arm for short periods of time. He seemed completely taken with his niece, and found excuses to hold her and make silly faces at her to get the baby girl to smile. And though Devil watched him closely, he was unable to detect any of his cousin's normal restlessness.

Chance, meanwhile, had believed in Angeline's sensitivity immediately, and took pains to keep the restless, caged feeling that threatened to smother him in check. He turned his need to do something to constantly scrutinizing any small, silver cars he happened to see on the street. His frustration grew steadily with each day as his search for the driver who ran him off the road continued to be fruitless.

Angeline met with Joe Carter, and in a shorter time than she anticipated, began working as a full partner at the veterinary clinic. Her life was falling into place again, but she couldn't help but worry if it was about to just fall apart; there was nothing that she was able to pinpoint as the source of her paranoia, simply a niggling feeling that things were about to go awry. What began as an occasional ping on her radar, soon developed into an annoying buzzing at the back of her senses. She became easily distracted. She found it more difficult to maintain an even temper. She began to lose sleep.

By the end of the third week, Angeline simply thought she'd go mad if she didn't get out. She felt claustrophobic by the routine of her life, caged by the restless need to do something different. She returned home from a quiet morning at the clinic, nervous energy spilling through her system, and in an effort to distract herself, set to work preparing a lavish meal for her family. Midway through the chopping of an onion, she realized tears were streaming down her cheeks; tears that had nothing to do with the bitter, acrid smell of the onion. She felt a weight pressing down on her, making her heart feel as if it were laboring for every beat, causing her lungs to struggle to draw breath. She stared at the raw ingredients for the meal through a veil of tears, not quite sure why she was bothering.

Nothing changes, she thought miserably, *it's work, the baby, Maddie, Devil. The same thing day in and day out.*

Delirious desperation seized her then. She threw down the knife in her hand and pivoted on her heel. Not knowing why she did it, she ordered Maddie to pack a bag and went to do the same for herself and Caytie. Within twenty minutes, she and the girls were driving out of Bounty Cove. She'd decide where they were going when they got to the airport. But for now, the knowledge that she was taking action and changing things up was enough to sustain her. Before she left the house, Angeline left a note for Devil.

All it said was *'I've got to go before I lose my mind.'*

~CHAPTER THIRTY-FIVE~

By the time Angeline had booked a flight for Portland, Oregon, Devil was walking in the door to find dinner half completed, and a cryptic note waiting for him on the kitchen table. It was written on white notebook paper in pink ink, the pen lying next to the note. The note itself was held in place by the salt and peppershakers. He read the nine words hastily scribbled on the page and let out a strangled roar.

"What the *hell* is this?"

Chance entered the room at his cousin's words and froze for a moment, the look of rage and disbelief on Devil's face causing him to give his cousin a moment to pull himself together. When Devil noticed him, he handed the paper to Chance.

"Do you know anything about this?"

Chance read the words and felt a fist sucker punch him in the gut. They were the exact words he'd been thinking just a few hours before, when he'd finally found the car he'd been searching for. He'd needed to get away, to gather his thoughts and come up with a plan of attack before he confronted the owner. He wondered suddenly just how much more Angeline had picked up from him.

Devil saw by the look on Chancc's face that he knew something, and didn't wait to let the man do his own explaining. Seizing Chance by the shirtfront, he shoved his cousin up against a wall, managing to knock a kitchen chair onto its side in the process. "What did you do to her?" He snarled, slamming Chance's head against the wall. The impact made the phone on the wall nearby chime in protest.

Chance didn't fight back; though he hadn't intentionally done anything, Angeline's flight was his fault. "I didn't mean it," he said as calmly as he could, "She told me about what she could do, that she picked up on the emotions around her. I tried really hard not to let anything out, in case I hurt her feelings." It was difficult to remain calm in the face of the fury radiating from Devil, but he managed to do it, to hold onto to his temper by the skin of his teeth; if they both lost control, it would only waste time when they could be getting to Angeline. However, the impact of Devil's fist on his jaw changed things and quickly. With a bellow, Chance shoved his cousin back and swung his own fist hard. He felt a bite of satisfaction when he connected and allowed his temper to bleed off; Devil landed on his ass in the kitchen floor, and Chance wasn't the kind to kick a guy when he was down. He wiped the blood trickling from his mouth away with the back of his hand and offered his cousin a hand up.

"Beating me to a pulp isn't going to help," he told Devil calmly. "Where would Angeline go if she needed to, no matter what?"

Devil shook his head as he tested his jaw to see if it was broken. "I don't know," he said slowly as he fell into a chair, "She's never taken off with the girls before, so we can rule out the beach, and even if that's where she intended to go first, she wouldn't keep Caytie at the beach after dark." He closed his eyes for a moment, and Chance remained silent, certain an answer would come if Devil simply stopped and thought things through. Minutes later, Devil suddenly stood. "She's gone to Portland," he said with certainty, "Her grandmother and sister live there." He gave Chance a grin that his cousin returned, and within the hour, they were headed to Portland.

Angeline breathed a heavy sigh of relief as the plane touched down at Portland International; it had been tough going during the six-hour flight to keep herself under control enough to not let loose and simply start bouncing off the cabin's walls. Common sense told her at the very least the flight crew would duct tape her to her seat, and at worst, the sudden outpouring of energy could cause the plane to crash.

Once she and the girls were through the gate and had collected their bags, she called Cassandra and rented a car. After dropping Maddie at home, Angeline continued on to her grandmother's house, arriving on the doorstep frazzled, exhausted, and unable to think straight from the strain. Constance took one look at her granddaughter and immediately took Caytie into her own arms.

"Let me take care of the baby," she told Angeline firmly. "You need to take care of yourself right now."

Angeline nodded, numbly grateful, and managed to stagger her way up the stairs to the room she'd always called her own. She fell, face first across the bed, and simply lay, her eyes closed, her mind whirling dizzily. What had been so important that she had to come to Portland on the spur of the moment? What had been so bad about staying in Bounty Cove? She managed to roll over and pull herself into a sitting position before reaching out to pick up the phone on the nightstand. She dialed her home number, but got the answering machine. When she tried Devil's cell, she got his voicemail. She hung up without leaving a message, knowing whatever she said at this moment wouldn't be enough to adequately explain her actions. With a sigh, she got to her feet and stumbled to the bathroom, pulling her clothes off as she went; she'd decided a hot shower couldn't hurt and might be just what she needed.

By the time Constance had settled Caytie in for the remainder of the night and checked on her granddaughter, Angeline was sleeping heavily. She frowned, shaking her head as she closed the door, not understanding what had possessed Angeline to drag her daughter and niece cross country in the middle of the night. As she returned to her own room, the phone rang, and she wasn't surprised to hear Devil's voice on the line.

"Don't worry," she soothed in a quiet voice, "They arrived here safely just about an hour ago. Maddie's at her mother's house, and both your wife and daughter are sound asleep."

Devil made a relieved noise that came out choked. "Chance and I are on our way," he said finally, once he'd swallowed the lump in his throat.

Constance promised to try and keep Angeline there until he arrived, and then hung up, wondering just how she would do that if her granddaughter changed her mind and decided she needed to be back in Bounty Cove. With a sigh, she turned out the light, and pulled the covers up.

~CHAPTER THIRTY-SIX~

Angeline awoke with a start late the next morning. There was a commotion somewhere below her, but before she could figure out what was going on, she heard her name roared. She shivered; the anger in Devil's voice was something she couldn't ignore, nor could she honestly say she didn't deserve. For the first time in her life, she cowered under the covers, hoping that if she pretended to be asleep, she could put off the coming confrontation. It was not to be. She gasped and bolted from bed as the bedroom door flew open and slammed back against the wall. Eyes wide, body trembling, Angeline watched her husband storm into the room like a wrathful god and slam the door shut behind himself. Though he was obviously exhausted and rightfully angry with her, he was, at that precise moment, the most beautiful person she'd ever seen.

So while he ranted and raved at her for being selfish, irresponsible, and flat out stupid, she simply stood there and watched him. Took in the breadth of his shoulders, the way the denim of his jeans hugged the long, lean lines of his legs as he paced in agitation, the way the light coming through the window gilded his hair until there were red tints in it. As she watched and listened to him, the claustrophobic feeling of being caged dissipated, leaving her clear headed for the first time in weeks. She sighed in relief as the weight lifted off her, then jumped when he whirled on her and roared her name again.

"Do you have anything to say at all that might explain what you've done?" He reached out and grabbed her arms. Her teeth rattled as he shook her. "Do you know how freakin' worried I was when Chance and I realized what was happening and you'd taken off?" Almost as if against his will, his hands came up to cradle her face. "Why, Angel? Why would you leave like that?" The anguish in his voice pierced her heart and tears rose in her eyes. "You promised to never leave."

"I didn't know what was happening," she whispered, "I couldn't think straight; nothing like that's ever happened to me. It was like someone else was in my head." She shook her head between his hands. "Devil please, listen to me," she pleaded as his eyes grew dark and the pressure around her head increased. She raised her hands to his, her nails digging deep in an attempt to free herself. She was completely unprepared for his kiss. His mouth was hard, brutal upon hers, allowing no avenue for escape. An iron bound arm dropped and clamped around her waist, jerking her hard against his unyielding frame, bending her back over his arm until she was certain her spine would snap. And all the while, his anger roared around her, through her, seizing her in its teeth.

Devil tried to stop, tried to reign in the relief-born temper that roared through him, but it was raging beyond his control now. It was no longer a contest between his relief that she was all right and the anger that she'd risked so much over an impulse she admitted she couldn't control. He knew how frightened she was, could hear it in her frantic whimpers, could feel it in the rigidity of her body against his, realized how dangerous it was to be so close to her with so much emotion boiling through his veins, and hoped she didn't incinerate them both to ash where they stood.

Devil, please, don't do this.

Her voice rang loud and true in his mind, and it stunned him, freezing him where he stood. His head lifted and he gazed down at her face, at the tear tracks on her pale cheeks, at the way her nails dug into his arms, and closed his eyes against the sight.

I don't want to hurt you.

She trembled in his hold, her small body tense and vibrating, as she poured her thoughts into a burst of emotion and fed it to him. It stilled him and when he opened his eyes again, he found hers open and glowing silver. Her skin was growing hot as the air temperature around them cooled. A slight breeze teased his hair.

Moving slowly, gently, he gathered her against him as she absorbed his anger and internalized it. He kissed the tears from her cheeks, his mouth now gentle and tender instead of bruising, and brushed golden curls from her face. "Look at me, Angel," he coaxed, his voice low, "Stay with me, don't let it go."

Her head shook slightly. *It's too late. There's too much of it. Let me go, Devil.*

His arms tightened around her as he read her thoughts in her expression. "I almost lost you once," he whispered in her ear, "I'm not risking it again." She was almost too hot to hold now, but his arms remained in place. He'd sworn to protect her, and he was going to finally fulfill that promise. He experienced a moment of disorientation as the pressure around them rose and his ears popped painfully and though he expected it, he felt a dizzying wave of vertigo when their feet left the floor. He heard her gasp and felt her small body tighten further than he thought possible. A low cry escaped his lips as the sensation of electricity raced through his body. Then, not knowing what else to do, he did the only thing he could think of in what he thought was possibly his last moment on earth:

He kissed her.

With everything in his heart, he kissed her, pouring every ounce of love he felt for her into it.

Angeline's eyes flew opened as she registered the gentle sensation of his lips on hers. It was like no other kiss she'd experienced with Devil. It went beyond the toe-curling kisses they'd shared when they made love, beyond the gentle expression of love they shared in quiet moments, beyond the parting kisses they shared as they began each day, the silent wish to return to each other safely at the end of the day. This kiss gave her all of that and more; it gave her hope, gave her strength, and gave her the will to stop this before it was too late. Before she went too far to ever come back.

Slowly, her grip on him relaxed, and her arms rose to twine about his neck. She returned his kiss with her own, suddenly able to let go, to share the burden that pressed against the insides of her skull. She felt Devil stiffen and groan in reaction as the emotional overload hit his system; it was almost a sound of pain. She instinctually pulled back, to spare him the agony of the energy roaring through her, but he wouldn't let her.

"No, Angel," he murmured against her lips, "Not this time." He deepened the kiss again, overwhelming her, taking over, softening the harsh edges of the emotion he'd generated and she was feeding back to him. As she gave over to the power of the kiss, the pressure around them lessened, slowly releasing the almost crushing grip that had wrapped around them. Her skin cooled, though she was still warm from the passions rising in her blood. They both staggered a little as their feet touched ground again.

When the kiss finally ended, many long minutes later, they were both breathless. Devil's skin tingled as the last remnants of energy flowed from his body and he gasped for breath as if he'd been running. His legs felt wobbly, and it took greater effort than he expected to turn them slightly in order to sit back on the bed. He kept his arm around Angeline's shoulders, and was relieved when she leaned into him, resting her head on his shoulder. Several minutes passed before either of them could speak.

"Well," he sighed, kissing the top of her head, "We're still here."

A ghost of a chuckle slipped from her lips, and she pulled herself into an upright position. She looked at him askance then sighed. "Trust me, it was close." Her head turned until she looked him in the eye, her expression serious, her gaze haunted. "Why didn't you let me go?" She demanded, slugging his shoulder before jumping to her feet. "Do you have any clue how close you came to being nothing but a smear on the floor?" It was her turn to be angry, to pace in agitation. She spun to glare at him. "If I hadn't figured out at the very last moment that I could share it with you, one of us, probably *both* of us would have been dead."

It was Devil's turn to simply watch her as she stormed around the room, angry and put out. Her anger was solely based in her belief that he almost died, and it told him more than she would ever know; it told him just how deep her love for him was. He looked up as she said his name sharply.

"You could have died, do you understand that? Do you have any idea at all how serious this is? I could have stopped your heart," She continued, her face flushed, her eyes suspiciously wet, her chest rising and falling as she continued to breathe heavily. "I could have stopped it just as easily as I did Jessop's," she continued, doing her best to loom over him. Devil was momentarily distracted by the sight of his tiny wife doing her best imitation of a Valkyrie. "Don't you ever do that again!" She demanded when she came to end of her tirade. Devil reached up, snagged her hand, and gently pulled her onto his lap. He curled a finger under her jaw and tilted her face up to his.

"Sweetheart, as long as I can spend my last moments on earth kissing you, I'm going to do it every time." He kissed her to still the protest he sensed lurking on the tip of her tongue.

Angeline tried to hold onto her anger at his cavalier attitude, but the meaning of his words sunk in and scattered her wits.

When Chance pressed his ear to the door an hour later, the sound of husky laughter and sighs reached his ears. He suppressed the urge to knock and interrupt, and took himself off in search of breakfast instead.

~CHAPTER THIRTY-SEVEN~

They returned to Bounty Cove that evening, Maddie once again in tow. The girl managed to pack most of her room's contents into two large suitcases, and Devil wondered aloud if she'd remembered the bathroom sink. Maddie simply laughed, rolled her eyes, and ignored her sadly unenlightened uncle. Her aunt however, understood, and gave Maddic a conspiratorial wink behind Devil's back as they piled into the taxi Chance had hired to take them to the airport.

When they finally arrived at home just after midnight, Angeline felt as if she would go to sleep standing up; the prospect of digging through haphazardly packed bags left her feeling more exhausted and she gave Devil a grateful smile as he took their sleeping daughter from her arms and carried her to her crib. Angeline stumbled along in his wake, yawning widely and trying to not bounce off walls along the route or stumble over Nico as he loudly meowed his happiness to see her again and tried to wind himself around her ankles. Her husband didn't seem at all effected by the back-to-back cross-country flights, and she secretly envied him; she suffered jet lag no matter how short a flight she took, and she prayed there wouldn't be any reason for her to go into the clinic for the next twenty-four hours. She briefly looked in on Maddie and smiled to find her niece already in bed and out cold. She made her way to her room, and managed to get as far as the bed before she gave up the fight to keep her eyes opened. She sat down on the edge of the bed and fell back, asleep before her head hit the mattress.

Devil finished putting Caytie to bed, and poked his head into the door of his room to look in on Angeline, and smiled when he found her sprawled, still clothed, across the mattress. Moving carefully, he quickly undressed her and slipped a nightgown over her head, juggling her limp body until he managed to get her arms through the sleeves. He maneuvered her under the covers and tucked them close before he placed a soft kiss on her forehead, and smiled as she sighed and snuggled deeper into her pillow. Closing the door quietly behind him, he moved into the living room and ran into Chance as he came from the kitchen. The fact that his cousin wasn't wearing his sling wasn't lost on Devil. "Shoulder feeling better?' He asked.

Chance grimaced as he flexed his sore shoulder. "It's bearable," he replied, rubbing at the soreness. "I'm tired of doing everything with the wrong hand," he added, twisting the cap off a bottle of beer. He handed another bottle to Devil and the two men wandered out onto the back patio. Neither spoke for a long time, each enjoying the quiet of the night and the pleasure of being home again. Chance drained his bottle before glancing at his cousin. He cleared his throat and spoke.

"It was my fault." He watched Devil out the corner of his eye, and knew when he had his cousins attention. "I knew the minute I read her note. It's exactly the same thing I was thinking a few hours earlier when I found the car I've been looking for." He blew out a breath and turned to Devil. "I was sitting in the diner, and happened to look out the window and saw it parked in front of the flower shop. I thought I had to get out of there before I lost my mind and did something stupid."

Devil shook his head. "It's not your fault."

"Yeah, I think it is," Chance countered, heading back into the kitchen for more beer. When he returned, he handed Devil one and twisted his open. He took a long swig before continuing. "I knew she could pick up on stuff, on what people were feeling, and I didn't want to hurt her feelings." He drank again. "So I tried to keep things under tight control, but obviously I wasn't doing a good job of it. I might as well have poisoned her, Dev; all these weeks I thought I was being careful, and it turns out that I wasn't. Then, when I saw that damned car, I felt like all my frustration just rushed out of me; who's to say, after all these weeks of living in the same house, Angeline hadn't grown sensitive to me? And if she did, that last rush is what set it all off, made her forget what's important to her, and made her feel trapped. Made her desperate to escape." He stopped speaking and watched as, after a few minutes of thought, Devil nodded slowly.

"It's possible," he admitted quietly, turning away from Chance to look out over the dark yard, "And right now there's nothing to say you're wrong; I suppose it's the best answer we'll get for now." He sighed heavily and turned back to Chance. He started to say something about turning in, when a shudder, a ripple, a stirring of energy rushed toward them from the night-darkened tree line along the creek. It blew over them, pulling at their clothing and hair as it poured through the opened patio door into the house. A moment later, the two men heard feminine voices cry out.

Devil dropped his bottle, not stopping to check if it broke on the flagstones of the patio or not and tore through the door. The house was unchanged; everything was in its place. Maddie and Angeline had not uttered another sound after the first time, and he felt a shiver of unease crawl down his spine. As he glanced at Chance, he moved, headed for his wife, somehow knowing Chance was going to Maddie.

He stepped through the bedroom door, and found Angeline asleep, tossing and turning restlessly, the covers tangling around her slight body. Devil moved swiftly to the bedside and fell to his knees, his hand reaching out to touch her shoulder. He drew his hand away with a hiss; Angeline's skin was ice cold. He reached out to her again, this time saying her name and shaking her.

Angeline gasped as she sat bolt upright, her silver eyes wide and confused. Her breath came in ragged gasps and Devil could see the pulse pounding heavily in her throat. Devil couldn't tell if she was actually awake or not until he spoke her name again, and she didn't respond. He heard a sound behind him and turned to find Chance standing in the doorway.

"Maddie's fine," Chance said in a low voice. "She woke up the minute I touched her; she said it was a bad dream."

Devil looked back at Angeline. Her breathing and pulse continued to be erratic. He reached out to her again, intent on pulling her into his arms, but she shrank from his touch and scrambled out of the tangle of sheets and blankets that twisted around her hips. Before Devil or Chance could react, she was at the sliding glass door that led to the private patio off the bedroom. Devil caught a look at her face as she did, and the blank, wide-eyed stare on her face chilled him; she was most definitely asleep, and didn't know what she was doing. He managed to reach her before her fumbling fingers figured out how to unlock the door.

Devil wrapped his arms around her from behind, and grunted when she struggled against him, little sounds of desperation escaping her lips. He lowered his head until he could whisper in her ear. "Angel, it's me. You're safe; nothing's going to hurt you." He pinned her arms to her sides with his arms and held her tightly. She strained against him, seemingly desperate to escape. Stark terror etched her expression.

"No!" She moaned as she collapsed against his chest. "No! Don't let them die! We have to help them!"

Devil's hold relaxed out of surprise and in that moment, Angeline wrenched herself out of his grip and ran across the room. She barreled into Chance, and Devil heard his cousin's breath rush out of his lungs at the impact. Angeline's tiny form disappeared through the door.

"Stop her!"

Devil's voice was low, ragged, and Chance responded to it immediately. His cousin's voice was laced with something he couldn't identify completely, but there was an urgency that he instinctually responded to. With Devil right behind him, Chance chased Angeline through the house and outside, her pale form glowing in the weak moonlight of the night. A part of his brain marveled at how swift his cousin's wife was as Devil sprinted past him.

She had to get to them. They were being stalked, hunted, and she was the only one who understood, who knew what was happening. Shadows loomed up, dark and menacing, to engulf the people; they were strangers, people she didn't know, but somehow, in her mind, she knew each and every one of them. They were as dear to her as her own husband and child, as loved by her as any of her family. She had to find them, to warn them, to protect them somehow before the shadows carried them away from her forever.

So she ran. Ran until her lungs strained and her legs felt hot and leaden; ran until her heart threatened to pound through her ribs. She had to find them, had to reach them, yet she didn't know where they were; no matter how hard she tried, these strangers, these pieces of her very soul seemed always out of reach, always shrouded in those seething, hungry shadows. She could hear those shadows, those twisting, writhing pieces of dark; they whispered, their voices blending into each other until there was no individual sounds, but one voice, menacing and terrifying.

Something plowed into her back and once again, she felt the bonds of steel clamp around her, holding her arms against her sides as she struggled to get away. She screamed, her terror, her urgency making themselves heard in her voice. She heard his voice, calling her back, and she turned to it, knowing it was a dream, yet unable to break the vision's hold on her. His voice was worried, afraid, loving and she reached out to him, climbing through the morass of befuddlement caused by sleep. Yet as she reached for him, a second voice became known, and Angeline shrank back from it, pulled in on herself to hide from it.

"They're mine."

The strangers' faces flashed in her mind, and Angeline felt the terror, the denial, the pain of loss rise up and choke her. She knew these people. She had to help them. She felt herself go still as the shadows engulfed them, and reached for her. She struggled to get away, but the bands of iron that held her tightened more, holding her immobile. Terrified, she watched the shadows creep slowly, stealthily up her body. She screamed.

Angeline screamed again, her voice tortured and anguished, and her body suddenly went limp in his hold. She slumped against him and would have slid through his arms had he not reacted quickly enough to sweep her body up into his arms. He'd reached her as she came to a sudden halt at the edge of the creek, her toes barely an inch from the water. She'd stared across the water to the other side, her hands raised in entreaty, as if she were trying to reach out to someone, to bring them back. She fought against his hold, snarls and growls erupting from her throat as she did. He'd whispered in her ear, words of love, assurances of safety, and entreaties for her to come back to him until she seemed to be responding; she'd slowly stopped struggling against him, her body had relaxed. She'd turned herself into him, tucking her body against his, snuggling closer to his warmth, his strength. Her face had been tucked in the crook of his neck when she screamed. His ears were still ringing when he carefully deposited her back in bed. As her head settled in the feather pillows she favored, her eyes opened and she frowned up at him, her body tensing in alarm.

"Is something wrong?" She asked, struggling to sit up. She frowned more when Devil held her down. Her gaze shifted to the sight of Chance hovering in the door of her bedroom, his expression carefully blank. Yet she could sense the worried, tense set of his emotions radiating through the room. From Devil, she felt a sense of relief, yet she could almost taste his worry.

"Don't you remember?"

Angeline returned her gaze to her husband's face, focusing on his voice. She felt an odd pull in her belly, reaching for him, seeking him out. Slowly, she shook her head as the pull faded. It flared back to life the moment he spoke again.

"You were dreaming."

That's all he had to say, and the nightmarish vision rushed back into her memory, hard, sharp, and clear. She drew in a sharp breath, feeling the blood drain from her face. "Maddie!" She gasped. "Maddie was there!" She shook her head, trying to find words to explain. "We were together, in town, and we heard people screaming. I turned to her, and she was suddenly gone." She ignored Devil and scrambled out of bed. "I have to see her!"

Chance hesitated a moment before stepping out of Angeline's way as she rushed to her niece's room.

Angeline opened the door and as the light from the hallway spilled into the room, she slumped against the doorframe in relief; Maddie slept peacefully in her bed, her cheeks sleep flushed, her hair tangling about her head on the pillow. As she watched, Maddie sighed a little in her sleep and shifted, a small smile gracing her features. Angeline stood and watched Maddie sleep for a few more minutes as her heart rate slowed to a normal pace. She sighed as Devil joined her, and leaned gratefully back against him. Once again, that pull surged through her as his arms curled around her protectively.

"There were people," she began slowly, her voice low, "They were in danger. I don't know who they were, but somehow, in the dream, I did, and I was terrified because they were dying."

She didn't mention the menacing voice she'd heard in her vision, and though Devil felt there was something she wasn't telling him, he didn't press the issue. And though he wasn't sure he wanted to hear the answer, he asked the question foremost in his mind:

"Was it one of your premonition dreams?"

Her eyes were wide and frightened as she nodded and he felt a chill crawl up his spine.

"Something's coming," she whispered, her fingers twisting together at her waist, "something's coming and it's going to hurt a lot of people I know." She turned frightened eyes to her husband. "Sue already knows." The connection between them flared brightly one more time before fading. Instead of a feeling of emptiness or loss, Angeline felt a distant glow, a warmth that seemed to be a part of her very soul; it was then that she realized just how much Devil was a part of her, just how firmly entwined their hearts and souls really were. The knowledge left her more strengthened than she ever been. A shiver stormed up her spine as she wondered just how strong she was going to have to be in the future. She buried her face against his chest, seeking every shred of warmth and protection he offered.

In the distance as the first fingers of dawn touched the horizon, a shiver of energy swept across Bounty Cove, as something stirred and raised an awakening head.

For several nights the premonition haunted her dreams. By the third night, she was no longer crying out, but simply awakening herself the moment she fell into the dream. And though she never mentioned the reoccurring dream to Devil, he knew every time she awakened from it. When she did, he made sure to hold her just a little closer, a little tighter, in a wordless quest to reassure and comfort her.

The fourth night was definitely the worst; once again, Angeline was driven from her bed in a vain attempt to help people she only saw in her slumbering mind. This time, Devil was able to keep her indoors and she began to calm quickly. However, the moment her eyes opened, she let loose an unearthly scream and her body bowed backwards as if electricity was coursing through her frame. Devil winced as more light bulbs and the television went up in a shower of sparks and smoke. She didn't awaken as he returned her to bed. As he tucked the blankets around her small frame, he heard Chance clear his throat behind him. "How is it that Caytie and Maddie can sleep through all of this?" It was a question that Devil had asked himself on more than one occasion in the last several weeks, but he'd yet to find an answer. For whatever reason, his daughter and niece remained undisturbed no matter how loudly Angeline cried out in terror, no matter how much turmoil erupted during a nightmare. Sighing heavily, he kissed his wife on the forehead and silently left the room, closing the door behind him.

He and Chance sat up until the sun rose, neither talking. As the rest of the house began to stir, Chance rose from the kitchen table. "I have some business to take care of in town," he told his cousin, absently flexing his shoulder as he rubbed it. "And I'll be heading out tomorrow." Devil nodded and watched Chance leave the room, knowing his cousin's business had something to do with the silver car he'd seen in town the week before. Chance had taken delivery of a new motorcycle, and Devil had had the feeling that he'd be saying adios to his cousin sometime soon; Chance had never been the kind to stay too long in one place if he could help it. Devil simply hoped he wouldn't have to bail Chance out of jail after he confronted the driver who'd run him off the road.

Angeline entered the kitchen, her face drawn, dark circles under her eyes. She gave Devil a half-hearted smile in greeting and shambled across the room to get herself a cup of coffee. Neither spoke until she'd sat down across the table from him.

"Chance is headed home tomorrow," Devil said, his voice loud in the quiet. Angeline's only response was to nod as she stared into the depths of her coffee cup. "He thinks he's found the car that ran him off the road," Devil continued, fulfilling a deep need to fill the silence.

Angeline sighed heavily. "I had the dream again."

Devil nodded. "I know," he told her. "Is there any way of making it go away?" To his dismay, he saw Angeline's lower lip begin to tremble and her fingers clutched convulsively around her mug as she shook her head slowly.

"I've never had a dream more than once; I don't understand why I keep having this one, especially about people I don't even know."

A thought struck Devil, and he leaned forward. "Is it possible you're dreaming about people you meet in the future?"

Angeline shrugged. "I don't know. Probably." She took a sip of coffee and swallowed slowly. Before she could say anything else, Chance reappeared, clad in his riding jacket, his helmet in his hand. "So, you're ready to fly the coop?" She asked him, trying to smile, "We're too boring for you?"

Chance grinned, his green eyes laughing. He reached out and ruffled the top of Angeline's golden head affectionately. "Naw," he drawled as he pulled her out of her chair to give her a brotherly hug, "It's just time for me to move on."

Angeline patted his leather-clad shoulder as she moved out of the embrace. "Be careful," she murmured, kissing his cheek, "And don't be such a stranger; you always have a room here."

Chance nodded wordlessly as he went to his cousin; before meeting Angeline, he hadn't met a woman who gave such love and affection so freely without expecting some kind of payment for it; his wife certainly never did anything without a reason. His jaw clenched as he thought about Vanessa; in the six weeks he'd been laid up, she'd never once called to check on him, to make sure he was all right, even though Devil had made a point of calling her after the accident against Chance's wishes. Not wanting the anger he felt whenever he thought of Vanessa to infect Angeline, he stifled his thoughts and hugged Angeline and shook Devil's hand once again. He made his goodbyes swiftly and left, not wanting to linger and run the risk of never leaving again. He had business to take care of, and once it was complete, he had business to take care of at home.

Devil and Angeline watched Chance motor away, each wrapped in their own thoughts. Silently, Devil curled an arm around his wife's waist and pulled her against his side, offering his protection and support wordlessly. A year ago, had someone told him he would soon find this measure of contentment and love, he would have been hard pressed to believe them. Yet, here he stood, a husband, a father, an uncle, and he wouldn't trade places with anyone in the world. He kissed the top of his wife's head and held her just a little tighter, vowing without words to never let her go, no matter what awaited them in the future. He felt her move and glanced down into her gently smiling face. The look of love in her eyes was mirrored by his own and he bent to place a kiss as gentle as spring rain on her soft lips, absorbing her sigh as if it were the very breath of life and a warm, golden glow seemed to envelope them, to cradle them. The man, called Devil by his friends, had found his own angel, and he would never let her go, would go to his grave loving and protecting her.

As for Angeline, she was unafraid of what her dreams foretold; she knew that as long as she had her devil by her side, there was nothing she couldn't face, nothing that could harm her. For deep down, she knew that no matter what obstacles lay ahead of them in the future, their love would sustain them, and, like a Phoenix rising from the ashes of death, their love would be reborn, stronger and more powerful than before. She laid her head against his shoulder and sighed contentedly, smiling as she felt him kiss the top of her head. Without a word, she took his hand and led him into the house; Maddie and Caytie continued to sleep, and she didn't want to waste a single moment with him. Without speaking and smiling a come hither smile, she led him into their bedroom.

As Devil and Angeline fell together into the arms of passion, a ripple of energy swelled, reaching out to taste the air, to test the boundaries. It seethed and pulsed, unseen, unheard by the handful of mortals it encountered, but still, it left behind an invisible mark that those it touched were vaguely aware of; the humans shivered as though someone or something was watching them. The sensation passed quickly, and they shook it off as they continued on with their lives.

Its curiosity satisfied, it retreated and gathered around itself; the timing wasn't quite right, but soon, yes soon, it would be perfect...